Red Jade

The First Avery Shepard Detective Mystery

J.H. Graham

Malice Books

Published by Malice Books
P.O. Box 188045
Sacramento, CA 95818

ISBN: 0692501479
ISBN-13: 978-0692501474

So fleet the works of man
Back to earth again.
Ancient and holy things
Fade like a dream.

—Charles Kingsley, "Old and New"

PART I

CHAPTER 1

They say the air in Los Angeles once smelled like orange blossoms. It may well have. All I remember, though, is formaldehyde.

Stepping off the train on a November morning about a week before Thanksgiving, I stood blinking in the glare of their much-advertised winter sunshine. The next moment I plunged into darkness again, down into a subway that took me under the tracks and up to the passenger station.

Before I'd crossed the length of the waiting room, I'd had the chance to buy shares in an oil well; the homesite of my dreams in the subdivision opportunity of the decade; a poultry farm ("Home of the Happy Hens!") and a cemetery plot. At least two people had offered to save my soul. And it wasn't that large a station.

No one seemed in a particular hurry. I elbowed past red-cap porters, messenger boys, delivery men and shoe-shiners, other passengers coming and going, and got outside where I scanned the assemblage of vehicles waiting at the curb. I caught the eye of a fellow in a brown wool suit and a snap brim hat who was polishing the fender of a green Ford coupe with the seat of his trousers; he tossed his cigarette away and came ambling over.

"You Shepard?" he asked amicably. I said that I was.
"Frank Ricketts." he said, offering his hand. "Got any bags?"

"Just the one." I said. "They'll send it over to the
hotel."

"You eaten? Want a cup of coffee or anything before
we, uh– head over there?"

"I had breakfast on the train." I lied.

Ricketts shook his head. "That *Limited* must be swell.
You're in Chicago Tuesday night, and here you are on the coast
already. Wish I could do it."

"This isn't exactly a pleasure trip." I said.

"No, 'course not. I'm a dope." he said. "Well, this is
our chariot."

Ricketts got behind the wheel of the coupe. I stepped
up into the passenger seat and held on as he pulled away from
the curb– making a sweeping U-turn in front of a streetcar–
and headed west up a side street that intersected at a right
angle. He swerved around another car going the opposite
direction then slammed on the brakes as a grocery van in front
of us came to a dead stop, keeping up a steady stream of
chatter all the while.

"I come out here in 'twenty-one. The doc
recommended it for my health. I was Chateau Thierry– you
know?"

I gave my escort a sidelong glance. Ricketts had a
freckled, pale face, thinning brown hair and a wide mouth that
seemed to fall naturally into a grin. He was about my age,
medium height with a slight build. He looked healthy enough.

When the signal turned green, a sign reading GO
clanged down and Ricketts took off like he was Barney
Oldfield, cutting around the van, to the obscene objection of its
driver. He turned the wheel a hard left at the next corner,
narrowly missing a couple of jay walkers, and drove south. The
street was an endless blur of unremarkable buildings housing
squatty garages and automobile showrooms, with the

occasional church steeple or a modern skyscraper standing tall and proud above it all.

All at once we were pulling into the driveway of what looked like a pleasant, middle-class home of brick and stone and white concrete; only a blue Studebaker hearse, parked conspicuously near a set of extra-wide double doors, spoiled the illusion. Ricketts brought the machine to a halt and we went inside, through a reception room furnished not unlike my mother's parlor at home, to an elevator that carried us up to the fourth floor. As we stepped off the car the smell hit me.

Formaldehyde.

We were met in the hall by a Mr. Abrams, the assistant mortician, who looked ready to be laid out himself; his skin was stretched tight over the jutting bones of his face and his old-fashioned black frock coat hung on him as if still on the hanger. He took us into what he called the viewing room.

It was decorated like a theater lobby, all overstuffed davenports and stiff-backed chairs, smoking stands and thick Wilton carpets. A pair of green velvet curtains hung from heavy iron rods. Nice– but the show on the other side of them wasn't likely to get any return engagements.

On cue, Abrams drew back the drapery, revealing a picture window. Through the glass I could see a body, reclining on a day bed, covered from the neck down with a sheet. A young woman with light brown hair. Pretty, maybe, once.

But me? I had never seen her before.

This all started almost three months ago when I got a letter from my younger sister Katherine– Kit we called her in the family– postmarked Los Angeles, announcing that she'd left home to study dance there. She had found an apartment and was looking for work. Mother sent terse letters demanding that I bring Kit back to Kansas City. I ignored them. Kit sounded very happy and, once I'd got over my surprise, though I still didn't much like the idea of her being on her own, I was glad for her and kind of proud.

We wrote each other regular, and I made plans to come out and see her at Christmastime. I got a picture postcard from her saying she'd found a job. After that– nothing. It wasn't like her. She was arty but she'd always been dependable. I was worried enough to telephone her, long distance. The manager of her apartment house said she had moved out, giving no notice and had left no forwarding address. That was definitely not like Kit.

I got in touch with the Los Angeles police, a Detective Lieutenant Frank Ricketts of the missing person detail, sent him Kit's photograph and all the particulars. There'd been no news from him for a couple of weeks. Then he wired me that the body of an unidentified young woman matching Kit's general description had been found, and could I come out and identify her?

I'd taken the next train, and here I was, and it wasn't her.

Ricketts took me to an early lunch at an Italian joint he knew, one of those wood paneling and red-and-white-checked tablecloth joints. The entrance was on an alley, in the cellar of a building that housed a cobbler and a Painless Parker dentist. The paneling looked greasy, the tablecloths were sauce-spattered and the whole place reeked of fermenting vegetables. In the way of atmosphere, there frankly wasn't any, Ricketts admitted, nor was the food anything you'd go out of your way for. But they'd put a slug of the real stuff in your coffee if you asked for it. I found myself warming to Ricketts. He had a dish of raviolis with mushroom sauce and coffee; I just had the coffee.

"We must get fifty missing person queries like yours a month or more." Ricketts said, out of the blue. "Most are women, girls. You wouldn't believe how many come out here to be in pictures. We're a two-man detail– just my boss and me is all. I don't even get a car assigned to me– fact, I borrowed that flivver to come get you. But we follow up on every single one."

"Do you ever find them?"

"As a matter of fact we do, mostly. The thing of it is Shepard, a lot of the time, they've gone missing on purpose, don't want to be found. They're married, or went off somewhere with a fellow, for fun. Look at this McPherson woman, the preacher. You heard about her?"

I nodded. It would have been hard not to. The Los Angeles evangelist's disappearance, her presumed death by drowning off the coast, and her seemingly miraculous reappearance a month or so later had been making headlines for months. She claimed to have been kidnapped, but now it looked more likely there'd been a man in the case, and the whole thing was starting to sound like some kind of stunt.

"What about Kit's bank account?" I asked. One thing Ricketts had been able to find out was that Kit had opened a savings account at the Pacific-Southwest Trust and Savings. The account still had thirty-two dollars deposited in it and had not been drawn on since early September, when Kit must have paid her hotel bill and the rent on her new apartment.

Ricketts hedged. "Well, suppose she *is* married– husbands and wives don't always tell each other about their little nest eggs, do they?"

"I guess not." I said. If my wife, Ruby Alyce, knew about the pile I'd won on a longshot at Saratoga in August, I'd be lucky to have the price of my cup of coffee.

"It's like this, Shepard: we never officially close a case until the person's found, one way or another. But we can't spend a whole lot of taxpayer money looking if there don't seem to be evidence of foul play."

5

"I get you."

He stabbed the air with his fork. "Know what I'd do if it was my sister? I'd hire a private dick."

I stared at him. "What– like Nick Carter?"

He gave me a blank look. "Harry Price is the man you want. Runs his own outfit. He used to be on the force, long time ago. They still talk about him downtown. He went after fugitives in Mexico with Wyatt Earp. And way back when he was a deputy U.S. Marshall, he once jumped off a bridge handcuffed to a robber. A couple old timers who were in the Klondike with him say he made more money as a prizefighter up there than panning for gold."

"Sounds like a lot of bullshit to me." I said.

"Maybe some of it is. He's the goods, though. I've met him. I dunno where his office is these days, but you can find him most afternoons at this joint over on Spring Street." He wrote down the address on the back of an envelope.

Ricketts dropped me outside the Fifth Street entrance of the Rosslyn Hotel on Main Street. We shook hands, and he asked me how much longer I figured I'd be in town for.

I shrugged. I hadn't really thought about it. If that body had been Kit's–. But as things stood, I was in no particular hurry to go back east, had nothing, no one, I really cared to go back to.

"Well, if you're going to stick around a while, you oughta get a car." he said.

I said it seemed to me there were already too damned many cars in Los Angeles, and too many rotten-ass drivers behind the wheels of them. The drive back had been even worse than on the way over. I'd wondered a couple of times if we'd wind up back at the mortuary– entering through the rear doors this time. That made Ricketts grin.

"If you're still here at Thanksgiving and want some company, my landlady makes an Irish turkey you'd swear was the McCoy. She won't mind one more." he said.

I thanked him. "For all of your help today, too, while I'm at it."

I found my grip waiting for me upstairs in my suite. It looked like it had been gone through. The bellhop loitered about, opening windows I didn't want opened and generally trying to earn his two bits. After I'd got rid of him I had a look inside. All I'd brought, besides the usual toilet articles, were a couple of extra shirts, pajamas, a wool cap, and some clean linen. And my gun, a nice little Colt 38 Army Special. I'd wrapped it in a piece of oilcloth and stashed it inside the lining of the bag. It was there, along with all the rest of it. I started to unpack, then sat down suddenly on the bed and closed my eyes. "Goddamn it all." I said. After a minute or two I got up and went into the bathroom and ran some cold water over my face. Then I changed into a fresh shirt and went out to try to find him, this private detective, Harry Price.

The joint Ricketts sent me to turned out to be a narrow, three-story building from the nineties. At its north end a narrow stairwell lead up to rooms and beds for rent. Straight ahead at street level a small, hand-lettered sign mounted to a pair of stained-glass doors read CAFÉ.

The inside of it hadn't been changed in twenty years, with its stamped tin ceiling, green and white tiled floor, and brass chandeliers with etched-glass globes. A moose head gazed down at framed photographs of the likes of Corbett, Sharkey, Fitzsimmons and Jeffries in their best fight poses. Below them, in one of the high-backed private booths, a couple of old men were waving their cigars around, rehashing the Ad Wolgast-Joe Rivers fight of 1912 as if it had happened yesterday. The piece de resistance was a hulking mahogany bar with brass rails and a mirrored back advertising the specials of the day.

Three men leaned up against this relic, offering a boozy rendition of "Farewell My Bluebelle."

One last fond look into your eyes so bluuuuue;
'Mid campfires gleaming,
'Miiiiid shot and shell.
I will be dree-eeaming
Of my own Blue Belle.

There was a man in an apron at the end of the bar, slouched over the *Daily Sporting Times* and smoking a cigar. He looked up as I approached, spat into a dented cuspidor and went back to his reading.

"I'm looking for Harry Price." I said to no one in particular. "Frank Ricketts told me I could find him here."

"Never heard of him." the bartender said, shifting the cigar to the other side of his mouth. I wasn't sure if he meant Harry, or Frank. "Try upstairs." he added after a pause. With a motion of his head that was barely perceptible, he indicated a narrow flight of stairs, at the back of the room.

I went up, and came to a heavy wooden door, locked. I pounded on it. Someone opened it a crack and peered out at me.

"Yeah?" a man's voice said.

"Harry Price?"

He opened the door just wide enough to let me in, then a second lookout slammed it shut again behind me. They held sawed-off shotguns. He nodded in the direction of another door.

This one wasn't locked, and I walked in. It was a long room lit by a couple of brass chandeliers like those downstairs. Across the back was a bank of windows, boarded up or bricked over on the outside, and a fireplace with a chipped marble mantle. In the center there were three green baize poker tables, with men seated around each one. Along the side wall was a bookmaking counter, and beyond that a door marked *Toilets*.

A large, burly man in shirtsleeves and a green visor was perched on a stool just inside. He held up his tree branch of an arm to stop me going any further.

"Not so fast, Bub. Whadda ya want?" he growled.

"Harry Price."

He squinted at me a little longer just to show me what a tough customer he was. Then he waved vaguely in the direction of the tables.

"Over there." he said.

I looked at the men playing cards and tried to figure out which one of them was Harry Price. One fellow nodded at me over the top of his cards. He was in his late forties I guessed, with clean-cut features. I started over his way and he watched my approach with a keen interest, as if he'd been expecting me.

When I got close enough, he drew my head down and said in a conspiratorial whisper: "Bring me an East Side, will you, kid? I'm dyin' a' thirst."

"You're– are you Harry Price?"

"Who? Say, what's the gag? Ain't you the waiter?"

"No." I said.

A man at the next table caught my eye. He hadn't moved, or even gestured, but somehow I knew *he* was Harry Price. He was a very tall, broad-shouldered man in a blue suit, obviously custom-tailored for his build, silver-gray hair and a clean-shaven, reddish-bronze face with razor-sharp cheekbones like an Indian, and a long, crooked nose broken who-knew how many times. He was well into his fifties, easy. The gun-metal blue eyes, though sharp, had bags under them. I could read nothing in their expression.

"Who are you looking for?" he asked. The thin lips of his mouth hardly seemed to have moved. His voice matched the face– raspy and haggard.

9

"My sister." I said.

"Oh." he said. "I thought I heard my name."

"C'mon, Harry." one of the other men at the table said. The tall man tossed a chip on the center pile without looking at it.

It was foolish of me, but for a second I'd thought that he'd been able to tell by looking that I was seeking a missing person, the way Sherlock Holmes would tell everything about a man by a cigarette ash. I frowned, and shook my head. Harry Price was just an old man, getting hard of hearing. Maybe he had once been a good detective, if any of what Ricketts' colleagues had to say was true, but that had to have been a long time ago. He looked more like a criminal, and not a very successful one at that. He couldn't help me.

Price watched me for a moment with narrowed eyes, then shrugged and turned back to his game.

I felt hollow, somehow. For a moment I'd let myself think there might be something to this Harry Price, after all, but it was just another dead end. I shook off the feeling. It was still a good idea Ricketts had had, and Harry Price wasn't the only private detective in town. On Monday I'd go to one of the national agencies and hire a reliable man.

In the meantime, since I was in town, I thought I'd visit Kit's apartment house. Ricketts had been there on official business, of course, but I wanted to see it because Kit had been happy there and it was my last link to her.

I asked my pal the door monitor which way to the 700 block of West Fourth Street.

He shrugged. "What am I, a *Gillespie Guide*?"

I heard a throat being cleared, as daintily as was possible for that task to be performed. The throat was a pretty white slender one and belonged to a girl curled up in an old leather armchair. She was maybe twelve or thirteen, with a boyish figure, dressed in a schoolgirl's middy blouse and skirt with a blue scarf wound around curly, bobbed golden-blonde hair. Her face had all the loveliness of a Henry Hutt girl, but with more character– a dimple in her chin, high, prominent cheekbones, a wide, full-lipped mouth. The eyes that were turned up at me were large, almond-shaped and green. A book rested in her lap and she had a finger tucked between the pages to mark her place. I couldn't imagine what she was doing here, but I didn't much like it.

"Just go back out that way, and up the hill." she said, shyly, pointing west. She had a soft, low voice that carried through the din without being shrill.

"Thank you." I said, then hesitated. "Uh, look kid, you aren't here all by yourself, are you?"

"I'm waiting for my father." She glanced in the direction of Harry Price then nodded at me, as if to say "don't worry."

I thought of myself at her age, and even younger, waiting for my father at the barber shop– the kind with three chairs out front and five in the back. I hadn't known what was going on at first; I just thought the old man got an awful lot of haircuts.

Downstairs, the boys at the bar had left Blue Belle behind and were singing "Then We'll All Go Home." The barkeep was still studying his racing papers. He didn't look up.

CHAPTER 2

It was on my last visit home, back in early summer, that Kit first told me of this ambition of hers to be a dancer. I hadn't put much stock in it, to tell the truth. She had always gone in for arty stuff. A couple of years ago it had been poetry.

"What– in the Follies?" I teased.

"No, silly." she'd scoffed. She meant serious concert dancing, like Ruth St. Denis. Who? I'd said. She showed me a picture of a woman, in classical Greek costume, from a tattered theatrical magazine. Then she'd pulled me into our father's library– never mind he died in 1922, it was still his library– where our old phonograph was kept, and locked the doors. She said she would dance for me, show me what she meant. Dance, apparently had to be seen, felt. It couldn't be explained in words, she'd insisted in the young, earnest way that she had.

"Would you put that record on when I say, Ave?" she asked. I wound the machine and dropped the needle at Kit's signal; a classical tune I didn't recognize came scratchily to life. Then Kit came out from behind the Japanned screen, stripped of all but her white chemise, barefoot, with her long brown hair loose, and had performed her kind of dancing.

It was all fluid, graceful movement. Her young body flexed backward and forward like a reed, and raised her slender arms over her head, arching, neck and back muscles taut, legs doing the serious work. For the finale she dropped to the floor with a little cry, legs tucked under, arms outstretched, hair fanned out around her just as the music warbled to an end. I'd held my cigarette between my lips and applauded. I wasn't just kidding her along. She was really good.

She got up, laughing. She was breathing heavily and holding her heavy hair out away from her neck. Her body shone a little bit with dampness and the chemise clung to her legs and her young bosom. She turned the record off, then flopped down in the armchair across from me and looked at me expectantly.

"Well, I don't know what the hell that was but it was damned beautiful." I said.

She thought for a minute. "It's a poem. Only, you write it with your body."

"I never understood poetry much. But I liked it."

"Thank you." she said, smiling, shyly.

"Where'd you learn to dance like that?"

She blushed. "I taught myself. I've seen it done. I practice in here, when no one's at home. Can I have one of those?"

"A cigarette? Since when do you smoke, baby?"

"Oh, ages." I gave her one, and lit it for her.

She took a drag, watching me, then started to cough, holding the cigarette away from her face.

I hid a grin. I knew she was no smoker. "This tobacco's probably just stronger than what you're used to." I said. "Inhale it lightly– like this."

She did it the way I showed her, and smiled. "I wish you'd come around more often Ave. I miss you. You're the only one I can talk to, about dancing and things like that. You never laugh at me, or tell me I ought to look for a husband and get married."

"I miss you too, Kitty. And I think you should do whatever you want to do. I mean it." I said. "Besides, I'm not exactly an advertisement for the joys of wedded bliss."

"From what I saw, I'd say Ruby Alyce isn't much of a wife." Kit said, sniffing.

"We just weren't suited." I said.

She rested her cigarette on the edge of Father's brass ashtray stand and started rolling the ends of her long, thick mane, pinning it at the nape of her neck.

"I'm glad you never cut your hair." I said.

"Oh, bobbed hair is– unromantic." she said, shoving in the last pin. "So how long do I have you for?"

"A couple more days" I said.

"Then where are you going?"

I shrugged. "I've got a job in New York for a few weeks. After that, Saratoga for the racing."

"Take me with you– to New York. Please?"

"New York is no place for a beautiful young girl. It's a wicked city. They take baths in champagne."

"Now you sound like Mother."

"God forbid."

We sat smoking in amicable silence. Then she said, "You were the one who first taught me to dance, remember?"

"That was only the one-step. You know a lot more now."

She jumped up again and went over to the pianola. "Play something, Ave." she begged.

To please her I fooled around with some of the old tunes: "I Wonder Who's Kissing Her Now," "Row, Row, Row," "I Ain't Got Nobody." Kit sat with me on the bench singing along, until Roberta, our older sister, knocked on the door to call us to supper. Only Bert could put so much disapproval into a knock.

"She hates me." Kit whispered.

"No, she doesn't." I said. "She's just afraid somebody in this house might be having fun."

14

I played "Somebody Else Is Getting It," loud. Kit stifled a giggle.

Bert had been married and out of the house by the time Kit was born; I was eight, almost nine. Kit was like a doll, tiny, fragile– and terrifying. She was still a kid when I joined the army. Then, hardly back from the war, I'd married. I actually saw more of Kit then. She would take a streetcar downtown to the store where I was working and I'd slip away and take her out for ice cream so she could tell me her troubles, or her dreams, as the mood struck. I was her only ally, especially after our father died. But my marriage wasn't a success, and I separated from my wife, found work that took me out of town more and more. The last two or three years, I didn't come home regular at all, and then it was only to see Kit.

"Look, Kitty." I said. "I know how rough it is for you here. Hell, I went to France and got shot at to get away. But not from you. If I had a home, you know I'd have you with me, don't you? I just couldn't stick it any more with Rube."

She stepped out from behind the screen dressed once again in her yellow afternoon frock, looking as fresh and young as a daffodil, and came over to put her arms around me.

"I know, Ave. I love you."

"I love you too." I kissed her on the forehead and gave her some money, folded in a clip. "Tuck this in your corset, or whatever you gals wear these days."

"As if you didn't know." she laughed.

That was the last time I saw her.

I was in Atlantic City where Jack Dempsey was training for his bout with Tunney, when I got her letter from Los Angeles. I sent her some money, but she returned it with her next letter.

15

You're a sweet, good brother, but I can't take it. I want to stand— or dance rather— on my own two feet. I used most of what you gave me before to get out here and get settled and still have some of it left. I'm going to pay you back, every cent, eventually. I've been looking for a job!!! (Don't faint). I'm going to earn my tuition so I can start classes this winter at the Denishawn School. It's so wonderful here. Only, so far no one seems to want to hire me because it seems I can't actually do anything! I found the ideal apartment, at least. It's so romantic— not to mention cheaper! I'm moving in at the end of the week so when you write, use the new address. Please <u>do</u> write, Ave, and <u>soon</u>— I live for your letters. Isn't it marvelous how fast the mail travels nowadays? (If one <u>does</u> write— hint).

All my love—
Your Kit

I did write, and for a while got regular replies from her, describing her neighbors and telling me how much she liked the place. Only once did a little discouragement creep in, toward the end of September, when she still hadn't found a job. Then there'd been the card, the last word I'd had from her. Postmarked October 7, it showed a snowcapped mountain. The message read:

Guess what, Ave? I got a job today, my first!!! I'm to be a dance instructress. Can you beat it? XO Kit
P.S. Hope Old Baldy looks like this while you're here. You <u>are</u> coming aren't you?

A walk of less than ten minutes brought me to Kit's apartment house, perched on the crest of an embankment on one of the hills just west of the downtown. The crowds on the sidewalks thinned out as I climbed and traffic noise faded. It was a mostly residential section with blocks of apartment houses and hotels, and old wood-framed houses, much cupola'd and gingerbreaded, holdovers from the last century– mansions some of them could rightly be called– set on large lots with palm trees and lush shrubbery and sloping green lawns and flowerbeds. Some places had discreet signs in windows hung with lace curtains, advertising furnished rooms to let, dressmaking, piano lessons. It felt like a remote suburb here, quiet and almost peaceful without the rumble of streetcars. Folks were sitting out on porches in rocking chairs. A nurse in a crisp blue uniform rolled a bundled-up patient along the sidewalk in a wheelchair. Some small boys chased each other through a garden, playing Indians. From inside an apartment house an opera singer went through her scales.

Kit's was a fanciful towered and turreted place with a slate roof that would not have looked out of place in the French countryside. I could see now how it would have appealed to her. The interior was bright and cheerful enough, with its dark woodwork painted shades of blue and yellow and cream and the high ceiling of the lobby had been adorned with stars and moons. No one was about.

...There are a lot of other artists living here (not that I can call myself one– yet), and nobody bothers anybody else or lectures....

I found a small group assembled in the parlor: an old woman in black silk with a high neck and floor-sweeping skirt banging out Schumann on a rosewood piano, a young woman in orchid silk lounging pajamas half-reclining on the davenport reading the latest number of *The Outlook*; and two men, one middle-aged in dungarees– the other young, in a herringbone wool suit, a red bow tie, and a Van Dyck beard, sat across from each other in easy chairs by the fire playing checkers and arguing.

17

"…a finite mind can't even begin to grasp the infinite. What you want is…." the bearded one was saying.

"What I want is for you to shut yer yap and make yer move." the other man said. "It's not a theory, it's a science. You take embryology now–"

He broke off as a man with a full head of snowy white hair above a young pinkish-complected face that was going to fat came in carrying a laden silver tray.

The young woman looked up from her magazine and sighed. "Henry, must we have embryology with our tea?"

The older woman caught sight of me in the mirror over the fireplace and stopped playing. She had to be Miss Emily. Kit had written of her often and of her cat, Queen Bess. She was in her seventies, Kit said, and had lived in this building for as long as Kit had been alive.

"Young man, come over here." Miss Emily commanded. complied. She peered at me near-sightedly over a pair of silver nose glasses. "Why, how extraordinary. You are the spitting image of Charlie Pearce."

"I'm not him." I said.

"I certainly hope not. He drowned in 1894."

"Was he your beau, Miss Emily?" the young woman asked.

The old lady fixed her with a gimlet-eyed stare, then turned back to me and said dreamily. "Remarkable. I must to try to contact Charlie."

"Oooh, you mean a séance– like Sir Conan Doyle?"

"Hush, child. I do not. Such things are pure chicanery."

The snowy-haired man, having laid his burden on a side table and arranged cups and saucers and cake plates around it, straightened up and winked at me. He would be Mr. Greene, the manager, the man I wanted to see. We went out into the hallway.

"We adored having Kit here. She fit right in to our little family." he said after we'd introduced ourselves. He had an English lilt to his voice. "I'm sorry now I didn't get in touch

18

with you sooner– as soon as she left. If I'd had any idea there was anything wrong about it–. It's just that I get folks, artist types you know, who move around a lot or take themselves off to Laguna or Carmel at the drop of a hat. Then they show up here three months later shocked to the core that I rented their room out from under them. Not that Kit seemed the flighty type."

"Had she seemed worried or upset about anything lately?"

"No– she seemed very happy here. That last week though, fact is, I didn't see her. I heard her in her room but I had the notion she might have been avoiding me." He looked at me with sympathetic blue eyes. "The rent was coming due, you see. I know she was trying hard to find a job. A lot of folks here are sometimes a wee bit– late, shall we say– with the rent. They always pay up as soon as they can. I wasn't going to press Kit for it. But I thought maybe she was short and kind of ashamed to face us."

"How did she leave here?" I asked. "I mean, did she go by cab?"

"I suppose so." he replied. "She kind of just– slipped out. We, none of us, saw her go."

I felt for my wallet. "Did she owe you any money?"

Greene waved his hands. "No, no, no. Not a bit of it."

I asked if I could see Kit's old room. It had been rented to another tenant of course, Greene said– but if I thought it would help, he was happy to show it to me. I followed him up the stairs to the top floor, to a quaint arched door of a corner room at the front of the building.

"Don't think anyone's home at this hour, but I'll just check." he said, tapping on the door. When no one answered, he opened it. "Most folks don't lock their doors here" he said at my surprised look. "I'll leave you to it. Take as long as you like." he said, and left me.

The room was like the rest of the place– quiet, slightly eccentric, with slanted ceilings and walls at odd angles, painted a soft orange, the color of sunset. The furniture looked like walnut, old and a little scuffed but good quality. The turret in the northwest corner was equipped with a new velvet-upholstered easy chair and a floor lamp. I could picture Kit sitting there, reading, or dreaming.

...I'm like The Lady of Shallot in my tower bedroom. It looks out over the trees and the mountains (also a billboard for Post's Bran Flakes– but never mind). It's lovely....

"Hello." someone said behind me. I turned to see a woman leaning against the frame of the hall door smoking a cigarette. She wore a plain, sack-like dress of vivid purple with an elaborately embroidered sash tied loose around her hips; the short hemline revealed bare, rather sturdy legs. Her coarse, dark brown hair was cut in a severe blunt bob that didn't flatter the broad planes of her face and thick jaw. I knew her, too, from Kit's letters– an artist of some sort. Her brown eyes lit up with recognition of their own.

"You're Avery– the brother." she said. "Your photo stood on the table, right there. Is Kit come back, then?"

"No." I said. "I came out to– to look for her myself."

"Lena Parrish." she said, offering me one of her hands– wide palmed but with elegant tapering fingers, though the nails were broken and jagged.

"A sculptress's hands." she shrugged. "The skin you love to touch they're not."

Her voice was soft, deep, with a hint of sex about it.

Something brushed against my ankles. I glanced down. It was an enormous red tabby-striped cat.

....Miss Emily's ancient puss more or less rules us all. She has the run of the place.

"Queen Bess." I blurted. The next thing I knew my

eyes had filled up with tears. I turned away, but not before Miss Parrish saw them.

"Come along." she said, and, taking a firm grip of my hand, hauled me across the hall into her own room. It was arranged like Kit's except the bed was pushed into the corner and heaped with embroidered cushions. There were photographs and charcoal sketches tacked up all over the walls and bits of clothing strewn everywhere.

"Not very tidy, sorry. I wasn't expecting company."

She smoothed the coverlet of the bed and invited me to sit while she went through an arch into a dressing room. I heard a bottle clinking around and she came back carrying two glasses filled with a dark reddish-purple liquid, handed me one.

"Bottoms up." she said, touching my glass with hers. It was some sort of wine– a little bitter for my liking but welcomed.

"Okay?" she asked, watching me.

"Yeah." I said.

"I can offer you something more stimulating, if you like."

"No thanks."

"Kit is a real sweet kid." she said. "I've missed her. She talked about you all the time."

"She wrote me about all of you, too. It sounded like she loved it here."

"I thought so. Not that she wasn't a little homesick at times."

"Did she say anything to you at all, about where she was going?"

"No. I'd have told that police detective straightway if I had, though I'm not keen on having any truck with cops. We're very close here, in this building, almost like family. But you know how it is– people get wrapped up in their own lives, don't pay as much attention as they ought to. The last week Kit was here, I don't think I even spoke to her. I was getting ready for an exhibition, spending all my time at the studio; sleeping there too most the time– if I slept. I wasn't around much. Still, I thought she'd have left some word for me before going."

"Did Kit have any men friends here that you know of?"

"There was one man who used to phone up here for her but it wasn't anything romantic. We ragged her about him nursing a pash for her, but Kit laughed and said he was just someone who might know of a job for her."

"You believed her?"

Miss Parrish nodded and took a sip of her wine. "Kit sparked a lot of interest from men. And from women." She looked up at me through her eyelashes. "She didn't do anything to encourage it. Kit was welcomed into our little group here with open arms, but I think we're very– different than what she was used to at home? We tend to be a little jaded, maybe. It was novel and charming to meet a girl who could still blush. Kit's no prude, but we tried to keep our most debauched talk from her virginal ears. I think she enjoyed hearing new ideas though. She came out here to, you know, spread her wings, after all. This is a good place for it."

I finished my wine. She took the glass and looked down at me with her head cocked to one side then the other. "I wonder if you would pose for me sometime? I warn you though, I have to make love with all of my models. It helps my work to know their anatomy, intimately." She grinned at me.

I didn't answer but rose and gave her my contact information- in case she should get word from Kit before I did.

"Look, Miss Parrish–"

"Lena."

"Lena. Thank you for talking to me about Kit. I just want her to be happy. I'll never take her back to– our Mother. I promise her that. You'll tell her if you hear from her, won't you?"

"Yes." she said, and stood on her tiptoes to kiss me on the cheek. "Now, I had better go and join the mad tea party."

CHAPTER 3

I found my way back down to the noisy, frantic corner of Fifth and Main. In front of the hotel, a newsboy with a terrific hustle was making no secret of the fact that he had copies of the evening paper for sale. He was around fourteen or fifteen, a good-looking kid, tall– maybe five-seven. He was dressed in a brown suit that was slightly too small for him but more or less clean and neat.

"Paper, mister?" he asked. He advanced one toward me that had been folded back to the sports pages, meeting my eyes with a clear, steady gaze. His eyes were a remarkable shade of turquoise blue, framed by long black lashes.

I took the paper from him and gave him a quarter. "Keep the change."

"Holy fuck, thanks!" he whooped. The face, which had looked rather stern in repose, was transformed by his grin. I couldn't help grinning back.

"How'd you know I'd want the sports sheets?" I asked.

He pushed his cap back off his forehead. He had black hair that wanted cutting; he pushed it away where it flopped into his eyes. "I dunno, mister. In this job you get real good at sizing folks up. It's the shoes, mostly."

I looked down at my feet. I had on calf leather brogues in two shades of tan, with wing-tips. I guess a lot of sporty fellows were wearing them in the east this season.

"A banker, or your stock-broker types always have black leather, mirror shine– they want the financial pages." the lad went on. "A guy with scuffs on his shoes, holes in the toes, he wants the help-wanted ads– I give that fellow the paper. Maybe he'll buy one from me when he gets a job."

"That's pretty smart, kid."

I glanced over the headlines absently and noted Tod Morgan, the little world junior lightweight champ, was due to defend his title yet again in New York tomorrow.

The lad watched me for a minute with his head cocked then asked, "You like the fights, mister?"

"Yeah, sure." I said. "Why?"

"Well, there's a show Monday night, at the A.C." he said, noting that it was in the nature of a fundraiser to put on a Thanksgiving dinner for all the newsboys. "There's going to be a vaudeville, and Mushy Callahan and Paul Berlenbach and some other guys will be there."

"They're good boys." I nodded. Callahan, "the Newsboy's Idol," had recently won the world light welterweight title, and Berlenbach had until lately been the world light heavy champ. I didn't figure on going, but the cause was a worthy one; I gave him the money and told him to leave me two tickets.

"Thanks a lot, mister."

"What's your name, kid?"

"Robert McElmon, sir." he said, offering me a slightly ink-smeared hand.

"Avery Shepard." I said. We shook. "My pals call me Shep, or Ave if you like. What do the fellows call you?"

"Buster." he grinned again.

The signal at Fifth changed, sending a surge of pedestrians toward to his corner, and he darted off to attend to them. The ladies, I noticed, all bought their papers from him; it didn't matter what kind of shoes they wore. We chatted for a few more minutes during the next lull, then I left him to his business and went back up to my room.

I was named after a dead man: my mother's brother, Avery, who died when she was thirteen. We used to visit his grave, in the Langbourn plot, every year on Decoration Day. No one had been expecting me. My mother almost died having her firstborn, a girl. There wouldn't be any more babies, the doctor said. My father, himself a doctor, agreed. They called the baby Roberta, after him. She was an only child for twelve years, until I came along, and mother dredged up poor, long-gone Uncle Ave. They gave me Robert as a second name but no one ever used it. Then there'd been Kit, but that was another story.

I had just taken off my coat and sat down when someone knocked at the door. I opened it and found a man standing there. He was biggish, with a round-jawed face and a little toothbrush mustache. He wore a poorly-fitted checked suit at least three years behind the mode.

"Shepard? Harrison." he said. "House detective."

I ignored his tendered hand. "Anything the matter?"

"No, no, I just like to meet all the new outter town guests, you know." he said. "I come in?"

"Have I got any choice?" I shrugged.

He sauntered in and he reached into his coat pocket for a cigar. "Mind if I smoke?" he asked as he lit it and took a long draft. "Here on business or pleasure?"

"Personal business." I said.

"Not from Chicago by chance are you, Shepard?" he asked.

I stared at him. "Why do you ask that?"

"Call it a hunch." he said.

Hunch, my ass, I thought. I doped him as the one who'd

gone through my bag earlier. Most of the labels on my clothes were Chicago tailors, either that or New York. It didn't take any Sherlock Holmes.

"I happen to know you've got a rod with you." he went on.

"If you know that, then you also know I've got a permit for it, and that I wear green silk pajamas."

He chuckled. "Hey, you know what they say about Chi? Four out of five folks there carry a revolver—"

"Yeah, and the fifth one has a machine gun." I said.

His face fell. I'd spoiled his joke. So what? That one had whiskers on it in the east.

"As it happens," I said "I'm not from Chi. As you goddamn well know from the hotel register."

"I saw it." he nodded. "I'm just checking up, routine. It ain't like folks never lie on hotel registers."

"What have you got against Chicago anyway?"

"It's them gangster wars they're having, got people jumpy. Our chief of police is afraid some of 'em might come out here."

"Can you blame them? It was snowing like hell back there when I left."

He grinned. "I guess you're awright, Shepard." He took something out from inside his coat and thrust it at me. "Here— compliments a' the house."

It was a bottle of brown-colored liquid, labeled Canadian Whiskey. I looked at him, questioningly. This was a new one.

He shrugged. "It ain't no crime to give booze away. It ain't no crime to drink it in private, neither. Management figures, guests are gonna anyway, better it's the pure quill. Some a' the bootleg they bring in here takes the varnish off the furniture."

"Well," I said, shaking my head, "it's mighty white of them."

He hung about, waiting for me to invite him to sample

26

the stuff with me, I suppose. I didn't, but as soon as he'd gone I had a couple quick ones myself. It was far from rotgut, but the hotel had been rooked if they'd shelled out for uncut stuff. Then I stretched out on the bed and closed my eyes.

I dreamed of Kit. She danced about in her chemise, her wild hair flying everywhere, singing "Waltz Me Around Again, Willie." Then she stopped the record and looked at me, her big hazel eyes filling with tears.

"I'm nobody's baby, Ave." she said. "And everybody knows it but me. Why didn't you tell me?"

When I woke the room was in semi-darkness. For a second or two I couldn't remember where I was, and, squinting at the hands of my wristwatch in the dim light, wasn't even sure if it was morning or night. I sat up and caught a glimpse of my face, tanned but drawn looking, in the mirror of the dressing table. I got up and went to the window, looked out across an expanse of rooftops, the hulks of a few modern buildings, and beyond them, the hazy undulations of purple-blue mountains. The streetlights were on. I could hear Buster below on the corner, still calling his papers, the dull rumble of passing streetcars and auto horns blaring at each other like strange, ancient beasts.

I found I was hungry. Back east, I'd have had supper already, and would be getting ready to go out to the fights or a show. I wasn't up to the formality of the hotel dining room, though. I took the elevator downstairs to the lobby and went out to the corner, where the rush-hour crowds were thinning out and Buster was unloading the last of his sheets.

"Hey, Buster– know any good places to eat around here?" I asked.

The lad expressed himself on the subject at length, pointing and gesturing up this way and that way until I was dizzy.

"You had your supper yet?"

He hadn't, so I invited him to come along with me. We walked up Fifth to Broadway and turned into a coffee shop he'd suggested. I ordered us hot roast beef sandwiches with mashed potatoes, apple pie and coffee. Buster wolfed his down before I'd even had three bites of mine, so I caught the waiter's eye and gestured for him to bring another plate.

"How old are you, kid?"

"Nineteen."

"Bullshit." I said.

He grinned good-naturedly. "I just turned fifteen."

"That's more like it." I said.

I asked him how long he'd been in Los Angeles.

"About a year I guess, maybe a little more."

I thought I detected a hint— a slight one— of the country boy about him. I hadn't heard cursing like his outside of a trench but somehow, in his pleasant, lilting voice it didn't sound half as bad as when some half-literate truck driver screamed the same things in traffic. And he was smart. His vocabulary, while profane, was well developed for his age and he spoke well.

"You go to school?"

"Mmmhmm. The junior high." he said.

"Like it?"

He nodded, swallowing a mouthful of potatoes. "Only I catch hell for falling asleep in class sometimes. And I have to ditch a lot."

"Got any folks out here?"

"Nope." he said, with his mouth full. "You?"

I found myself telling him all about Kit, her dancing, and coming to Los Angeles, and her disappearance. I hadn't meant to. Maybe, something told me he could help. After all, newsboys knew everyone, and everything that went on in their part of the city. I showed him Kit's photograph.

He studied it intently, but shook his head. "I'd remember seeing her around." After a pause, he added, "You say she had a job as a dance instructress?"

"Yeah. The police checked all the dancing schools around here, though. None of them have seen her."

He took another bite of his sandwich and chewed it, thinking. "Maybe she meant a taxi dancer." he said at length.

"A which?"

"A girl who works at a taxi-dance hall. They call 'em instructresses, but that's bullshit. Fellows are really just paying a lady to dance with them."

I just looked at him. "Have you been to any of these places?"

"Gosh— hell no." he said. "I knew a girl worked in one, though."

I drank my coffee, deep in thought. I was fairly sure Frank Ricketts had only investigated legitimate dancing schools. I would never have thought of the taxi-dance halls, myself. There had been dance halls of a sort like what Buster described back when I was his age, only there was no pretense about the girls being instructresses. I couldn't picture Kit going for anything like that, but it was a new angle, worth looking into.

When the waiter brought the check, Buster reached into his pocket. I shook my head. "That's cute, kid, but this is my party."

We paused under the restaurant's marquee and chatted for a few minutes while Buster nimbly rolled a cigarette. On the sidewalk, office girls strolled in packs of three or four, pausing now and then to look at displays in the shop windows; they all turned to make eyes at Buster.

"So where are you off to after this?" I asked.

"I work at the K of C bowling alley tonight, tomorrow night too." he said, and glanced up at the clock above the marquee. "Holy fuck! I almost forgot the time. I'm gonna be late. Thanks again, Ave. I'll see ya."

Back at the Rosslyn I got hold of a phone book and took it upstairs into the reading room, deserted at this hour. There, I jotted down all the names listed under "Dancing Academies and Teachers." They filled two and a half sheets of hotel note paper, but once I used a Gillespie city street guide to cut out the ones that weren't right downtown, there were only a couple odd dozen. I whittled them down still further by crossing off the legitimate schools, those that Frank Ricketts had already visited.

Then I made a new list of those that were left over, and called up Frank just to make sure I was right, that he hadn't already gone around to these other dance halls.

"No, no– 'course I didn't." he'd said. I could feel him blushing over the phone. "Those aren't– well, they only call them instructresses to stay within this side of the law– they're not allowed to supply dance partners for a price, but if they call it a dance lesson, it's okay."

"So I gather. And if they only happen to hire young and good looking ladies for these lessons no one squawks?"

"That's about right. I– well, I went to one of the taxi halls myself a couple of times, when I didn't know anybody here. I tell you, a fellow may learn something at one of those places, but it's not dancing."

"I thought I'd go around to some of them, ask around about Kit."

"Did you go and see Harry Price?"

"Oh, sure I saw him."

"Didn't I tell you he's the goods?"

I read him the names of the places on my second list, and marked off the ones that Frank said were regular public dance halls– the kind where you could take your sweetheart, or your wife, or even your grandmother– and those he said had closed since the book came out. When I was done, I had a list of ten places, with names like the Paradise Dance Academy, Wonderland, Danceland, The Pink Pagoda, The Silver Palace, The Moonlight Ball Room.

I used the street directory again to map out the places that were left and saw that a couple of them, Danceland, and the Moonlight Ball Room, were only a couple blocks away. I could visit them tonight.

I put the list in my pocket next to Kit's picture and went downstairs. People milled about the lobby on their way to the theater or out to supper– an overdressed middle-aged, middle-western couple; parties of young men in dinner jackets– salesmen if I had to guess; a pompous-looking man in evening dress, pacing among the furniture. I bought a pack of Old Golds from the cigar stand and ventured out onto Main Street.

I walked: past half-lit office buildings, cut-rate drugstores, men's haberdashers that sold clothing by weight; a bank, a shooting gallery, a Turkish bath house; a hotel where old men sat in wicker rockers in a lobby of brass-potted palms and velvet portieres; signs that said "We Never Close" in the windows of darkened shop-fronts; Buster's A.C., quiet tonight; used bookstores, tailors, barbers, knife sharpeners, pool halls, and painless dentists; dark stairways that led to rooms and beds for rent; pawnshops with Money to Loan on Anything; Greek cafés, Mexican cafés; barkers selling patent cure-alls; ballyhoo artists out front of burlesque and vaudeville houses touting the greatest show on earth for the money; "For the wise or the otherwise;" picture theaters with deep-set foyers ablaze in white lights and lurid posters advertising the coming attractions. It was a little like Forty-Second Street in New York only cheaper and with fewer tall buildings. The weather was almost balmy. People were out strolling: young gobs with their dates, lone men in loud plaid overcoats, men in pairs, packs of young boys

31

in gaudy sweaters and bell-bottom trousers.

I came to Danceland, which was on the second floor of an aged brick building, above a lunch room. Shadows flitted across the tall, narrow windows, and a bright red and white electric sign promised "75 Beautiful Lady Instructors." It had its own entrance, up a narrow wooden staircase. I could hear an orchestra playing frantic jazz. It stopped abruptly, like someone lifting the needle off a phonograph record. Before I'd gone more than eight steps, it started up again. At the top of the stairs was a cashier's cage. I paid the admission fee and left my hat and coat in the check room then looked around.

It was a large, open room, not unlike places where I'd gone to high school hops, only the dance floor had a railing around the front of it. Corralled on this side of it were men– Chinese, Mexican, Japanese, Filipinos, Italian, mostly, and a few white men. In age they were anywhere from fresh-faced boys in shiny silk suits to old men in their Sunday finest. They ignored each other and gazed intently at the dance floor, where couples fox-trotted and black-bottomed in syncopated time. I saw maybe thirty ladies, some possibly beautiful, but if their partners were being given any instruction in the terpsichorean arts it was being done through telepathy. It was no dancing school.

When the music stopped again, some of the men on my side of the rail bolted through a little swinging door, out onto the floor and made a bee-line for the girls who, in the split second, had abandoned their partners and were standing around, idle. The new men went up to a girl of his choice and handed her something. Then the music started up and they trotted off. It takes longer to describe than to watch in action.

I couldn't picture Kit in a place like this. However much wing-spreading she'd wanted to do, she wouldn't have liked it. It certainly wasn't her kind of dancing.

The room was warm and the air felt heavy. The smells of the place– face powder, perfume, hair oil, sweat, feet, and what all– were overpowering.

Off to one corner there was a long oaken bar, advertising soft drinks. I walked over to it and was immediately attended by the barmaid, a highly-rouged woman with drugstore blonde curls.

"Hi, handsome." she said. "I never seen you in here before. Ya new in town?"

"Yeah." I said. "How does this place work?"

"Well, honey, it's like this: ya buy your tickets at the cashier's. Then ya pick out the gal ya wanna dance with and ya give her a ticket. That's all there is to it."

"How about learning how to dance?"

She winked at me. "Don't ya know how to dance already, a great big fella like you?"

I took the photograph of Kit out of my pocket and showed it to her. "Ever see this girl working here?"

She looked at it, curious, and handed it back to me, shaking her head. "I ain't seen her. You her old man?"

"She's my sister." I said. "She was living here on her own. It's been a while since we've heard from her."

"Gee, that's rough." she said, and patted my hand. "You could ask some of the other gals. But I'd of seen her if she'd been working here. All the gals gotta go through me to sell the fellas their soft drinks."

I believed her. There didn't seem any point in staying and the place was giving me a headache, so I retrieved my hat and coat again and went out to try the second joint on my list.

CHAPTER 4

B y half past midnight Saturday, I'd visited all but two of
the taxi-dance halls and had come around to thinking
that if I heard "Baby Face" or "Sunday" one more
time I might commit murder and no reasonable jury
would convict me.

There was a dispiriting sameness to the places, and to
the girls. In both cases, some were shabbier or livelier than
others; some of the girls were quite pretty, some had engaging
personalities. All wore an air of detachment, a professional
friendliness with no emotion behind their words, their smiles,
their mild flirtations. I was used to New York girls who
affected sophisticated, world-weary poses, but these girls
were, I thought, just plain weary. None of them admitted
knowing Kit.

The Pink Pagoda was my next stop. It was on Hill
Street between Ninth and Tenth in a two-story building of no
particular style, wedged between a three-story electrical
appliance wholesaler on one side and a modern ten-story
office building rendered in green terrazzo on the other. The
Pink Pagoda occupied the entire second floor and had its
own entrance, marked by a small bronze marquee. Suspended
vertically over the sidewalk, a narrow electric sign spelled out

D-A-N-C-I-N-G in pink, green and white. The ground floor housed a men's hat shop and a cafeteria, both closed now.

Someone had put money into the Pink Pagoda. It was designed to impress before a sucker ever got near the ballroom. I pushed through its heavy bronze doors and crossed an expanse of checkerboard patterned floor to a graceful, curved marble staircase. It took me to a mezzanine, which overlooked the colored glass ceiling of the cafeteria dining room below. Here I traipsed along red plush carpeting and mirrored panels set in pink damask-covered walls until I came to an arched doorway framed by columns and gold velvet portieres. Just beyond it was another marble staircase, carpeted in flame-red, orange and jade green, with a scarlet-velvet rope across the bottom step.

A Geryon in a dinner jacket sat at the foot of it. He gave me the once over before letting me give him the half-dollar admission charge. I did and he unhooked the rope and held it back for me to pass through.

Jazz music spilled down the stairs as I made my way up to a large inner lobby. It was all done up in an oriental theme, with more mirrors, and potted palms, and red, black and yellow light fixtures made to look like paper lanterns. Fresh air circulated through church-like, arched windows that looked out over Broadway; they were inset with stained glass that depicted not saints but flowers, and birds and Chinese maidens. A wrought-iron rail with elaborate scroll-work separated the dance floor from the non-ticket holders. The ballroom had a tented ceiling, of green and yellow silk and was twice as long as a high school gymnasium. It appeared to be operating at capacity. The orchestra– piano, two trombones, a banjo, trumpet and saxophone, all going at top speed and volume– performed from a good-sized platform in an alcove at the rear of it, framed by a peaked arch. There was a ticket booth and a coat check room attended by blondes with Chinese headdresses, decked out in black silk pajama coats with Mandarin yellow trousers. I bought a string of blue tickets from the cashier and asked to talk to the manager.

He squinted and looked me up and down. He must have pressed a buzzer or something, because the next moment, a man in a dark suit with a cauliflower ear sidled up to me.

"Is there a problem?"

"This guy wants to see the boss." the cashier said.

"What about?"

"A girl. She's my–"

"You a cop?"

"I'm her brother." I said. "I'm looking for her."

"That so?"

Cauliflower Ear looked at me, and suddenly caught my wrist. He had about three inches and thirty pounds on me, most of the latter around his middle, and an expanse of chest as wide as No Man's Land. I tried to jerk my arm free but he held on, and wrenched it behind my back. "Let's go, pal."

"Where?"

"We aim to please here. Customer wants to see the boss we take him to see the boss."

Cauliflower Ear marched me along through an arched door marked "private" at the far end of the ballroom. Keeping his grip on me, he paused and rapped on a green baize door. A man answered it. He was short and wide, about forty in both age and waistline, with a double-chinned bulldog face and wavy brown hair, heavily pomaded. He raised his thick eyebrows at my escort, who shoved me inside.

It was an office, bare except for a huge desk, a leather chair, and a wooden bench. It had a small, high-up window on the inside wall that must have overlooked the ballroom. A curtain was drawn in front of it now. I could hear the jazz band quacking and barking away, faintly.

"What is this?" the fat man asked.

"This one's raising a ruckus." Cauliflower Ear said.

"About what?"

Out of habit, with my free hand I reached for the photo of Kit in my coat pocket. The big guy came around the desk in a flash and lunged at me while Cauliflower Ear gave my other arm a twist, nearly bringing me to my knees.

"Pat him down." the fat man said.

I didn't carry my gun with me so they found nothing except the photograph, my billfold and a silver cigarette case. They looked inside the billfold, which held nothing but cash, and some state athletic commission licenses. They tossed the billfold and case down on the desk. The second man still held the photo in his pudgy hands. He nodded, and Cauliflower Ear let go of my arm.

"I'll take that." I said, holding out my hand for the photograph.

"What kind of racket you running?"

"I just want to know if she worked here."

He looked at Kit's image again and shrugged. "I never seen her."

"Who does the hiring here?"

"Don't get nervy." he growled, moving closer. I could smell his bay rum shaving cream, the sharp scent of his pomade. "I say I ain't seen her. Too bad. I could use a doll like her."

I reached out to grab the photograph and he took a swing at me, landing a haymaker square on my jaw that I didn't see coming until it was too late. I staggered back and let loose with a left but was hampered by the tight sleeves of my overcoat. Cauliflower Ear grabbed my right arm and spun me so that the punch went wild anyway, and the force of it threw me stumbling into the edge of the desk. He'd taken another swing at me in the meantime and it caught me on the shoulder. I swore, and in a burst of pain shoved my full weight at him, hitting him in his gut. I expected the blow to find soft, yielding flesh. Instead, it was like hitting a tree, and had about as much effect. Cauliflower Ear tried to grab me but unlike Dempsey, I remembered to duck. Just then, I thought I caught a glimpse of a third person in the room, small and pale. Startled, I stood still for a half a second. Something hard hit the back of my head, and I blacked out.

The face hovering above me, framed by ink black hair, was a woman's— oval shaped and milk-white, with brows that were two sloping black slashes above eyes dark as anything. She put something up to my lips. A cup. It had a strange odor. I cursed and shook my head; warm liquid ran down my chin, onto my neck. She started to blur. Maybe I only imagined her.

When I woke up again, I was alone. Someone had laid me out on a leather day bed, with a wet cloth across my forehead. There was a potted fern in a stand, just to one side of my head. A few feet in front of me was a paneled, lacquered screen, painted with scenes of birds and trees. The walls were hung with silk tapestries. Over in one corner was a sink, mounted to the adjacent walls. A light came from somewhere behind me, a lamp. I wore my pants and an undershirt, but my shirt, tie, vest and coat had been removed along with my overcoat and hat. I tried to sit up and fell back, feeling dizzy and slightly nauseous. I heard movement above my head, a faint tinkling of bells, and a woman appeared at my side.

She was in her early twenties, tiny, with a shining black bob that waved softly around her jaw line, showing off an elegant, slender neck. Her mouth, with a too-short upper lip and a full lower one, was bare of any lipstick. She wore ear drops of green jade that nearly swept her bare shoulders and two jade bracelets on her dainty wrists. Rather plain, I thought. Her eyes were the most striking thing about her— their darkness set off by her pearl-white complexion, with heavy lids, deeply shadowed, and curling black lashes. They had an anxious look in them now.

"Oh good. You're awake." Her voice was very sweet, musical. She lifted the cloth off my forehead and placed her hand in its place. It felt soft and cool– her hand, not my head. I recognized the scent of arnica.

"Where am I?"

"Don't you remember?"

"I remember they were beating me...."

"I am sorry about that." she said. "The management here does get a little– overzealous at times. I make no excuses for them, but I will say it's so easy to lose your license in this business. It makes them an easy target for gangsters and shakedown artists."

She spoke perfect English, with no trace of an accent.

I felt my shoulder and groaned. "I'd like to meet those fellows again sometime soon."

She peered at me closely. "Your pupils look normal now. I thought I might have to call for a doctor."

"I'm okay. How long have I been out?"

"About half an hour."

She went over to the sink, and busied herself with a spirit-lamp. The tinkling sound I'd heard was her frock. It was black velvet trimmed with silver beads; the modish, abbreviated skirt had little bells at the hem. She returned with two dainty, handle-less cups and handed one to me. It was warm.

"What is it?"

"It's an herb tea. Drink it this time. It will help you to feel better."

"Who are you?"

"I'm Helen Sing." she said. "I work here as a matron to the girls. This is my private dressing room."

"Where are my clothes and things?"

"Over there." she said. "I'm fixing your shirt up for you. Why don't you rest a little longer?"

Behind me was a hard pressed-back chair and a brass-topped table with a reading lamp on it. Helen Sing sat down in the chair and took up my shirt.

I sat up on one elbow, sipping my tea. It tasted like dirt.

"I never saw cups like these before." I said. "Are they from China?"

"No." she said, amused. "North Los Angeles Street."

I watched her profile as she sewed. Her expression under the lamplight was serene, inscrutable. The jade bracelets clanked with the motion of her arm.

"You're not oriental." I said after a while.

"No," she said, looking at me strangely. "And you're no gangster."

We looked each other over for a moment.

"Maybe I ought to ask them for a job here."

She smiled. "You've got the build for it. Under better circumstances, no doubt you can take care of yourself. I don't think you'd like the work, though."

"I was thinking more like piano player. The one they've got can read music but he can't play it."

"Are you any good?"

"Some people think so."

"You do look... capable." she said, with a little smile. Then she snipped a thread with a pair of little sewing scissors and held up my shirt. "*Et voilà.*"

She handed it to me, and took away my empty tea cup while I sat up and dressed. Helen Sing's handiwork was hardly noticeable. She must have removed the shirt while I was out, and applied the arnica; I imagined the cool soft hands, touching me, then shook my head. I was still a little punch-drunk. She came back with my coat, vest and tie draped over one arm, the photograph of Kit her other hand, to my relief.

"Pretty girl." she said. "Your sister, I think?" I nodded. "I see the resemblance— in the eyes mostly."

"I was trying to find out if she ever worked here."

She looked at the picture again. "The turnover rate is rather high. The girls come and go. But I would remember if I'd seen her before. I haven't. I'm sorry."

Helen watched me while I finished getting dressed. "Are you sure you're all right?" she asked. I nodded. "Then come, I'll show you a way out."

She brought me my hat and overcoat and went to peer out the door. When it was clear, she beckoned to me and we stepped out into a dimly lit hallway, carpeted in red. Black painted doors with ornamental gold scrollwork lined one side of it. I could hear girlish voices, chattering to each other, laughing.

"Them was my last pair a' stockings 'til payday…"

"And then he sez to me…"

"I got it on sale at Blackstone's…"

Helen Sing whispered, close to my ear: "We're closed for the night. The men will be busy up front, counting the money." I could smell her perfume, an exotic, sensual scent.

I followed her up the hallway, which gave out into a wider corridor. There was a door at one end of it, but Helen led me around the corner, down another short hallway. We stopped at a steel door and Helen pushed on it. It swung open with a rusty groan. Cool air rushed in; it helped revive me. I stepped out onto the grated metal landing of a flight of fire stairs. They led down the outside wall of the Pink Pagoda building in a passageway not more than four feet wide between it and the building next door.

She gave me her hand, and I took it in mine. It was the softest hand I'd ever felt. My own palm felt rough, raw.

"You have nice hands." she murmured. "They've done honest work. You weren't serious about getting a job here?"

"No." I said.

"Goodnight– and good luck. I hope you find your sister."

She went back inside, pulling the door closed behind her. I made my way down the steeply pitched stairs and came out onto Hill Street. A party of merrymakers in evening clothes went by on the sidewalk; they'd come from a show–

were singing snatches of songs, repeating jokes they'd just heard, deciding where to go for a late supper. They didn't pay any attention to me. I walked back to my hotel.

CHAPTER 5

"Murder 'im!" somebody screamed.

"Hit him in the slats, kid!"

There were muffled thuds.

A floorboard creaked under my foot.

There was a roar of laughter, followed by applause.

"Okay folks, you had some socks– now time to dip into your sock. All for a good cause. C'mon, cough up." someone was saying into a microphone.

I could hear a volley of metallic clinks as silver dollars and lesser coins were tossed onto a canvas. Boys scurried around sweeping them all into sponge buckets. Smaller boys went around passing a hat for folks who were too far back or had poor aim.

It was Monday night, and I was witnessing Buster's newsboy club boxing show.

The Main Street Athletic Club was in a huge old barn of a building hemmed in between a burlesque house and a bookstore. It had a café on the ground floor where I checked my hat and coat. A winzied, flat-nosed, foghorn-mouthed barker hawking programs and fight magazines at the bottom of a flight of grubby stairs directed me up to the gym floor. Not that any directing was necessary– I could have found it blindfolded– but he seemed to think it was part of the service. It had that combination of liniment and arnica, sweat,

43

dried blood, rosin, stale cigar smoke, and plain old grime that existed only in fight gyms.

There had been an exhibition bout underway in the ring, which was positioned in the center of a large, high ceilinged gymnasium floor. I'd arrived, not by accident, late enough to miss the vaudeville acts. There were wooden chairs several rows deep on all sides, all of them full of men and quite a few ladies. Men were standing along the back wall. I recognized the tall figure of Harry Price towering head and shoulders among them, and looked around for the girl, his daughter. I didn't see her. A blue haze of smoke floated above everyone's heads.

A dapper young man with patent leather hair and a dusting of white rosin across the knees of his dinner suit was introducing Baby Joe Gans.

I heard my own name called out above the din and looked up to see Buster, in the balcony that ringed the main floor. A minute later he had scrambled down the stairs and was standing next to me, and we shook hands.

"How goes it with the dance halls, Ave?" he asked.

Between his jobs and mine, we hadn't talked for more than a few minutes since our meal together the other night. I told him, including my own fistic encounter at the Pink Pagoda, though I glossed over it for the most part. Even so, when I mentioned that I planned to go back there tonight after the show, he frowned, and pushed his cap back off his forehead.

"I better come along with you." he said. "I'm not working tonight."

"That's okay, kid." I said. "You ought to get some rest. You got school in the morning?"

He nodded. "Yeah, but Ave…"

"I'll be fine, kid." I said.

A couple of his pals came up then and asked him to help collect coins; he looked at me, but I waved him on, nodding. I stood and watched the next exhibition.

At the foot of the marble stairs leading up to the Pink Pagoda, I pulled my hat down low over my forehead and raised my overcoat collar around my neck; I handed my fifty-cents to the Geryon and got past his red velvet rope. I shoved a dollar across the counter to the cashier without looking at him and he shoved a string of tickets back at me. Then I gave my hat and coat to one of the blonde Mandarins and stood behind the wrought-iron railing with a few dozen other men. I waited for the music to end. When it did I picked out the first girl I saw and danced with her. She was a brunette and chewed gum. She didn't recognize Kit.

At the song's end there was another great rush for girls. I spotted a cute, lively girl to my right, a pale blonde, but someone had already snatched her up– a paunchy man in a blue silk suit. I quickly found an unoccupied girl and handed her a blue ticket. The music started up. We danced, mechanically, to a fox trot. She stared, blinking, at the photo of Kit but shook her head. The music ground to a halt. Thanksawfully– g'bye.

The third try, I made a beeline for the lively blonde, narrowly beating out a young man in a plaid suit. She wore a white spangled gown and silver slippers, and had shapely legs in flesh colored stockings.

"Well, hello." she said, assuming the fox trot position with a friendly grin. She had a long, graceful neck topped by a plump-cheeked round face, liberally powdered and rouged, and wide, blue eyes that wore an ingenuous expression.

"Hello yourself." I said. We introduced ourselves. She was "Gladys." I was "Ave." Girls weren't hard to get to know at these places, I'd found. The music started at a frenzied pace.

"Say, yer some swell dresser." she shouted over the din. "You ain't from around here, are ya?

I showed her the picture of Kit. "Have you seen this girl around?"

She glanced at it, curiously. I thought there was a

flicker of…something, behind the naïve gaze, but only for a second. Then she looked up at me, making them wider. "I might've done." she said. "I don't remember so good when I'm thirsty."

I tried to keep my voice even. "Will you come out with me after this joint closes, then?"

Gladys assumed a prim expression. "The matron don't allow us to make dates with customers." she said.

"So, what's a fellow to do if he likes a girl?"

She leaned forward and whispered near my ear: "Meet me in the auto park by the corner. After one."

The song screeched to an abrupt end just as I was saying "You recognized the girl, didn't you?"

Gladys let her arms fall to her sides. "Sorry– I can't dance with ya unless ya gimmie another ticket." she said, making it sound as if she really, truly regretted this fact.

I fished one of the little blue tickets out of my vest pocket and started to hand it to her but was beaten to the punch by the man in the plaid suit who had danced with Gladys earlier. He was surprisingly nimble for a large man, and quick.

"Hiya 'gain, toots." he said, ignoring me.

"Pick another lady." I said. "This one's taken."

"Oh yeah?" he sneered, and turned toward Gladys. The music started up.

I tapped his shoulder. "Cutting in."

"Vamoose, pal. This ain't the junior prom." he said.

I wanted to take a swing at him then, but Gladys winked at me over his shoulder and nodded her chin toward the door. I turned to see a bouncer, my cauliflower-eared friend from the other night, advancing toward us. I started to make a run for it but wasn't quick enough; he caught me and wrenched my arm into a vice hold.

"Damned if it ain't Peck's Bad Boy, back again. Well this time we won't be so friendly with you."

He marched me not toward the office this time but out of the ballroom and into a hallway. I had been down it before, with Helen Sing. We rounded the corner and stopped at what I recognized as the exit to the fire stairway. He pushed the metal door open and shoved me out. I pitched forward onto on the metal landing.

"I don't have to tell you what'll happen if I catch your mug here again. Or then again, mebbie I do. You're don't seem too bright." he said, and hit me in the gut.

The door closed with a bang from the inside. There was no moon and almost no light from anywhere else. I stood there a minute, trying to get my wind back. Glancing down I felt the ground spin so I shut my eyes and clutched at the metal rail. I was chilled; my coat and hat were still in the checkroom. Still dizzy, I started down the stairs and had got about halfway when I thought I heard the metallic scrape of the door opening behind me. I started to turn around, but as I did, something hit my right shoulder. I let go of the hand rail. Then I was falling, down the stairs. I made myself go limp. I kept on falling.

They used to say when you Go West, there's a bright light. I saw one now. But only for a moment. Then everything went dark again.

The next thing I knew, someone was mopping my forehead with a wet cloth and swearing, badly. I half-opened my eyes and groaned.

"He's come to." the someone said. It was Buster, crouched down next to me.

The person with him was also on his knees. It was Harry Price. He held a flashlight that cast weird shadows over his granite features. The thought that it had been Harry Price behind the bright light I'd seen earlier struck me as high hilarity. I started to laugh. Or at least, I think I did. My chest hurt with the effort.

I must've passed out again, because when I woke up, this time I was undressed and in a bed. It was my bed, at the

47

Rosslyn. A man, a doctor by his white coat, was looking me over.

"...may have a brain concussion. Nothing seems to be broken, but I wouldn't rule out–" he was saying. Then he noticed I was awake, and introduced himself as Dr. Williams, the house physician. "How are you feeling?"

"Just peachy." I said.

Someone snorted, over to the right of my feet. Harry Price sat in the arm chair, in the corner by the window, smoking a cigar.

I tried to raise my arm to look at my wrist-watch and winced as a sharp pain ran through it. It was probably too late to meet Gladys, anyway, even if I could get up, which I wasn't sure about.

"Try to keep that arm still for now." the doctor said. I had several abrasions on my head, he told me, and some bad scrapes and bruises, mostly on my upper body, but no serious damage that he could see. "Some of those bruises didn't get there tonight." he said. "What are you, a prizefighter?"

"I feel more like a punching bag."

"Mr. Price here thinks you were robbed. Did you have your billfold on you?"

"Yeah– and a silver cigarette case, a signet ring, and a wrist-watch. Shit." The wrist-watch was a Waltham Khaki, Army model, a gift from my father, and the signet ring had belonged to him. The other things I was sorry to lose, but were replaceable.

"I don't know what things are coming to today." he said. "I hope you won't hold it against Los Angeles, and enjoy your visit anyway. Lucky for you, Mr. Shepard, you must have a hard head."

"I'm lucky alright."

"We'd better let you get some bedrest for the night." Dr. Williams said, adding that he would give me a prescription for some liquor if I needed it. He'd be back to check on me in the morning.

Harry didn't follow the doctor out right away. "That's

the problem with you elevator babies." he said. "You're soft. You can't even go down a little flight of stairs without getting windy."

"How'd you find me?" I asked.

"The kid told me what you were up to. He was worried, and I didn't like the sound of it, so we went after you."

He came over next to my bedside and placed my cigarette case, ring, wallet and watch on the night table. "I told the doc that story and said I found you in the alley here. I didn't think you'd like him getting too nosey. What's the real dope?"

"It was dark. The stairs were wet." I said. "I slipped."

"Uh-uh. That won't wash." he said. I ignored him. "I know your sister was living here, and she's been missing over a month."

"Buster– the boy– told you."

"Naw. I went through your coat while you were out." he said. "You think she had some connection to the Pink Pagoda?"

"I'm handling it." I said.

"That's going real well for you, I can see." he said. "This isn't like the east. Things operate different here."

My head hurt and I was fed up with him treating me like a kid not yet dry behind the ears. I'd been earning a man's wage since I was fifteen, and fought in a world war.

"Look, I appreciate you being on the spot tonight, but I've been wearing long pants for a quite a while now." I said.

I turned away, onto my bad shoulder, and held back a groan.

Harry didn't say anything. I listened, waiting, wondering why he didn't take a hint and leave me. "I'd like to get some sleep–" I said finally. No one answered. Harry was gone.

CHAPTER 6

I stood outside in the drizzle leaning up against somebody's Oakland-Six sedan in the auto park that took up a lot of valuable real estate just down the block from the Pink Pagoda. There was again no moon. A pair of mushroom-shaped outdoor lights mounted on poles around the perimeter of the lot couldn't cut through the gray fog of the night. My body ached all over. My head was okay, though. The doc had checked me out. No brain concussion. I'd stayed in bed, like a good boy, for most of the day. Buster came up to visit me in the late morning and brought the papers. I'd told him I planned to stay in and rest all night. I didn't want him to worry.

My hat and coat had been sent over by messenger this morning from the Pink Pagoda check room. I figured I had Helen Sing to thank for that.

All that time on my back had given me time to think. Despite what I told Harry Price, that fall of mine had been no accident. I'd had help down those stairs. The fuss that had been kicked up over my asking questions at the Pagoda– that too was strange. Maybe it was true what Helen said, that they thought I was trying to shake them down. All of the other places I'd visited were in the same boat, though, and none of them had minded my asking questions, in some cases had been anxious to help. Then there was Gladys's hint that she recognized Kit. Maybe she'd just been stringing me along, and maybe not. It was the best thing I'd had to go on so far, though.

So I waited for her. I had company. The attendant sat hunched in his little shed, hunched under an umbrella and reading a dime thriller by flashlight. There was a purple and lavender custom Cadillac sedan parked at the curb, with a uniformed driver pacing around on the sidewalk, smoking and idly watching the people going by. At least a dozen other men lurked about in the shadows. Some were in cars, parked out at the curb; I could see the driver of one, the tip of his cigarette, now and again and the gleam of a silver flask and wondered what kind of husbands, or boyfriends, or brothers let a girl they cared anything about come to places like this and dance with other men for money. I'd never have let Kit do it, if I'd known. But, if she had, I hadn't known. I was too busy working– and having a good old time– to bother finding out.

With effort I could hear the Pink Pagoda band through the ballroom's open windows, muffled like a Victrola with the speaker doors closed. They sounded like a barnyard, all quacks and barks. Then, finally, they played "Goodnight" and after that the second floor fell silent. Men came out of the front doors and went their separate ways. About a quarter of an hour later, bevies of girls started streaming past along the sidewalk. Horns ahoogaed. The auto park slowly emptied. For a minute I thought I must've missed Gladys. Then I spotted her– wearing her hat and coat with a little silver bag, like chain mail, over her gloved wrist.

I threw my cigarette away and fell into step with her. "Hello. Remember me?"

She gave me a dark stare. "Sure I do. You're the feller stood me up last night." she said. Then she noticed my face. I had a pretty nice bruise on one cheekbone, and a gash above my upper lip. "Lord sakes, what happened?"

"Just a little accident." I said. "That's why I couldn't

51

meet you. I'll do my best to make it up to you tonight, though, if you're game."

"I already got a date." she said, casting her eyes around the auto park.

"Give him the air." I said. "Come out with me instead."

She hesitated and bit her lower lip. "Whaaal, I guess so." she said, eyeing me sidelong. "Ya got a nice mug, 'spite it bein' all bunged up."

"Yours isn't bad either." I said.

"Where's your bus?" she asked, looking around the now nearly empty auto park.

"I haven't got one." I said. She sucked in her lips and glared like I'd said I forgot my wallet at a restaurant when the bill came. "I'll get us a cab." I added quickly. "A taxi in a taxicab?"

That broke her up.

"Never mind, big fella." she laughed. "A bunch of the gals has been talking about a new place that's got cocktails and an orchestra and it stays open all hours. It's not far— I guess we kin walk to it" she said. "It's supposed ta be expensive, though."

"Anything to oblige a lady." I said.

We strolled north along the mostly empty and dark street. The next block was livelier with heavy foot traffic. A crowd on the west side of the street huddled under a vaudeville house-picture theater marquee waiting for a cab or their drivers. Electric signs blazing white, and red, green, or orange reflected off the wet pavement; drips of rain hissed off their light bulbs. I had a glimpse of Buster, rounding the corner in the other direction with a couple of girls— flashy, chorine types by the look of them. Gladys's building was on Eighth, The Bamboo Garden. It was two stories high and had Roman arches along the upper level; an electric sign mounted to one of the columns read "Chop Suey." The inside was done up in an oriental motif like the Pink Pagoda with red carpeting and painted tapestries in bamboo frames on the walls, and big brass pots planted with, I supposed, bamboo. The staff was oriental and male; they wore uniforms of embroidered Chinese silk. I checked my hat while Gladys went to the ladies rest room to powder her nose. Then I tipped the head waiter, or whatever he was called here, and we were escorted through a large Roman arch into the main dining room. It had banks of red-plush upholstered divans along the side walls with little tables for two dispersed in front of them, and larger tables for four ringing the dance floor. It was lit overhead by a huge art glass dome. A mezzanine ringed the room on three sides, where the Roman arches had been disguised by elaborate bamboo panels and railing. There was a stage, elevated like a minstrel's gallery, at the back of the room where a Hawaiian dance orchestra played "Baby Face."

Gladys looked all around, gaping unabashedly. She turned back to me with a smile. "Gee, this place is as swell as the girls said."

"It's the gnat's knickers alright." I said. Her hair smelled of roses and cigarette smoke. Gladys had looked exhausted from her night's work but now seemed to have caught a second wind and wanted to kick up her heels and play. If this had been a real date I might have played along with her, but all I wanted was to find out what she knew about Kit, if anything.

"You were going to tell me about this girl." I showed her the picture of Kit again. "Did she work at the dance hall? Her name's Kit Shepard– Katherine."

"I want a cocktail first."

I sighed. "Which one?"

"Oh, I dunno. How 'bout one of the naughty sounding ones?"

"Between the Sheets?"

She giggled and blushed while I ordered one for her. I didn't care for cocktails, didn't want to drink tonight in any case, but I asked for a rye, neat, for myself, and two plates of

53

noodles.

While we waited for our food, I made small talk.

"Why do you work in the dance hall, kid? You like it?"

She shrugged. "I dunno. I like ter dance, and a lot of nice fellers come in- like you. Some of 'em are nice anyway."

I tried to ask her again about Kit but she started to get mad. Her "Don't rush me, big fella" was delivered lightly, but there was an edge to it that told me she might be one of those who got stubborn if pushed. I forced myself to be patient.

When our food came Gladys asked me to get her a second cocktail.

"Okay." I said easily. "Want another Between the Sheets?"

"Are ya getting' fresh with me?" Gladys asked, good humor restored.

While we ate Gladys prattled on about manicures, about what this girl had said to her, and what she'd said back, about her wardrobe. "I wanna get me one of them velour coats with a genuine beaverette collar. I saw one last week in the window at Coulter's. Gee, it was swell...."

I was only half-listening. A waiter in heliotrope silk was seating a couple at a table on the mezzanine almost directly opposite our table. The woman was Helen Sing. I could see only see the black-clad back of her companion. Helen looked down and glanced our way just then. Her eyes met mine and she smiled, bowing with a little nod. I nodded in return.

"Saaayy, buddy boy, ain't you even listenin' to me?" Gladys cut in.

"Sure I am. I heard every word. I'll buy you that coat tomorrow, if you want."

"Ya mean it?" Gladys squealed, and kissed me, impulsively. "Gee you're nice. You don't hafta. It's sweet of ya though."

"Isn't that the matron from the Pagoda, up there?"

"Where?" Gladys said, craning. Her face went white under all the rouge.

"She's seen us." I said. "Don't worry– I'll go square things with her."

"Oh, no, ya ain't gotta–." she started to protest.

I ignored her and shouldered through the throng in the lobby then made my way up the stairs, over to Helen Sing's table.

She was alone now, smoking a thin, dark cigarette in a jade holder inset with red stones.

"Mr. Shepard." Helen said, offering her hand.

She had on a plain black sheath made out of some kind of clinging stuff, with an orchid velvet wrap draped over her shoulders. Her black hair gleamed like a cap. She wore the jade ear drops, and no makeup except for a little red lipstick. Compared to her, Gladys– and most other women in the place– seemed like over-painted dolls.

"This seat taken?" I asked.

"Not for the moment. Sit, please."

"Thanks, I'm still a little woozy." I said.

She surveyed my face. "Now you do look like a gangster." Her expression turned serious. "I am sorry about what happened. I've complained about the bouncers."

"You know, I'm getting the feeling I'm not welcome at that establishment." I said. "Obliged to you for sending my coat and hat back to me."

She didn't reply, but took another cigarette out of an enameled case, and inserted it into the holder. I lit it for her and one for myself. A waiter brought her a cocktail, something with crème de violette in it.

"Would you like anything?" she asked.

I shook my head. "I just came over to say the girl didn't want to come out with me tonight. I more or less forced her to. I hope I haven't made any trouble for her."

Helen smiled, and glanced down at Gladys. "She's a very attractive girl."

55

"It isn't like that. I only took her out because—because I think she might know something about my sister."

I don't know why I said it. A fellow could do worse than Gladys. She was a little flashy, maybe, but I didn't hold that against her.

"Your love life is none of my business." Helen shrugged, and undid the clasp of her little silver beaded handbag. She took out a handkerchief, and dabbed the corner of my mouth with it. "One of your cuts must've opened up. You're bleeding." She said, showing me the cloth. It was tinged with red. Not blood, after all, but Gladys's lipstick.

"Going out with the customers is a serious breach of my rules, Mr. Shepard. All a place like the Pagoda needs is for some religious crank to find out about it and scream to the papers about it being a pit of immorality. But I do feel I owe you a favor. I'll let it go."

"Thank you." I nodded to her. I stood up and turned to go. Down below, through the dancers, I glimpsed my own table. There was a man sitting with Gladys. I could see his tuxedo-clad legs stretched out in front of him under the table, and his face, with a round, almost completely bald head, in profile.

Helen spoke again. "If you think that girl can tell you anything except what the bottom of a glass looks like, you're nuts. Alcoholism is a hazard of the job, I'm afraid. One of them." she said.

I made my way back downstairs to Gladys, who was by herself. Her dress strap had slipped down off her shoulder. I put it back where it belonged as she snuggled up to me, clutching my arm.

"Who was that man?" I asked.

She gave me a slightly piffled smirk. "Whattsa matter honey, ya jealous? How was the old dragon?"

"Oh, everything's jake." I said. "She's not going to do anything."

Gladys gave a little smile. "Oh yeah? Well, as a matter o' fact, I might not be workin' there too much longer, I'll tell the big, flat world. I just might be gettin' fed up with the crummy joint."

She sipped her cocktail, her third if I was counting. When she turned away to watch the dancers out on the floor I poured half of it into a poor, innocent potted bamboo plant. I hoped they would give it a proper burial. She didn't notice, and nodded when I suggested that it was time we made our exit.

I went to retrieve my hat and pay the check. As I left the cashier's, I collided with a woman coming out of the hallway that led to the ladies' rest rooms. She was a stunner, fairly bursting with pulchritude, with white-blonde, marcelled hair tied 'round with a silver bandeau and a pale, mask-like complexion setting off blood-red lips. She looked up at me sullenly.

"I'm– uh– er, beg pardon." I said.

"Why don't you watch where yer going?" she snapped.

Just then, her companion came along from the direction of the check room to collect her. A black derby covered his baldness now but I recognized him as the gent who'd been sitting with Gladys. He was an older man with a neat gray goatee. He wore impeccably tailored evening clothes, with a mother-of-pearl collar button and shirt studs and platinum cufflinks inset with diamonds. He glanced at me with thunderous black eyes, and the two of them swept past me out into the lobby.

Gladys had fallen asleep at the table; her head was pressed back against the divan cushion and her mouth gaped open a little. I shook her awake and got her up on her feet. She sagged her full weight against my body and I put my arm around her waist, half dragging, half carrying her up the few steps to the front doors and out onto the sidewalk. There was a break in the rain. For a minute Gladys seemed to revive in the fresh damp air.

"Where do you live, baby?" I asked. She gave me her address; it was a rooming house a few blocks away. I looked around for a cab; all of them coming around the corner were engaged. I held Gladys around the waist, and she leaned on me with both of her arms around my middle. I finally managed to flag down an empty cab, and poured her into it. She fell back against me with a giggle as the cab lurched forward. I rolled the windows down for the short ride, hoping it might sober her up but it didn't. The cab driver delivered us to the corner of Sixth at Hope, where Gladys lived.

"Good luck, pal." he grinned at me as I lifted her out. I didn't tip him.

Gladys roomed on the second floor. I lugged her up the stairs and leaned her against the wall while I fished the key out of her bag. Then I carried her inside, like a bride, and eased her onto a lumpy davenport.

It was an older apartment with a kitchenette and another alcove leading to a tiny dressing room and bathroom. There was a disappearing bed already pulled out from its hiding place in a china cabinet. I went around it into the bathroom and brought back a tumbler of water. Gladys had flopped forward, her face pressed against a pink satin boudoir pillow. I shook her, and pulled her shoulders back. I splashed some of the water on her face and slapped it, gently. She opened her eyes.

"C'mon, kid, wake up so you can go to bed." I said.

She opened her eyes a little and stared at me, open-mouthed. "I could rilly go fer you, daddy." she said. Then she passed out.

CHAPTER 7

The light rain of the night before had turned into a regular downpour by the next morning. When I went downstairs to get a shave, I saw Buster hard at work, neither his hustle nor his cheerful nature dampened outwardly by the weather. With typical boyish bravado, he wore no raincoat or rubbers himself but had his papers protected with a sheet of oilcloth. I bought one from him and read that Russ Whalen, of Chicago, won his fight against the local boy, Turkey Thompson, on points.

I told Buster, briefly, about my adventures with Gladys. He listened, frowning. "I wish you'd a told me, Ave. You shouldn't even be out and about yet."

"I'm okay. The doc was just being an old hen" I said. "Besides, you were busy."

He looked surprised and ducked his head, flushing. By the bluish circles under his eyes, it had been a late night.

"You can come along with me now, if you want to." I said "I was going to take the lady out to breakfast. Maybe you can get something out of her."

He'd just have time before he had to get to school, he said. So after he'd sold out his papers, we walked over to Gladys's. The apartment building looked shabby in the gray morning light. A couple of small boys in knee pants and galoshes were splashing around in the puddles between parked automobiles. A large, heavy-lidded man in overalls and a cap, with a dinner pail over his arm, came plodding up from the opposite direction at the same time we were arriving and let us in to the lobby with him. The upstairs hallway, outside Gladys's door, rang with the sound of pipes rumbling as folks drew their morning baths, and the air was thick with the odor of bacon cooking. Gladys didn't answer my knock. Still sleeping it off. I tried again, louder.

The door of the room across the way flew open and a woman poked her head out. She looked startled to see the two of us there, and stepped out into the hallway. She was maybe in her late twenties, thick-necked and stout, with brown bobbed and marcelled hair. She was dressed in a starched white uniform, like a nurse and held a plump, blond baby in her arms.

She looked back and forth from me to Buster, then asked, guardedly: "You looking for Gladys?"

"Yeah. I'm a friend of hers." I said and hoped I wouldn't have to admit I was such a good friend that I didn't even know Gladys's last name.

"I've got to get to work and I didn't know what to do about Charley." she said. "My man's asleep and I don't like to wake him."

I shook my head. "I'm not sure I follow you, missus uh–?"

"It's Earl." she said. "Mabel Earl. This is Charley." she added, bouncing the baby a little on her hip.

I introduced myself and Buster. Buster grinned at Charley, who smiled back. "So, Gladys watches your baby for you while you're at work?"

"It's the other way 'round." Mrs. Earl said. "I watch him for her. She works nights, you know, just like my man. When she didn't come for him first thing like usual, I went ahead and gave him a bottle. I thought I'd let the poor kid sleep in a little, Gladie I mean. She works hard. An' she's never neglected Charley. I don't like to get her in trouble. She didn't answer when I knocked. I don't know what to do. I can't be late for work."

I turned back to the door and pounded on it this time. There was no answer. I looked up at the transom; it was closed.

Buster and I shoved our combined bulk against the door and heaved. But the lock had been made to last and wasn't going anywhere just yet.

"Which way 'round to the service entrance?"

"Through there." Mrs. Earl said, pointing to a side hall door. I raced through it, Buster at my heels. There were stairs here and a window that gave out onto the fire escape. We found Gladys's door unlocked. I dashed through the kitchenette into the living room.

After Gladys passed out, I'd taken off her hat and coat and her shoes and put her to bed, in her dress and stockings, pulling the blanket up over her. She was still in bed as I'd left her but she wasn't sleeping, not exactly. No one, no matter how big a tear the night before, sleeps that soundly. I tried shaking her, anyway. She didn't move. She felt stiff. Her skin was bluish white, and purplish around the lips and nostrils. I leaned my ear down toward her mouth but couldn't hear any sound of breathing.

Buster came up behind me. "She's not dead is she?"

"No." I said. "Not yet."

I unlocked the front door from the inside and opened it. Mrs. Earl stood there with the baby.

"Where's a 'phone?"

"In here." she said, gesturing across the hall to her own apartment. She peered past me at Gladys's prone form. "Is she–? Oh my Gawd!" she screamed. Charley, frightened then, began bawling his head off.

I had already brushed past them and found the telephone. A cheerful-voiced operator connected me to the emergency hospital and I told them to send a police ambulance.

Mrs. Earl had come in and was seated on the

61

davenport; she said nothing but kept smoothing the skirt of her dress with her hands, perfunctorily. Buster held the baby, who'd stopped his crying and looked at Buster with wide blue eyes. I went outside to wait for the police ambulance. Within a minute or two I could hear the wail of a siren, getting louder. It came to a halt out front and four men in white came in with their stretcher. I directed them upstairs.

A few neighbors— schoolchildren, women in bungalow aprons or wrappers, and a couple of men in work clothes— were hovering around in the hallway outside Gladys's room. They parted, silently, for the ambulance crew.

A fifth man had raced up the stairs on their heels, and entered the apartment now as if he belonged there. He surveyed the scene at a glance and whipped out a pad of paper from his coat pocket and a pencil from behind his ear and began writing.

"What is it— a murder?" Vargas asked, trying to peer around the white-coated men who were working on Gladys.

"Get out of my way, Vargas." one of them said, glaring at the interloper.

"What— oh hell, the goddamn Press here already?" said another.

"She isn't a stiff— yet."

"Looks like alcohol poisoning."

"Another one?"

They loaded Gladys onto a stretcher.

"Get back all of you, damn it."

The crowd in the hall had increased, all pressing closer to Gladys's doorway, buzzing. There was a gasp and some excited screams when they came out with Gladys, covered with a sheet up to her shoulders. A couple of tough-looking types came up the stairs in their wake. One was tall, with an athletic build. The other was short and slight. I couldn't help but think if they switched suits they could've made a swell vaudeville act.

The taller of the two flashed a city police detective badge and addressed the assembly in a strident, flat-toned voice. "Any of you folks got anything to say? If not– beat it."

The curiosity seekers slouched off, back to their rooms or off to work. The reporter stayed put. I stayed put. Buster stood in Mrs. Earl's doorway holding Charley. The detectives looked us over.

"Good Lord, Vargas– how'd you beat us here?" the man who hadn't spoken yet asked the newspaperman, looking at him in disgust.

I couldn't blame him. Vargas was around my age– late twenties– and probably my weight, though he was at least four, maybe five inches shorter. His eyes were bloodshot and he was several hours overdue for a shave. He wore a battered and creased felt rolled brim hat that had once been green– probably– now the worse for being rain spattered. His suit looked like he had slept in it, and his tie, which flapped loose on the outside of his vest, was either a very clever modernistic design or he'd been using it for a pen wiper.

He didn't seem the least daunted by the cold reception but grinned and pushed the offensive hat back off his head, revealing a thick crop of unruly brown hair. "I was heading home when I heard the meat wagon and thought I'd come have a look-see." His mouth turned down. "It's a bust, though. An alchy poisoning don't even rate the third page anymore."

"No one's beggin' you to stay." the short detective said, gesturing toward the stairs with his thumb.

"Who says it's alchy poisoning anyway?" the tall one growled. Vargas went, and they turned their attention to me.

"You the one called for the ambulance?" the tall one asked.

"Yeah." I said.

I followed them into Gladys's vacant apartment. They glanced around and the short one raised the blinds. It was a typical rooming house room, better cared for than some, maybe, with the usual golden oak furniture, fading floral wallpaper, woodwork hidden under layers of paint. The bedclothes were torn apart where the ambulance men had worked on Gladys and somebody had knocked over the cane-seated chair just inside the front door where I'd placed her gloves and bag last night, but otherwise the place was tidy. Gladys had attempted to give it some personality– there were photos of film stars tacked up on the walls, and a newspaper rotogravure likeness of Rudolph Valentino, a piece of black crepe pinned over it; on the bed-china cabinet was a goo-goo-eyed Kewpie chalk doll in a painted-on bathing suit and artificial flowers in green glass Woolworth vases. Cheap machine-made lace tatting covered the back cushions of the lumpy davenport, which also held satin boudoir pillows and a hideous flapper doll with a curled blond wig and absurdly long arms and legs splayed every which way. The lamp table was covered with a pile of confession magazines, a couple of novels with lurid paper jackets, a theater program, and a religious tract of some sort. Gladys's coat, draped over the arm of the davenport where I'd left it looked threadbare and much mended in the daylight.

The tall detective turned back to me. "So who are you, Mac?"

I came out with the whole story, most of it anyway– about going to the Bamboo Garden, how Gladys acted pretty lit up after three drinks, how she'd passed out, and that I'd put her to bed and gone home to my hotel.

"Had she been drinking before she met you?" the short one asked.

"She didn't act like it." I said. "She'd been at work."

"Where's that?"

"The Pink Pagoda– it's a taxi-dance hall."

The two of them exchanged a glance and nodded.

"So, you didn't give her anything to drink?"

"Not personally, no."

"Didn't you have the same stuff?"

"No." I said. "Hers was rum. Mine was supposed to be whiskey. I didn't drink much of it anyway."

"What time did you say you left here?"

"I didn't say. I did leave, though. The girl was passed out cold. It was about quarter-past three." I said. "She seemed okay– just going to sleep it off I thought."

"Did she seem upset about anything last night?"

"No." I said, honestly. "In fact, she seemed awfully pleased with herself, now I think about it. She said she might not have to work at the dance hall much longer."

They exchanged another glance. I hadn't put any sinister motive to Gladys words. She certainly hadn't talked like a girl planning to do herself in and I said so, for what it was worth.

I gave them a few more details– my name, where I was staying, what I was doing in Los Angeles. I mentioned Frank Ricketts' name.

The short one nodded. "Okay, Shepard. I guess that's all for now. You'll have to come down to headquarters and give a formal statement."

I waited while they went into the bathroom and came back with a collection of bottles: brown ones of syrup of figs and iodine, clear ones of Danderine hair tonic, Listerine, Djer-Kiss perfume. The kitchenette yielded a bottle of bluing, a jug of Clorox disinfectant and a tin can of gasoline.

They chatted as they worked– the short one went on about his Thanksgiving day plans to go to the midget auto races and wondered whether they would be cancelled on account of the rain, while the tall one complained about having to dress up and go to his in-law's. Their mood sobered, though, when Buster came in with Charley and I told them that he– the baby– was Gladys's child. Suddenly she wasn't just a "dance hall girl" but a young mother.

"What'll you do with him?" Buster asked, tightening his grip on the infant.

The detectives looked at each other and the tall one swore under his breath. Neither seemed keen to take charge of the baby themselves.

"She got any family local? What about the father?"

65

the short detective asked me.

I shrugged. "It didn't come up in conversation."

We went across the hall to ask Mrs. Earl. Gladys, it appeared, was separated from her husband "or something." She had a mother who lived in town somewhere, Mrs. Earl thought. The mother and Gladys didn't "get on."

Mrs. Earl glanced at the clock on the china cabinet. "It's just awful what's happened to Gladie, but if I don't get to work I'll lose my place." she said.

The detectives took down her information. She was a manicurist, at the Savoy Hotel barber shop down the street. Buster and I agreed to go along to police headquarters and bring Charley; they'd get a matron to care for him until Gladys's family could be located. Mrs. Earl thrust his bottle at us and hurried away to her job. Back in Gladys's rooms Buster found a warm dress and wool leggings and a little hat for Charley and dressed him while the detectives gathered up several of the liquid containers to take away. It seemed an unlikely thing to me that Gladys would have woke up from her stupor, taken something, replaced it, and crawled back into bed, but I guess they were just following procedures.

Police Headquarters was an old, rusticated stone building that had seen a lot of use. The emergency receiving hospital, where they'd brought Gladys, was adjacent. Inside, the waiting room smelled of mold, cheap yellow soap, sweat, stale cigar smoke and I don't know what all and didn't want to go on smelling it, trying to figure it out.

I left Buster in the lobby and wound my way up through a rabbit warren of grubby partitioned offices, past a switchboard, a teletype. Fat, black electrical wires were strung everywhere. I finally found the Homicide unit and sat down at a desk and wrote out my statement. I gave it to the tall detective, who was a Det. Lt. Hoyt. Then I wound my way through the rabbit warren once more to try to find Ricketts and say hello. His desk was empty. He was out on a case.

Back downstairs, I found Buster, solemn-faced, staring blankly at a picture calendar on the wall. Charley had been carried off by a police woman. We went over to the receiving hospital to check on how Gladys was doing. They wouldn't tell us anything, of course. There was nothing more we could do. Neither of us had eaten, so we walked down the hill to a café on the corner. I had a hamburger and coffee. Buster's appetite seemed normal enough for him— he ate corned beef hash with poached eggs, a basket of hot biscuits, and a slice of apple pie— but he was quieter than usual and smoked cigarette after cigarette.

"Look— they'll take good care of the kid down there, don't make yourself sick over it." I said. "You were sure handy with him."

"I like babies." Buster shrugged.

He insisted on paying for our meals. After that he had to get to school; he'd missed two classes already.

"I'll see you later." he said. "If you find out anything about Charley—"

"I'll try." I said.

He ducked his head against the rain and trotted off up the hill.

I did some unpacking back at the hotel. My suit case had arrived by train from the east. I'd sent for it.

Just after three o'clock I took a cab over to the receiving hospital. The lobby was all white-tiled and sanitary looking and smelled of carbolic soap. A nurse sent me upstairs, where I found a crowd of people in the hallway outside the surgery. One looked like a police surgeon, in a white coat over a dark gray suit. With him was a grim-faced Det. Lt. Hoyt.

Gladys had just passed away a little while ago, he told me. Her body was being transferred to the county morgue, where there would be an autopsy. The police surgeon agreed that it looked like alcohol poisoning but there would be no official cause of death for the record until the county chemist had done an examination of her stomach contents and other vital organs. It might take two or three days to get the results of that.

I spotted Mrs. Earl, still in her uniform, on a hard wooden bench against the wall, with her arm around a heavy-set woman in a cloth coat who dabbed her eyes with a handkerchief, occasionally letting out a sob. There was a boy with her about twelve, in corduroy knickers and a plaid lumberjack jacket. He was red faced, and biting his lips, trying not to cry.

I went over to Mrs. Earl and was introduced to Mrs. Watson, who was Gladys's mother. The boy was Gladys's kid brother. Mrs. Watson had just had to identify Gladys's body.

"They can't even tell me when I can bury my girl." Mrs. Watson said.

I asked her about Charley, and found out that Mrs. Watson would be able to care for him. She would collect him from the matron on the way out. That was some comfort, anyway. I offered my condolences and left them to their grief.

Mrs. Earl walked out with me. "I've got to run along and get my man's supper for him." she said. She looked all in, and it was still raining. I offered to take her home by cab and she accepted with a relieved sigh. "I'm dead on my feet after a shift. I dunno how Gladie did it."

Gladys, it seemed, had also worked at the Savoy as a cigar stand girl, the afternoon shift, then went straight to the dance hall from there.

"She sure had a lotta pep. Mebbie I ought to try some of them health tonics she got from that reverend of hers. I teased her something awful about him. I'm sorry for it now."

Gladys, it seemed, had set a store by this reverend, who wasn't a real reverend at all, as far as Mrs. Earl could tell, but some sort of soothsayer who claimed to have telepathic and healing powers that he used to helped people with their problems. Gladys began going to his readings and had followed his advice devotedly for months.

"What nonsense he told Gladie." Mrs. Earl said. "He

said she'd been a princess in a past life and had had servants and slept in a bed shaped like a golden swan, and before that she'd been a swan herself– that's how come her neck was so long." Mrs. Earl shook her head. "Ain't it the limit? He has a way about him of saying just what a body wants to hear– Gladie was crazy for swans. She used to take Charley to the park to feed 'em. If you ask me I don't think his interest in Gladie were exactly– pure-hearted, you know?"

Mrs. Earl had gone with Gladys to a couple of "readings" and thought "the reverend" was the bunk.

"He didn't want *my* body, that's for sure!" she chuckled. "But he did seem interested in my money. I'd just got a little windfall from an aunt of mine. I didn't say nothing about it to my man yet– I wanted to surprise him at Christmas with something really nice. But I tole Gladie, and she musta tole her reverend. He hinted none too subtle that if I'd just let him invest it for me he could make me rich beyond my wildest dreams. I made the mistake of saying I'd think it over. I was just trying to be polite."

"That type is like a dog with a bone."

"And how! I half expected to find him under the bed at night. He kept' sending me letters asking for donations. I tossed them right in the incinerator."

"Sounds about the right place for them."

A couple of weeks ago Gladys came into a little windfall of her own, and had treated Mrs. Earl. "She paid a gal to look after Charley and we went out to a matinee had a little snack at a tearoom after. It was lovely. We really had us a time. That's how I'm gonna remember her now– happy like she were that day."

After dropping Mrs. Earl, I had the cab take me on to Spring Street, and walked up to Harry Price's gambling club. I hadn't known Gladys long, but the sight of her young form, still and blue, had shaken me. She'd been so full of life the night before. I'd seen plenty of death, lives taken too soon, but that was war, and I'd been in uniform, far from home.

I'd meant to hire a reputable detective last Monday, but by then I'd got my hackles up about the Pink Pagoda and wanted to find out what it was all about, handle it myself. Now I felt I'd made a mess of things and let Kit's trail go colder. I thought, now, however belatedly, Harry Price might be the man who could pick it up again.

The boys at the bar were at it again, this time trilling "Where the River Shannon Flows" into their cups. I passed unchallenged to the upstairs where the sawed-off shotgun twins greeted me like an old friend. The poker games were in full swing, as before, but I didn't see Harry Price's tall figure among the players.

"Harry ain't here." the guard at the door said.

"Will he be in later then?"

"Naw– he went down to Tijuana. The races are on tomorrow."

"He'll probably be back in a couple of days." one of the men at one of the other tables piped up. "Sooner, if he loses."

"Do you know where he lives, here in town?" I asked.

"He were at the Stowell, I think. I dunno for sure."

I spent half the afternoon playing poker with them while the boys told me stories of Harry: he'd trained as a detective with Pinkerton; he'd been one of the U.S. Marshalls to get Bill Dalton of the Doolin-Dalton gang; he'd ridden with Buffalo Bill. I came out into the early evening twilight a grand and a quarter ahead and called up Harry Price at the Hotel Stowell as soon as I got home.

A pleasant female voice came on the line– an older woman, not the daughter– his wife, maybe– and said Mr. Price wouldn't be back until the day after tomorrow. Did I want to make an appointment with him? I did. I left my name and told her how to get in touch with me.

As I was about to hang up, I hesitated, then asked if Miss Price was in. I hoped Harry hadn't taken her with him, down to Mexico.

"Miss Price is in Hollywood, with her grandmother." the woman said, and rang off.

CHAPTER 8

It was still raining Friday morning. Parts of the downtown were flooded as high as a car's running boards. We'd be okay on Fifth Street, Buster said. He came along with me, after breakfast, to the Biltmore Hotel where I was to meet Harry Price.

As we walked, Buster told me about his Thanksgiving dinner, held at a cafeteria with more than a thousand newsboys sitting down at table. It had been a swell spread, he said. I noticed a small cut near his right eye and he confessed a couple of the bigger boys had tried to shove some smaller boys out of line, and he, Buster, had gotten into a scrap with them over it.

Thanksgiving Day for me had passed slowly. Around four, I ate a solitary meal in the hotel dining room— with turkey and dressing and all the trimmings— the works. It might as well have been a cafeteria meal for all I enjoyed it, though. I thought about Kit, wondering if she was eating dinner someplace too, whether she was cold, or sick. I thought about Gladys, stiff on the autopsy slab, waiting to be put on ice like the girl Ricketts and I had gone to see my first day in Los Angeles.

The rain had let up for a while so I'd gone for a walk afterward, to clear my head. I passed other hotels, their dining rooms glowing yellow and cheerful behind plate glass windows, filled with happy couples and families; waiters in black and white did a ballet between the tables, bearing gleaming silver trays. I ended up at a burlesque show, an old fashioned type with baggy-pants comedians and tired jokes and even tireder girls in the chorus line, but at least you didn't have to think.

There was a message waiting for me back at the hotel, from a Miss Austin calling for Harry Price, to tell me Mr. Price would see me at 9:30 in the morning, and that he was now at the Biltmore Hotel. Harry, I figured, must have done alright for himself at the races.

"...the little guys got their chow alright." Buster concluded his story, grinning. He was more like his usual, good-natured self again. He'd been relieved to hear that baby Charley would be well cared for among his own people, though of course saddened about Gladys. Her death, as Vargas had predicted, had appeared as a brief item in the back pages of his paper. A couple of afternoon rags picked up the story, nothing more than a rehash of what Vargas reported; most had carried nothing about it at all.

The county chemist had also got partial results back, and the coroner had scheduled an inquest for this morning. I would have to appear. Gladys's funeral service would be held in the afternoon.

A woman answered the door to Harry's suite. I couldn't have told you her age, maybe thirty-five. She was only a whisper over five feet tall, with a slight figure displayed to advantage in a trim, dove-gray suit. She had a tidy mass of bobbed auburn hair, intelligent grey eyes and a pointed chin. She reminded me a little of the actress Maude Adams. She welcomed us in and took my dripping coat and hat and Buster's cap.

"I'm Edith Austin." she said. I recognized her voice as that of the woman I'd spoken to on the phone. "Mr. Price's secretary and operative."

"Operative?"

"Detective." she shrugged, and dimpled at my surprised look.

It was a large suite, with a dining room to one side and sitting room opposite. The girl– Harry's daughter– was curled up on the davenport by the fire, reading a book just as she had the first time I saw her. The glow of the fire cast a beautiful light, catching the golden glints of her hair. She raised her head and looked at us, just as Buster caught sight of her. Their eyes met and held for a few seconds. She rose and Miss Austin introduced us. The girl's given name was Lyric.

"I've met Mr. Shepard before." she said, smiling.

When it was Buster's turn he muttered "how d'y do?" and shook her offered hand.

He hadn't shown any signs of shyness before. I figured he felt a little cowed by the place, which was pretty swank, alright, though not overly showy. He ducked his head and looked at the carpet. Miss Price, in her low, feminine voice, invited him to sit down and have coffee with her and look at her books.

Miss Austin bade me to come into the dining room where Harry, in his shirtsleeves, was finishing up his breakfast. He had shaved and had on a clean shirt with an old-fashioned stiff collar, and looked almost distinguished. He was pushing some eggs around on his plate with a triangle of toast and looking through a pile of mail next to it. He glanced up as we came in.

"Oh," he said. "I didn't recognize you standing up."

Harry gestured for me to sit and Miss Austin poured some coffee for me and took her seat opposite with a pad and several sharpened pencils in front of her.

I told Harry everything I could think of, about Kit and about the Pink Pagoda, and admitted that my fall down the stairs had likely been no accident– no news to him. Miss Austin filled up page after page of her pad with little lines and squiggles.

Harry made no interruptions. When I finished talking he fixed his flinty eyes on me and asked, "Is that all of it?"

"That's all." I said.

"What did this guy look like, the one in the back room who gave you the pasting?"

I described the wavy-haired fat man from the Pink Pagoda office.

Harry nodded and turned to whisper some instructions to Miss Austin. "And see if you can get a line on Miss Shepard's baggage." he concluded. Then he rose and put on his coat, which was draped over the back of a chair. Miss Austin put down her pencil, went out, and came back with Harry's overcoat and hat, a Stetson of the fifty-dollar variety.

"Edith will go over the rest of it with you." Harry said. "I've got to go out, got another appointment. Come see me again in the morning. Oh, one more thing—" he added, turning back. "Have you got a car?"

"No."

"Oh." he said. "Well you might want to get one."

"It's been suggested." I said.

I told him that I'd hire a car. He nodded, and went out with Miss Austin. She returned with some papers in her hand.

"I went ahead and drew up a standard contract for you." she said. "You read it over, and then we can discuss the particulars."

"Thanks, Miss Austin."

"Please, call me Edith." she said.

"Then call me Avery." I said.

I read the contract, silently. From across the hall, I could hear the rise and fall of the kids' voices, and their laughter. I gathered by Buster's loud guffaw that he'd gotten over whatever fit of shyness had come over him and was being his usual self.

Edith produced a fountain pen and I signed the contract. Harry was now officially my detective.

I turned over the photograph of Kit to Edith's care. She studied it for a moment, then said she would have copies of it made at a place Harry used.

Edith poured some more coffee for us. I admired the graceful movements of her hands and thought of Helen Sing, fixing tea over the spirit-lamp.

I asked Edith how she happened to come to work for Harry.

Her eyes twinkled. "I hired him." she said. "To work my divorce case. I got curious, and suspected my husband was up to no good, when he started leaving the house at eight instead of eight-thirty. So, I shadowed him one morning– straight to another woman's house. I came downtown and hired Mr. Price– Harry– that afternoon. He got me my divorce alright, and custody of Arthur, my little boy, too. I needed a job and he suggested I come to work for him– he said I was a natural. That was– mercy, how the time flies– nearly six years ago now."

"Is he really any good? On the level, I mean. I already signed the contract."

She looked at me with amusement in her grey eyes. "There are a lot of stories about him." she said. "How he captured the Dalton-Doolin gang single-handedly, and could beat Jack Dempsey with one hand behind his back– the first Dempsey, I mean."

"Well, I hadn't heard that last one." I said. "His poker pals did tell some whoppers about him, though. Is it true he got fired from the police force?"

"Not exactly," she said, "since he was never officially on it. Back when he was starting out, private detectives were hired out as sort of adjuncts to the police. Anyone could call himself a private detective and get a badge. Some of them abused the privilege, and no one– no one on the police force I mean– asked too many questions about how they got their evidence. Harry didn't like it. He had a partner who was corrupt to the hilt. He'd blackmail clients, or the party he was investigating, or both. Harry kicked, and this 'detective' and his cronies on the force tried to get Harry blacklisted but they didn't succeed. When the state passed the detective licensing law, nineteen-fifteen, Harry got one of the first ones issued."

She paused, chuckling. "You know, Harry wasn't at all the way I imagined a detective to be. All I knew is what I'd read in books– *The Moonstone*, Dupin, Sherlock Holmes."

"With me it was Nick Carter, and *The Police Gazette*. I never heard of a woman detective in real life, though."

"Oh, we exist, I assure you." Edith said with a smile. "But anyway, I don't have a detective license– I'm only an operative. That's another thing you should know about Harry. All detective firms hire women, but most only use them to entrap men, in domestic cases. You know, the woman gets him up to a hotel room somehow then comes out dressed in a nightie, and screams. That's the cue for a detective and the man's wife to burst in and a photographer starts taking flashlight pictures. Not Harry. He doesn't cheat. He doesn't need to. He's one of the best there is, honor bright."

I thanked her for everything and went to collect Buster. He was seated in an armchair across from the girl. They seemed to be engaged in a friendly argument.

"If they were really–" Buster was saying.

"Have you ever–" Lyric said at the same time.

They broke off, laughing.

Buster caught my eye and I nodded; he stood up, reluctantly.

Lyric rose too. She wore a blue knit sports dress and had long legs, like a filly; in her heels she was only a couple of inches shorter than Buster.

She selected a book from a stack on the lamp table. It was *Kidnapped* by Robert Lewis Stevenson.

"I think you'd like this one." she said. Their fingers touched briefly as she handed it to him. "It's yours– for keeps."

"Gosh, kid, thanks," he said.

Edith brought our coats and we said our good-byes. Once we were out in the hallway Buster stopped to take a handkerchief out of his pocket and carefully wrapped the book up in it. Then he placed it inside his coat, against his body.

"You and the girl seemed to get on." I said.

"I– I never had a girl talk to me about books, and poems and things before." he stammered. "I made a date with her, to go out for a soda. She said she has to ask her father."

At Fifth and Olive we parted. "Have you got a place to stay tonight?" I asked.

"Oh, sure. I'm working at the K of C. They usually fix up a cot for me in back." he said. "It's pretty quiet after everybody goes home. It's funny, though– I don't feel half so lonesome, thinking about having that book to read."

I thought about his last words as I rode up by cab to the coroner's office. Part of it was the book, but I suspected it was also to some extent the girl who gave it to him and the kindness in her eyes as she did it. I realized, what I'd stupidly overlooked at first, that for all the bravado, he was just a boy, alone in a strange place where, for all he knew, no one cared if he lived or was sick, or lonely, or scared. She, Lyric, had seen that right away. Maybe she was lonely too.

The Hall of Justice was a new building, all shining white granite standing temple-like against the low-hanging clouds of a gray sky. We met in the coroner's office itself. It was a large, high ceilinged room, stuffy with the odors of wet wool and stale cigar smoke. Det. Lt. Hoyt was there, along with Mrs. Watson, and the reporter Vargas. There were two men in suits, who turned out to be the assistant county chemist and the Deputy D.A., and a nervous young redheaded man in blue overalls. The jury came in through a side door, with the coroner, a court reporter, and a Deputy D.A. The coroner, an elderly bespectacled man, thanked us for meeting at such short notice. Mrs. Watson testified only that she had officially identified her daughter's body. I was called and repeated what I'd told the detectives. Neither the Deputy D.A. nor the coroner asked me any questions. Det. Lt. Hoyt told his bit, and of delivering the bottles collected from Gladys's apartment to the coroner's lab. The star of the show was the chemist, who testified at length about Gladys's stomach contents and tissues, causing Mrs. Watson to weep loudly from her seat. He gave her official cause of death for the record as heart failure ("don't all hearts fail when you've croaked it?" muttered Vargas, scribbling away next to me) brought on by alcohol cut with poison. His results weren't complete, so he hadn't yet been able to identify the poison– admitting frankly that he might never be able to determine it without testing for it specifically– but thought possibly brucine sulphate. "It attacks the heart, much like strychnine." he said. "We've seen several cases lately of so-called 'real' Scotch cut with brucine sulphate. It's used for making certain perfumes, so isn't hard for bootleggers to get, and for some reason the public will drink anything– even acid or kerosene– as long as it purports to be alcoholic."

I might have imagined it but seemed to me he– and the jurors– glared disapprovingly at me during this last delivery. I sat up straight and tried to look as if lips that touched liquor would never touch mine, or vice versa.

The jury filed out. I spoke to Mrs. Watson, briefly, asked about Charley, who was getting along fine, she said, then went out into the hallway to smoke.

The redheaded kid was already out there, pacing. He hadn't been called to testify. I offered him a cigarette and he took it, gratefully. He was Gladys's "ex" and Charley's father, Charles Taggert, Sr. He looked all of nineteen or twenty, drove a truck for a sparkling water outfit, and roomed at a men's boardinghouse. He regretted that he wasn't in any position to take Charley himself.

"Charley's grandmother'll take good care of him,

won't she?" I asked.

"Oh sure." he said. "The old lady never liked me much, that's all. She thought Gladie was too young to get married." He shrugged. "At least, I'll be able to see the kid Sundays. I used to look after him myself sometimes when Gladie went to her readings or whatever they was."

He said the last bit with no little amount of bitterness. I commented idly that I understood Gladys's had been seeking spiritual advice.

"I guess you could call it that. I'd like to knock that feller's block off for him, and that ain't all." Charles said. "We used to have good times, me and Gladie. We mighta got back together again when she turned eighteen if he hadn't put so many fool notions into her head. I wasn't good enough for her anymore."

"I thought Gladys was already over eighteen." I said. "I mean, I thought you had to be of age to work in a dance hall."

"She probably lied about her age like she did on our marriage license. Her ma went to the judge and got it annulled on account of it wasn't legal."

"How old was she?"

"Seventeen in June."

Oh, hell, I thought. Under all the harsh makeup, she had been a schoolgirl, practically. I hadn't planned to try anything on with her, even if she hadn't passed out, but still didn't like the idea of being out with a kid.

"I didn't know anything about her working in a dance hall. I'd of put my foot down." he said. "Thanks for the gasper."

The jury came back with the not very surprising verdict of accidental death, by poisoning. The D.A. said his office would wait for the full report of the county chemist but most likely would not order any further investigation. No arrests were planned.

Mrs. Watson was resentful. "They killed my girl with their poison and the law don't do a thing about it?

Charles, Sr. punched the wall and went out.

"For what it's worth, I think it really was just an unfortunate accident. It's not anyone's fault." I said.

Mrs. Watson wouldn't be soothed. "She was a good girl, my Gladie. They don't care. If she was one o' them society girls, always getting' their name in the paper gadding about, I guess mebbie then they'd care."

Vargas and I went out together. He looked a little bit hangdog. "It's true, what she said, you know. If she was some millionaire's daughter, all the papers would be giving this story more ink than the Armistice. What the hell difference does it make? A girl's dead. A baby doesn't have a mother."

I said I was surprised to hear him talking this way. "The other day, you didn't sound like you cared much, yourself. I never would've taken you for an idealist."

"Who says I am? I'll sue 'em for slander." he grinned. "I'm a newspaperman, that's all. My job's to sell newspapers. All the same, it gets my goat sometimes."

Outside under the arch of the entrance, he offered me a drink from his pocket flask but I waved him off.

A woman, a girl, had walked by us, headed east down Temple Street. She wore a green plaid coat and a smart brown cloche, and had a knot of thick, light brown hair at the nape of her neck. Something about her graceful walk, a familiar tilt to her head, caught my eye.

I ran after her, calling: "Kit! Kit!"

I almost reached out and touched her shoulder but before I could she turned around, with an alarmed expression on her face. I stopped short. Of course it wasn't Kit at all but some other young woman, who pressed her handbag against her chest and cast her eyes around as if looking out for a policeman.

"Sorry, miss. I thought you were somebody else." I mumbled.

She hurried away.

Vargas came sauntering up and paused next to me to

light a cigarette.

"That's the hell of it about women's hats these days. You can't tell if a Sheba's good-lookin' until you get right up close to her— an' by then it's usually too late. I'll see you around, Shepard."

Gladys's funeral took place in the small chapel of a mortuary on West Washington Boulevard. It was well attended for all its hasty preparation. Flowers— roses, sweet peas and gladiolas, flanked her coffin, which rested on a metal stand in front of the altar. There were a few wreaths of pine boughs and white roses. She had been dressed in a white satin frock with a high neckline and wore a small gold ring— her wedding band, or class ring, I supposed. Without her heavy lipstick and rouge she looked like the schoolgirl she had recently been.

Gladys's family filled the front chairs, surrounding a weeping Mrs. Watson in rusty black. Charles, Sr. sat with them, in a too-small suit, fidgeting with his stiff and probably unfamiliar collar and holding his small son on his lap. I spotted Mrs. Earl and a man sitting with a group of neighbors from the rooming house. There were some young men and women, school friends, maybe. A couple of rows back, sitting apart from the rest, sat Helen Sing and a handful of girls from the Pink Pagoda. Helen caught my eye and nodded. I nodded back.

As the lights dimmed, I noticed a figure slipping in to the very last row of seats— a dapper man, dressed in a dark grey sack suit and pearl-grey bow tie, holding a gray derby in chamois gloved hands. He had a goatee and a round, nearly bald head. I'd seen him before, at the Bamboo Garden. I wondered how he knew Gladys, or if he did— recalling the stunner I'd seen him leaving with, for all I knew he'd just been going around trying to collect stray blondes. For a gate crasher, though, if that's what he was, he appeared perfectly at his ease. He sat down and folded his hands in front of him, glancing around at the backs of the heads of other mourners, half-smiling. He noticed me looking his way and glanced up; the eyes were as I remembered– small, black, piercing. He didn't appear to see me, though he was looking right at me. There was something uncanny, almost sinister about the man.

After the brief services concluded those of us who weren't family filed out. The dapper gent had gone, I noticed.

Helen waited for me in the aisle and I walked out with her. She was dressed somberly, with black and white dotted kid gloves and a fur coat over a severely plain black velvet dress, and a matching hat with a wide brim.

"It's a sad day." I said.

"Yes, it is." Helen nodded. "Did you have to appear at the inquest?"

I told her about it, briefly.

"She was one of the hall's most popular girls. I hate to lose her." She looked sidelong at me. "You probably think I'm heartless."

"No." I lied.

"I'm not– not really. But the fact is, in my business, you can't get too attached to the girls. They come and go so often. Some aren't suited to the life." She nodded to the bevy of girls as they rushed past us in their discount-store mourning, almost glowing with conspicuous health, unaffected by it all. "The ones who do stay– you try to care for them, but they do what they want– go off with strange men, drink, get into trouble. You want to shake some sense into them, but it wouldn't do any good."

"Gladys's neighbor and husband both say she was under the influence of some sort of clairvoyant. Did she ever say anything about it to you?"

Helen shrugged, delicately. "Not that I can recall. But the girl was extremely secretive about her private life. Until today I had no idea she was supporting a baby– poor child."

I didn't know if she meant Gladys, or Charley.

"There was a man here earlier– dandy type. I saw him

before the night I was out with Gladys. I don't like the looks of him."

"What– here?" Helen looked around.

"He's gone." I said. "Odd person."

"I wouldn't put too much stock in it. These sorts of tragedies, when a young girl is involved, seem to bring out all sorts of curiosity seekers." Helen said. She looked up at me and gave a little smile. "Your face is coming along. You look almost respectable."

"Well, no one was ever going to ask it to sell any shirt collars, anyway, but would you be ashamed to be seen out with me?"

"Oh, I don't know. I might like it."

"Well, look– Helen– I was thinking of hiring a car for a day or two. Would you like to go for a drive Sunday afternoon? Your place is closed, isn't it?"

"Yes. That sounds divine– Avery. I'll be glad of some agreeable company– not to mention the chance to get out of town for a day." Helen said. She sighed "Even though Gladys's death didn't have anything to do with her being a taxi girl, I expect the police will nonetheless feel obliged to send someone out to the Pagoda, which means I'm in for a grilling– and a shakedown of course."

I realized between the inquest and the funeral I had almost forgotten about Harry Price's inquiries, and wondered if he too would be visiting the Pink Pagoda. I said nothing to her about that, though it made me feel a bit shady. She'd come to my aid, after all.

I helped Helen into the cab and rode with her back downtown as far as the Pink Pagoda. We chatted without really saying anything. She gave me the name of her hotel, and I promised to call for her Sunday.

CHAPTER 9

The modern detective is not the softshoe artist of the detective novels, with long black hair and a big black hat. Nor is he a swaggering individual with a gun on either hip, a knife in his shirt and a blackjack in his pocket. He is a quiet man, unobtrusive but highly efficient.
—William J. Burns, director, Bureau of Investigation, Department of Justice, Washington D.C.

The next morning was chilly for Los Angeles, or so I was told, but the rain had stopped. I went down to the hotel barber shop and got a shave, then had breakfast and afterward went up to the Biltmore to see Harry.

Edith wasn't there; the girl, Lyric, let me in. Harry was dressed and shaved.

He told me that the Pink Pagoda was managed by a man called Louis Morelli. "Not officially, of course. They got some front man to apply for the license. But Morelli runs the joint, alright. He's the guy who beat you up in his office. A thorough sonofabitch. Showed up here a few years ago and has run different kinds of joints— of the infamous sort. That's all I'll say about him for now." Harry concluded. "Have you got that car? I want to take you to meet someone."

I said I had; Harry told me to come pick him up out front on Olive Street at ten-thirty.

"Oh, Mr. Shepard." Lyric hailed me as I was letting myself out. "Would you ask Robert to come along with you? My father said he could. I'm going, too."

She was dressed for an outing, alright, in a tight, striped jersey sports skirt and cardigan– with sensible brown leather shoes and a wool tam. I wondered what kind of a crazy stunt Harry was pulling that could possibly involve having the kids along– a picnic? Nothing he did would have surprised me at this point.

"Sure, I'll ask him." I said. "You know, he sure likes that book you gave him. It was nice of you to want to improve him."

She looked up at me with her big, womanly eyes wide. "I didn't give him the book to improve him, Mr. Shepard." she said gravely, then broke into a grin. "He doesn't need any improving. But don't tell him I said so."

I arranged about the hire car– a blue, five passenger Chevrolet sedan– from the Hertz Drive-Yur-Self outfit across the street from the Biltmore. Then I walked back down Fifth to Main where Buster was finishing up his morning's work. He whooped when I gave him the news and the invitation, and redoubled his efforts to get rid of his papers. We walked up to the garage and got the car and were waiting in front of Harry's hotel well in advance of the appointed time.

Buster acted the perfect gentleman, helping the girl into the backseat and arranging a robe over her knees. Harry climbed in up front with me. He spoke little as I headed northwest out of town, except to issue traffic directions. The kids made up for it, talking of everything: books, school, poetry, the movies, baseball, tennis, motorcycles, and music.

The tall buildings fell away, and buildings in general became fewer, spread out between billboards and vacant lots as we headed up into hilly territory. After about a quarter of an hour Harry directed me up a steep hill; the Chevrolet's motor strained with the effort.

"Everybody lean forward." I said, only half-kidding. Just before the crest Harry told me to stop in front of a modest bungalow. It was set back on a large lot that sloped away from the street, set amongst lush shrubbery. There was a stone path leading up to the front porch and a stone birdbath in the center of a circle of rose bushes. There were views of the valleys and more gently rolling hills, dotted with houses, and of the more distant mountains.

Though not far in distance from the Biltmore– I could see, hazily, in the other direction, the downtown over the slanting roofline of a neighboring house– it seemed miles from the city. The only sounds were the shouts of some young boys, in sweaters several sizes too big for them, playing with a football in the vacant parcel across the street, and a truck backfiring now and then from somewhere down below.

"Whose place is this?" I asked.

As if on cue a woman opened the door in answer to Harry's knock. She was short, very round, and white-haired, in a neat, printed cotton dress and low, flexible-soled shoes. There was something solid and comforting about her presence.

She smiled warmly at all of us and clasped Harry's hand. "My, it's good to see you." she said. "Did you run into any traffic? Father's pottering around somewhere out of doors– you know how he is. Coffee's on– be ready in a minute."

Harry introduced us to the lady, who was a Mrs. Clara Breuner. She bade us to come in and escorted us into a parlor. It had a comfortable look, with a well-used Morris chair and a Turkish rocker, an overstuffed davenport crowded with embroidered cushions, lace curtains at the windows and a faded Brussels carpet underfoot. A fire crackled in a large hearth made of river rocks. There was a basket of knitting next to the rocker and a low coffee table in front of the davenport stacked with newspapers and magazines. An Atwater Kent radio set and speaker stood out in this homey setting like something out of a pathological laboratory, occupying a place of honor on a console table within arms-reach of the Morris chair.

Through an arch was a dining room and beyond it, glimpsed through an open swinging door, the kitchen. The cooking smells coming from that direction made my stomach rumble, though it hadn't been long since breakfast.

A man came in. We felt him as much as saw him— he had a vitality that drew people to him, though he lacked the imposing physical presence that often went with that type of personality. He was of medium build, as trim as his wife was portly, with a shock of white hair and furry eyebrows above merry blue eyes. He wore trousers and a soft collared Madras shirt with a sweater coat, its pockets bulging with a briar pipe and other whatnot.

He greeted us in a hearty, youthful voice. "Hello, hello. I was just out chopping some wood."

"Sawing logs, more like it." Harry said. Introductions were made once again.

He was the Reverend Doctor James L. Breuner, pastor of a modest Baptist church in downtown Los Angeles. It was beyond me how Harry knew him. Dr. Breuner saw my puzzlement and grinned. He suggested that Harry and I go into his study.

Mrs. Breuner showed the kids to a bookcase, next to the fireplace, where there were piles of jigsaw puzzles and patent card games and books that had belonged to "the children" that they might like; she would bring them some tea and gingerbread.

In the study, Dr. Breuner had a desk and a comfy leather chair and a floor-to-ceiling bookcase. Volumes, some I recognized from my father's library, were crammed into the latter willy-nilly: a worn leather-bound *Pilgrims Progress* rubbed shoulders with Spencer's *Essays*, J. Arthur Thompson's *The Outline of Science* and a set of Stoddard's *Lectures* were neighbors to gardening manuals and a fair selection of novels— Harold Bell Wright, Zane Grey, William Macleod

Raine, Arthur Conan Doyle, Arthur Somers Roche, Earl Der Biggers.

"I do enough heavy thinking during the week. In my leisure time, I like a good murder mystery or a western." Dr. Breuner said, laughing. "Though I expect it's all pretty tame stuff to Harry."

He offered me the leather chair; Harry folded his long frame into the window seat.

"Nice home you have." I said.

"Thank you. It's not fancy but it suits us. Mother and I built it ourselves when I first came to Los Angeles. You might not believe it but we had five children living here at one time– three boys and two girls. They're all grown now, and married. But enough about me– you must be wondering what this is about. Knowing Harry, he didn't enlighten you on anything."

"You've pegged that right." I admitted.

"It wasn't his wish to be mysterious, I assure you. It's just that he wasn't at liberty to discuss one client's case with another. He came to see me yesterday and asked for permission to bring you in on my business, and I invited you all out here. He didn't give out any information about your case to me."

I nodded, and told him briefly about Kit, including the strange encounters I'd had at the Pink Pagoda.

Dr. Breuner looked at me, his eyes full of tears. "Well, I will pray for your sister and trust in God, but here on earth I think you've done well to place things in Harry's hands. I see now why he thought we should compare cases."

"Some of my colleagues have been grumbling lately– on pure conjecture– about immorality in the taxi-dance halls. The fact is, some of them hold the view that all dancing is a sin and ought to be banned; others think only jazz music and the– what they call– lascivious dancing that goes along with it is immoral and that these dance halls where men pay girls to dance with them are a breeding ground for other vices,

89

namely– drinking, dope-taking, and prostitution.

"I don't hold the view that dancing itself is evil. Not that I exactly care for the kind of dancing young people do nowadays, but I remember my father complaining about the way we held girls in the waltz, and old folks said my generation was going to hell in a hand-basket– but we turned out okay, most of us." He winked at Harry.

"And back when my girls were young we were fairly shocked by their dances– the Turkey Trot, the Texas Tommy, the Bunny Hug, the Polar Bear and so forth. But they turned out okay, too. Isn't that right, Mother?" he asked, as Mrs. Breuner came in with coffee for us.

"Grizzly Bear, dear." she corrected. "But yes– how do you think I got this gray hair? The boys were far worse than the girls, though, and that's a fact, Father."

When she'd gone out again, Dr. Breuner continued. "That being said, my colleagues looked to me for guidance on this matter because a number of years ago when the city tried to pass a certain dance hall ordinance, I was quite outspoken in my opposition to it. The backer of this law was a dance hall operator and tried to sell it to voters on the pretense that it would impose stricter regulation, but in fact it was designed– with, I must say, devilish cunning– to do just the opposite. I was pleased to see it defeated for that reason, but the end result is I became generally knows as the decrier of dance halls.

"I've since come to believe– naïvely perhaps– that the public halls today are conducted properly, and are not necessarily the notorious dens of vice they once were. So, when my colleagues came to me about what they described as the taxi-dance hall problem, I thought I should have a look at the places for myself. Ignorance is the true mother of vice, I say."

I gave a low whistle, thinking of my own circuit, and how shocked I'd been at some of the goings on I'd seen– and I was no Sunday school teacher.

Dr. Breuner chuckled. "Does that surprise you? Well,

I can't say I enjoyed it, and I don't at all like the idea that the girls are getting paid to dance with strange men. That aside, I didn't witness anything base or untoward, and the dancing itself isn't any worse than at our church functions. But, the fact is my face– such as it is– is fairly well-known in the city, and I realized the places I visited might have been warned to be on their best behavior for me. So, a few weeks ago I hired Harry to investigate possible vice conditions." He looked at Harry. "Do you want to tell the next bit or shall I?"

"You're doing fine, Doc."

"Well, in general, Harry found the same thing I did– that most of the clubs were on the up and up, as they say. You wouldn't want your daughter, or your sister, to work in one, but there was nothing really objectionable going on. The girls have to be of age to work there, there's no drinking or any really lascivious dancing allowed, and a patron who doesn't behave like a gentleman is likely to get chucked out on his ear."

My face reddened.

"However, there was an exception to this otherwise sterling record." Doc went on.

"The Pink Pagoda?" I said.

Harry spoke up. "Yeah– even you cottoned to the fact that there was something not quite right about it."

I frowned. I didn't care for the implication of that "even you."

"Edith and I tried to find out about the place, only we couldn't get on to anything from the usual channels." Harry continued. "But once we traced the fact that Morelli is the real boss of the place it's impossible to think that it isn't crooked somehow. He's run places before– the kind where the help is mostly women and the real entertainment is upstairs."

I felt a little like I did when this Morelli hit me.

Dr. Breuner took up the story again. "I'm acquainted with a woman, through my work, who is– quite well known–

in underworld circles. Her name is Helen Sing."

My face felt hot. "I've met her." I said.

"Have you? Well, then you know, Mrs. Sing is a fine woman, very charming. Her father was French, and her mother was a white Russian, I believe. She hasn't had an easy life. She had an opium habit and did things she is ashamed of, suffice to say. She's had to shift for herself from quite a young age. She married a Chinaman, Sing, when she was still practically a child. Then he abandoned her. When I met her she had come to a pretty low state of things, but she got clean of the drugs and has been leading a blameless life ever since. I can't tell you how I admire her– her courage and her strength, her keen mind, her honesty. All of this is a long way of saying Mrs. Sing was uniquely well suited to help us in this investigation."

I turned to Harry. "You mean she's your operative, like Edith?"

Harry shook his head. "She doesn't work for me. She's more in the way of a so-called informant."

"I engaged Mrs. Sing and instructed her to get a job at the Pink Pagoda." Dr. Breuner continued. "With her reputation, those of the underworld trust her. I went down there and made a fuss about them needing to hire a woman, a matron, to watch over the girls and keep them on the straight moral path. To get rid of me and keep me quiet, they employed Mrs. Sing– Mrs. Sing having made it known she was looking for such work. From her position on the inside, she's able to see what all goes on."

"And– well, has she found out anything?"

Harry and Dr. Breuner exchanged a look.

Harry spoke first. "The Sing woman says her boss, Morelli, made it clear she's nothing but window dressing. She says she keeps her eyes open but claims she hasn't seen any illegal activity going on. The only thing she's given us, not long after she was there, in confirmation that the Pink Pagoda is a protected joint. We know Morelli has friends in the police department. She sees them come in regular, like clockwork, to collect their share– the officer in charge of the dance hall detail, and his deputy. They come in for a routine so-called "inspection" and go out again patting their pockets."

"Why not just get the landlord to evict this Morelli and shut him down that way?"

Harry told me that the building was owned by a W.H. Hillman, as in the Hillman Building, the big green structure I'd noticed next door to the Pink Pagoda. The Hillman syndicate owned a number of buildings downtown– offices, theaters, garages, auditoriums, and had a private club for realty men that had its headquarters in the top three floors of the Hillman Building.

"Henry Hillman is a developer primarily but he dabbles in oil." Harry said. "His latest venture is a beach club on the coast, probably on one of his old oil leases. He came here about four or five years ago. Belongs to all the right clubs and considers himself a pillar of the community, always hosting some charity stunt, one of those that goes around speaking to women's clubs and boys clubs and telling people how they ought to live."

"When are they fitting him for his halo?" I asked. I didn't like showy do-gooders; my mother was one. Behind closed doors she was bigoted, hard-hearted and mean. "I mean– if he's so strong for civic virtues and you tell him there's something shady, maybe criminal, going on in his building, he'd have to throw the bums out or show himself up as a phony." I said.

"He's the last person wants them shut down." Harry said, with disgust. "Why should he? He collects a nice fat rent and his hands are clean. He's probably got gambling clubs and speakeasies and brothels operating in almost all of his buildings. If anybody finds out about it, he'd just say he has so many properties, he can't know what all his tenants are up to. Meanwhile he goes to church on Sundays, and shouts 'amen!' when the preacher rails about the police not doing enough to curb vice and crime.

"So, Hillman *is* a phony?"

"I suspect some of his business dealings are shady, and I don't think his reputation with women would hold up in the wash, but he's very, very careful of his public image as beloved philanthropist and home-loving man. Nothing that suggests otherwise ever gets into the papers. You know him better than I do, though, Doc. What do you think?"

Dr. Breuner smiled. "I don't like to judge the man unfairly, but he always brings to my mind that line of Galsworthy's– 'he can't be a Christian because he has such a kind face.' No one is as virtuous as Hillman looks. The truly good always feel guilty about *something*. But, he claims to be a man of God. Brother Shepard had a good idea. Maybe I'll speak to Hillman about our problem and leave it to his conscience."

"Do me a favor, Doc, and keep it to yourself– for a little while longer anyway." Harry said. "I have my suspicions, but that's all they are so far. I'm not ready to tip my hand to Hillman, or anyone else, just yet."

Mrs. Breuner called us in to lunch. The kids had helped to set the dining table, which was laid with a lace cloth and flower-painted china.

"It's just soup and bread but there's plenty of it." she said. "Plain, simple cooking is what Father likes best. During the week he often has to eat out– all that rich food gives him a tummy ache."

Her "plain, simple cooking" could put any restaurant in New York out of business in a week. We ate gallons of the split pea and ham soup and endless baskets of her home baked bread. Dr. Breuner chatted easily with the kids about their schoolwork.

After lunch, the kids wanted to go exploring, as the rain had stopped. The doctor and I walked outside with them, and he showed me around the property. Even this late in the year, there were flowers blooming along the edges of the lawn, and a vegetable patch. At the edge of the yard was an enormous tree, a mission fig, he said. The rest of the property was dotted with fruit trees of every kind– orange, peach, apricot, pear– planted by the Breuners themselves, years ago.

"Mother will probably send you home with some of her preserves, I don't doubt it."

A clothesline stretched between the back porch and the garage, which housed Dr. Breuner's aged Saxon runabout and his workshop. We sat down on a green wooden bench under the fig tree.

"This is the shadiest spot in the yard, come summer." he said.

We sat a while, just admiring the view.

"On clear days, you can see Catalina from here." Dr. Breuner said. "Or so I was told when we bought the place. I've never seen it in fifteen years."

"It's peaceful here."

"It's my sanctuary. I confess, I sometimes feel closer to God here, working in my garden, than in church. Getting pretty built up around here to my eyes, but it's still pretty close to heaven."

I asked him how he had come to know Harry Price.

"James, our younger son, lost his way and got into some trouble a few years ago. I don't say that some of it wasn't of his own making, but the other boys involved had wealthy fathers and got a high-priced lawyer who tried to argue that my boy had been behind it all. His clients would have escaped with only a slap on the wrist. Our lawyer got Harry to investigate it, and Harry came up with irrefutable proof that the other boys had planned and executed the whole thing. James paid his debt for his part in it, but at least it was fair."

Harry hates cheats. Edith had said.

"How is your son doing now?"

"Fine, thank you for asking. He's turned himself around. Married a wonderful woman, and is even thinking of entering the ministry." he said. "I make no excuses for him, but the world is awfully full of mine-fields for young men these days."

"You know, Doc– I've been thinking the same thing. It's the boy, Buster. I worry about him, out on the streets by himself. He's a good lad, smart. I think he could make something of himself if he had a chance. I'd like to do something for him but I don't know what. He's proud, rightly so. He wouldn't take a handout."

Dr. Breuner pulled on his briar pipe and thought a while. "I've had a number of amateur and professional boxers in my flock over the years. I even baptized one." he said finally. "They're fine fellows. A lot of them came from less than ideal backgrounds but they all tell me the same thing– that learning to box made them better men. Not just improving their physical strength but their moral character, their minds. Jim Jeffries says if a boy's boxing, he takes care of his body, he's proud of it."

I nodded. "I dunno Harry Greb ever heard that, but for most boys it's true. Buster's got energy to spare, and he likes to fight."

"You know, Big Jim himself learned to box with the private athletic club here. They still have a boxing team, and give free training in the pugilistic arts to a few boys of their choosing, at no cost. The boys represent the club at amateur athletics contests. Some of them have gone on to the Olympic Games. I count a few club members among my congregation. I'm sure I could arrange a what-do-they-call-it, a try-out, for Buster."

"I think he'd like that. I'll talk it over with him. Thanks a lot, Doc."

As we strolled back to the house, he asked: "You aren't a church-going man, are you Brother Shepard?"

"To tell you the truth, I've hardly seen the inside of a church since I was in a velvet suit with knee pants and a lace collar."

"Mother used to dress up Hiram, our oldest boy, like

that, too." he said, chuckling. "You haven't lost your faith, though? I only ask because it may be of comfort to you, with your sister."

I turned to him. "I dunno, Doc. I was in the trenches."

Dr. Breuner nodded. He had gone to France, right after the Armistice, on a tour with some other American ministers, as spiritual advisors, to offer comfort any way they could. "It was part vaudeville, part old-time revival meeting, whatever was required." he said. "Those boys who could find their God again were the better for it, I think. What branch of service were you?"

"Army." I said. "Top kick."

"Hiram was navy." He turned to me with a mirthful smile. "I was planning to listen to the Army-Navy game this afternoon. Are you a betting man, Brother Shepard?"

"I am." I said, a bit taken aback. "I never met a preacher who was, though."

"Oh, I'm not." he said, with twinkling eyes. "But, let's say if the navy wins I would be very pleased to see you among my flock some Sunday."

"Well–" I hedged.

"Oh, have faith in the Army, Brother Shepard. I know I've got heavy competition. Most young fellows would rather spend Sunday at the pictures, I suppose, or out riding with their sweethearts."

I thought of Helen, and our date for tomorrow.

Back in the house we settled in the parlor, where Mrs. Breuner brought in coffee and gingerbread, "in case we'd worked up an appetite." Dr. Breuner turned on the radio set and let it warm up.

"Mother wouldn't have it in the room until I happened to tune in a cooking program one morning– then she became a convert." he whispered. He bent over the dials and tried for some time, unsuccessfully, to tune in the football broadcast.

"Jumping ginger! I'm not a man given to profanity, but this contraption has brought me closer to it than anything else, except maybe the automobile."

He was spared the temptation, though. Lyric and Buster came in from their walk and Buster took over the dials. Soon, the game came in, as loud and clear as if we'd been at Soldier Field– only warmer.

"My boy, you're a wonder." Doc said.

We relaxed the rest of the afternoon, listening to the game. Harry commented that football could be played by old ladies since the forward pass came along. I never heard anyone laugh as loud as the Doc did when it ended in a tie, 21-21.

We declined Mrs. Breuner's offer to stay for supper, knowing "Father" would need to work that evening; she sent us home with a basket of enough foodstuffs to last a journey of several days.

We stopped at a roadside café on the way back and had dinner– cream of celery soup and smothered steak with onions for me, prime rib of beef, au Jus for Harry; after Mrs. Breuner's cooking it was an insult. The kids had roast chicken dinners with slices of pineapple pie and vanilla ice cream and talked nonsense about books. Back in town, I dropped Buster first, as he had to hustle to get his papers. Then I took Harry and Lyric to the Biltmore. To my surprise, Harry got back in the car after helping the girl out and seeing her safely into the lobby. After a minute he told me to drive to the 200 block of Spring Street. I figured he wanted to go to the gambling club, but that was in the next block over.

"Do you mean the 300 block?"

"Did I say the 300 block?"

I drove to the 200 block and circled it until I cursed and said it would have been smarter to leave the car at the hotel and walk over; just then I got a parking spot. We got out of the car and I followed Harry up the block. He came to a stop in front of a five-story office building of sunset-colored terra cotta, in the style popular about thirty years ago. Most of the windows were dark, this being a Saturday night, but he strode into the lobby and pressed the button for the elevator as if he owned the place. He told the operator to take us to the fourth floor, where our footsteps echoed across a tiled landing; Harry went around the corner, on the north side, and producing a key from his pocket, unlocked one of the frosted glass doors.

It was a typical office. It had a pair of wooden desks, shoved together, with their narrower ends aligned against one bank of windows, overlooking Spring Street. One of them had a typewriter on it, covered by a leather cloth. An empty bookcase stood against the wall, and three or four file cabinets. Another frosted glass door led to a second office. This one had another desk, arranged so that its user had his back to the windows. There were more file cabinets, an assortment of hard wooden chairs, and a scratched and battered leather davenport. The rooms had the stuffiness of a space not lately used. The shades were drawn, but Harry made his way in the dark to the desk, switched on the lamp and raised the shades.

Harry still said nothing. He wiggled open a window and sat down on the edge of one of the desks and lit a cigar. On the wall a maiden with come-hither eyes and a slave bracelet advertised California Hardware Company; the calendar underneath her was torn to March, 1926.

"I didn't realize you had an office." I said.

"I don't." Harry replied. "I'm thinking of opening one though." he added after a pause.

"Business picking up?"

"It might be." he said. "So what were you and Doc talking about?"

I told him about confessing my worries over Buster, and Dr. Breuner's suggestion that he might take up boxing.

Harry listened, nodding. He was already two steps

ahead of me. He had asked around about Buster, given his daughter's interest in the boy, and from what Edith reported, the boy's obvious interest in her. He'd learned that Buster was well liked by his various employers and had a reputation as a hard worker. Everyone Harry talked to regarded him favorably as a good natured, friendly boy, popular with the ladies, for sure, but with the reputation as a gentleman.

"I'd like him to go to school." said. "It's hard for him with his newsboy work hours."

I expected Harry to say something about the younger generation being mollycoddled, and how plenty of youths in his day had been newsboys and went on to make something of themselves. Instead, he agreed with me.

"I'll need an office boy to run messages and that sort of thing. He could do his schoolwork here, and we could probably fix up a janitor's closet with a cot for him to sleep in."

"Would the landlord stand for that?" I asked.

Harry surprised me again. "My mother owns this building." he said.

Edith filled me in later about Harry's mother. She was a tiny octogenarian widow from Tennessee, whom everyone, including Harry, called Price Dear ("Though she's anything but!"). She had followed her son out to Los Angeles and started buying up real estate here and in Hollywood on what had been vacant land in the middle of nowhere. She was mean with money, however, and lived like a miser, alone in Hollywood.

Harry's closet idea would be okay, but I thought it would be lonesome for Buster.

"I might have Buster stay with me, at the Rosslyn." I found myself saying. The thought had just occurred to me.

"Planning on settling here then?" Harry asked.

I stared out the window, down at the web of streetcar cables. Electric lights twinkled from signs on rooftops.

I liked the feel of the place, its hustle and its wide streets so you didn't feel like the buildings were closing in on you. I even liked its newness. Rome had once been new. Being here was like watching one of those ancient civilizations being built, I thought.

I lit a cigarette. "Maybe I could go to work for you too."

I turned to look at Harry. His profile was half outlined by the lamplight.

"You want to be an operative, like Edith?" he asked.

"I know I have a lot to learn– "

"I'll say you do." he said. He fell silent. The only sounds were the street noises from below. "Detective work isn't like it is in books." he began finally.

The impulse to run headlong into something, the urge to action, could hinder an investigation more than it helped, Harry said; one of the most useful skills for a modern detective to have, he insisted, was patience. Sometimes you had to wait for a target to make a move, or a wire that would put the lid on a case. It might mean combing through old police reports and mugbooks, newspaper files, or real estate index books at the county recorder's office. It was hard, oftentimes tedious work, he insisted.

It was also important to know people, contacts, connections, people who could be called on to provide help or information.

"You're a natural when it comes to that, Shepard. You're good with people. You've got charm. People talk to you. I could use a person like that."

"So, you'll–"

"But, you've made a lot of mistakes. You've been foolhardy and bull-headed. You can unlearn those things, though. The important thing is your instincts are sound. Like the way you followed your hunch about the Pagoda– even though it was idiotic to go charging in by yourself."

"I agree I could have–"

"Good instincts and the guts to follow up on a hunch are skills that can't be learned or bought, and a detective isn't

101

worth a damn without 'em." Harry said.

"But?"

"But nothing." Harry said "My instincts tell me you're honest and I can trust you. I'll think about it." He closed the window and went around pulling the blinds down again.

"What happens now– about my case?"

"What happens is I keep looking for your sister." Harry said. "And you don't go to the Pink Pagoda by yourself and let them use you for a heavy bag anymore. If the Sing woman said she's never seen Miss Shepard there before, you can take her to the bank– about that anyway."

"You don't trust her otherwise?"

"I think that was a nice story the Doc told. Some of it might even be true."

After another long pause, I said, "Look, I've asked Helen Sing out for a drive with me tomorrow."

Harry shrugged. "Good idea, keeping tabs on her."

"That's not why I invited her." I said. "And I wasn't asking for anyone's approval. Anyway, I thought she was on our side."

"Let's just say, I'm not convinced that Mrs. Sing is telling us all she knows, and leave it at that for now." Harry said.

CHAPTER 10

Build thee more stately mansions, O my soul;
As the swift seasons roll!
Leave thy low-vaulted past!
Let each new temple, nobler than the last,
Shut thee from haven with a dome more vast,
Till thou at length art free,
Leaving thine outgrown shell by life's unresting seal!
—Oliver Wendell Holmes, "The Chambermaid of Nautilus"

I picked Helen up at her hotel the next afternoon. She was dressed in a green checked sports frock under a camel hair polo coat with tan leather walking shoes and carried a large leather handbag, an umbrella, and her hat. Her hair, I noticed, seeing it in natural light for the first time, wasn't jet black at all, but the color of polished rosewood. She looked sweet and wholesome in the winter sunshine, and highly decorative.

"Which'll it be?" I asked after getting her settled in the passenger seat up front. "Mountains or seashore?"

"Oh, seashore, definitely." she said, pulling her hat down over her head. We settled on Long Beach, where Helen said there were a couple of hotels that did a nice supper on Sundays, one quite new. I looked it up on the maps.

We spoke very little during the drive, only about the weather and other trivial things. Helen navigated and pointed out the sights to me, when there were any. I found that I was self-conscious around her, knowing all that I did but unable to say anything to her without Doc Breuner's okay. I'd thought of cancelling the outing, to be honest, but on the other hand felt that Harry, in giving it his approval, had intended for it to have the opposite effect, and I chafed at the idea of being Brer Fox to his Brer Rabbit. I tried to forget his suspicions of her. After all, she'd voluntarily agreed to help Doc. What was in it for her? I glanced at her sidelong and caught her watching me, her expression as inscrutable as ever.

When we arrived at the beach, I left the car at a garage on Ocean Boulevard and we strolled down to the seafront walk where sailors promenading with their girls shouldered past us, harried mothers darted across our path chasing after little ones, and an electric tram full of passengers glided by, tooting its horn impatiently. Helen's heels clicked along on the broad concrete walk, trying to keep up with me.

"Could you slow down, please?" she asked.

The salt air was tinged with other odors: fish, fried food of indefinite origin, creosote, vanilla. There were confectioners; Cream Do-Nuts; hot dog stands; root beer and orange ade stands; stands selling popcorn, roasted peanuts, old-fashioned pickles "like mother used to make;" barbeque and corned beef sandwich stands with long wooden picnic tables; ice cream and frozen custard stands; cafés and lunch counters. There were scales that told your weight and others that guessed your future; gift shops that sold oriental curios, wax flowers and razor strops, souvenir spoons, piggy banks, china bathing beauties and pin trays, painted seashells, leather belts, and needlework; a photography studio selling rolls of camera films, picture postcards and Your Portrait, Any Backdrop– two poses for a quarter; barbers, cigar shops, shoe shine stands; a sheet music shop; a tango game parlor, a penny arcade; a bath house and plunge; a vaudeville house. Jazz music poured out of a dance hall, mingling with the roar of the roller coaster, waves of music from a merry-go-round's organ playing "Oh! You Beautiful Doll," the crack of guns firing from shooting galleries, the strident tones of barkers hawking bags of hot nuts, the whir of a cotton candy machine, and the cries of the sea birds that swooped and dove overhead like the dips of the coaster.

We went out on the pleasure pier, where the swells of the ocean surf under the wooden planks crashed and roared in time to a hurdy-gurdy. Hatless flappers came staggering out of a fun house, adjusting their garters showily for their Kodak-wielding sheiks. Pairs of shingle-bobbed young girls raced past us toward a roller skating rink. Rival dancing pavilions pouring forth the likes of "Bye Bye Blackbird" and "Where'd You Get Those Eyes?" competed for the jazz hound's nickel. Young men played Skee Ball or showed off for their sweethearts at the shooting galleries, the bottle toss and other games of chance, spending a week's wages to win kewpie dolls, garishly painted chalk figurines, or purple and orange glass dishes worth no more than a penny. Hula-hula dancers swayed to Hawaiian guitars while the ballyhoo artists did their best to lure suckers into sideshow tents ("This way to the Pig-A Dilly Circus!" "C'mon up folks– see the GEN-u-wine baby ratt'lers!").

Comely clairvoyants with beaded eyelashes and bright headscarves wound around raven curls offered to crystal gaze and read our palms. Helen stopped in front of one of the stalls. She might have been a gypsy herself, with her dark hair and eyes.

"Do you want to have your fortune told?" I asked.

"Oh, no." she said. "They're nothing but charlatans."

There were people everywhere– waiting to board the Ferris wheel, watching the Dodg'em cars, resting on benches: packs of schoolboys arguing over the divvying up of their penny candy; old timers with sticks resting across bony knees;

courting couples who took no notice of any of it. A trio of deeply bronzed bluejackets contemplated Sailor Jack's tattooing parlor. Small children ran up to their parents and begged for more dimes, got them, and raced off again. For all the crowds, the place had the stale, washed out feeling of a resort out of season.

We wound our way out of it at last and came onto a landscaped area a little ways apart where there were benches facing out to sea. Helen tugged the collar of her coat up around her neck and sat down on one of them. I stayed standing. Next to us, a hotel's empty tennis courts looked desolate; from the other direction the sea breeze carried screams of laughter from unseen riders on the coaster.

"Why don't you just come out with it?" Helen said, "Or do you want to keep glaring at me the rest of the afternoon?"

I turned around. "I wasn't glaring at you."

"You were." She looked up at me and waited. "You've heard something about me."

I didn't respond at first. Then I blurted: "You're married."

It seemed to me she relaxed. She seemed almost amused. "Well– what of it? Aren't you married?"

I sat down on the bench with her.

"I'm separated." I said.

"I am too." she said. "Do you want me to tell you about myself?"

I stared out at the oddly peaked, gray silhouettes of the warships on the horizon. A few green and red lights flickered from fishing craft, heading back to the harbor. We were in for a storm.

"Look at me, please." Helen said. I turned to face her. The expression in her dark eyes was pained but frank.

"I met Jack when I was practically a child, dancing in a music hall chorus line to support myself. He was a visiting performer– he performed magic acts and sold cure-alls, that sort of thing. He was scholarly, very cultured, well-read. He educated me, taught me things."

"I'll bet."

"Do you mean my drug habit? That's one thing I can't lay at Jack's door. He helped me to get free of it. We became lovers and he made me part of his act. We travelled together and lived as man and wife, were billed that way– I took his name– but we were not married. I've never told anyone that. We couldn't marry, in fact, because Jack already had a wife. She would never give him a divorce, he told me. I found out later he had simply deserted the woman, and that she was not his first wife– another fact he neglected to mention. I don't believe now that he ever intended to marry me, even if he had been free.

Jack was chronically unfaithful, from the very start. He was good-looking, charming to a fault, and something of a local celebrity wherever we went. He never had any trouble getting women– and young women are so stupid. I should know– I was one. They were drawn to him like the proverbial flies to honey."

"Flies are attracted to other things besides honey." I said.

"Quite. In one town where we stayed for three weeks, he became particularly attached to a young girl who was all of fourteen. They eloped, taking all the receipts and the act with them. I was left there with no money, no real skills, no family. I came back here, to Los Angeles, where I was born, to try to start a new life."

"Are you still in contact with him?"

She shrugged. "No. I long since ceased to care anything for him, not even to hate him. I simply don't think about him at all. I kept his name because with it and my looks, I could sometimes get work billed as an oriental performer."

We stared out at the green-gray ocean; neither of us

spoke. After a little while I said. "We've both had pretty knockabout lives, sounds like." I said.

She looked at me and her eyes flashed. "I didn't tell you this to have you pity me."

"I don't, far from it." I looked her straight in the eyes. "But Helen– I have to know: were you on the level when you said you've never seen Kit– my sister– in the Pagoda?"

The black eyes really snapped now. "What do you take me for? Of course I was. I've been called some filthy things, but not a liar."

"I believe you." I put my hand on hers and she didn't pull it away. "I'm sorry."

"So am I." she said softly. "Well– what do you think? Shall we walk?"

I kept hold of Helen's hand and we strolled, skirting the amusement zone this time, past a gleaming fountain– a memorial to the recent war dead– and onto the midway again. The concession stands had bags of sand stacked in front of them but their striped awnings– green and orange or brown and red– stood out cheerily against the gathering gray clouds. We retraced our steps, past billiard parlors, a bowling alley, an aquarium of sharks and brightly-hued tropical fish, and more confectioners. Helen admitted to a weakness for salt water taffy so I bought her a box and we walked out onto a double-decked pier, strolling in companionable silence, and stood for a few minutes at the rail looking over at the pleasure pier and feeling the salt spray in our faces. Helen waved to the fishermen with their lines and buckets who stood at the rail below us, dressed in sailor's pea jackets and baggy sweaters.

It grew windier and we turned back, going out along the promenade and onto a protected sand beach where there was a band shell. A couple of kiddies in blue and orange bathing suits dug in the sand while their folks looked on from picnic blankets.

"I love the sea." Helen said. "There's something peaceful, almost spiritual about it, don't you think– the way it washes everything clean then starts over, fresh again. This sea in particular. It hasn't been tainted by war and tragedy." she added.

She was shocked when I told her I hadn't seen the Pacific before. "Well, how do you like it? Does it seem different to you– knowing out beyond is the exotic, the tropical. The call to adventure. Or didn't you read *South Sea Tales* and dream of jumping a tramp steamer to Malaita?" Her eyes teased.

"Who me? I get seasick if I hear "The Oceana Roll" played too fast." I teased back.

We watched the waves pound the fence that surrounded the beach, sending plumes of foam and salt water higher and higher– six feet or more– until the sky opened up and it started to rain, a real downpour. The picnickers darted around, gathering up their youngsters, scrambling for cover.

"…I cain't find my shoes, Mama."

"Well, where'd you leave 'um?"

"Dunno."

"Quick, Harold– go and look for your sister's shoes…."

I took Helen's arm and we made a dash for it, taking dubious refuge under the slatted roof of the band shell's pavilion, then under the awning of a café.

Helen wrenched her hat off with a jerk and shook her head, like a dog. Her hair stood out in unruly waves and her cheeks were flushed from the blustery salt air. "I must look a sight." she said, laughing.

Before today I'd pegged her as a hothouse flower, the kind that were only at home reclining on velvet sofas or slouching around swank night-clubs. I would never have pictured the *soigné* Helen of the dance hall racing along a beach and laughing about her own disheveled appearance.

"You look okay." I said. I took her up in my arms then, and kissed her. She kissed me back; her ardor matched mine. We sat down on a bench and stayed there, embracing like that for some time until Helen broke away, breathing

109

hard.

"You're one of those primitive males– all yang." she said, close to my ear.

"Is that good?"

"It can be. Ask me in the morning."

"You mean it, Helen?"

Her dark eyes met mine frankly. "I know what I'm saying. Can it be done?"

"I'll manage it." I said and kissed her again, hard.

When the rain let up enough we walked up the street and around the corner to The Breakers, the hotel where we'd planned to have an early supper. But instead of going to the dining room, I parked Helen in the ladies' lounge and went to the lobby desk.

"My wife's taken ill." I said to the clerk. "She's not up to driving back to the city tonight. Can we get a room with a bath right away?"

"Certainly sir." he said. He produced a register, and consulted it.

"Would you like to have the hotel physician look in on her?"

"I don't think that's necessary." I said. "She doesn't like to be disturbed when she's poorly."

I signed the register, A. R. Shepard and wife, Rosslyn Hotel, Los Angeles.

The room was a pleasant one, with windows overlooking the sea and all the modern comforts– built-in radio, hot and cold running sea water in the bath– and a double bed.

Helen put on an act for the bellhop that would have impressed Bernhardt. I congratulated her on it after he'd gone.

"Oh, I'm good at pretending to be a wife. I have practice."

"Don't." I said.

"Don't what?"

"Helen– I don't think you're as hardboiled as you

pretend to be. I like you the way you were earlier. I think that was the real you. This cynical act is just a pose."

"I'm not a cynic, but I am realistic. I have no illusions about the way most men– decent men– would view the way I lived."

"I'm not exactly a candidate for sainthood. I'm married. And here I am with you. What does that make me?"

"It's different for men and you know it." she said. "But for you and me, right now, the way I see it– we're both free, white and twenty-one. We want each other. Let's say we forget about what society would call it, forget our own troubles for a few hours, and just concentrate now on pure pleasure."

She looked me up and down, sensually, and could probably see what effect she was having on me. "I think you could please me very much." she said. "And I think I know what you'd like. I want to please you."

She unbuttoned her dress and wiggled out of it, showing me her pearly-white body clad only in a black silk teddy trimmed with cream lace. She had small, firm breasts, pert; the nipples were hard and showed through the lace. It was the best thing I'd ever seen. She had narrow hips and a tiny waist, with plump thighs and dimpled knees, and ankles– as I'd already observed– as dainty as a racehorse's. She kept her eyes on me while she unbuckled and kicked off her shoes, then peeled off her garters and filmy stockings.

"God, Helen…."

She came toward me. "Your turn, Avery. Let's get you out of those wet things–."

She undressed me, with my help, and pushed me gently back toward the bed.

"Lie back." she whispered. I obeyed and she stood next to the bed, just out of arm's reach, looking at me. "You're magnificent. I knew you would be." she murmured and slipped the teddy's ribbon straps off her shoulders, letting it slide to the floor.

Her hair, and her body, as silky as the sheets, caressed me. She traced my scars, old ones, and kissed my bruises, new ones, gently.

I'd never been with a woman who responded like Helen. Afterward, I felt weak, weaker than I had been after Morelli hit me. We slept.

It was dusk and the rain was still coming down. I stood looking out of the window at the lights that twinkled along the coastline as far as I could see. The occasional note of music– the carousel organ or the wail of a jazz trumpet, wafted across the water. The amusement pier was lit up like it was on fire, its lights reflecting off the sea, which was dark except when the beam from a searchlight tower made its sweep. In the distance pinpoints of light marked the battleships. Beyond, the outline of the purple mountains reminded me of Helen's lovely shape.

I turned around to watch her, walking about nude and unashamed, and admired her full, heart-shaped posterior as she leaned over to retrieve her damp stockings from the floor, draping them over the back of the desk chair, near the radiator. I ordered supper sent up to the room, a nice one– Lobster *a la* Newburg with cheese toast. We deserved it, Helen declared.

"I'm feeling particularly virtuous for having resisted the temptations of all that food on The Pike." she said.

"Except for the taffy."

"That doesn't count."

There was also champagne– good stuff, the McCoy.

"We want something sparkling to drink and I don't mean ginger ale– savvy?" I'd told the waiter, and tipped him plenty. He brought it up with the dinner, grinning, and said it was "fresh off the boat."

"He probably meant it quite literally." Helen remarked; Long Beach was, she noted, lousy with rum-runners.

We ate sitting on the floor, with pillows scattered all around, oriental style, and chatted about this and that– nothing very personal: recent shows we'd both seen, the now ex-champ Jack Dempsey, whom Helen saw quite often around town with his wife, who was a film star. We didn't discuss the dance hall, or Doc. Then Helen put her chin in her hand and asked me about my marriage.

"Can't we talk about something pleasanter– like Bright's disease?"

"Oh, come on, Avery. I told you mine. It's only fair."

"Well– okay. Where do I start? We split up about four years ago. That was by my choice, but I don't think she's too broke up about it." *As long as I kept sending the money.*

"When did you get married?"

"Right after I got out of the Army. She lived in the neighborhood. My mother knew her mother." *And what a mother.* "We went to school together."

"You mean– you and she were– high school sweethearts?"

"No. I went with a lot of girls. I took her to a dance or two. She was one of those pure, high minded types who thought if a boy kissed her, it more or less amounted to an engagement."

Helen smiled at me from under lowered lashes. "And did you kiss her?"

"Once, maybe. On the cheek."

"So you married her?"

"I joined the Army." I said. Helen laughed. "I don't mean because of her. I'd just turned eighteen and wanted to get away from home. There was no engagement. I didn't write. But, when I came back everybody– her and her folks and mine– seemed to expect that we would marry. I drifted along with it."

"You weren't in love with her?"

"No. I wasn't even in lust. She was too pure and high minded for that. Maybe– I never thought about it before–

113

maybe pure and high minded had its appeal after– the war and everything. Or maybe I was just drunk. Hell, I didn't know what I was thinking in nineteen-nineteen. I mean, I bought a jazz suit."

"You didn't!" Helen exclaimed.

"It was blue, summer-weight worsted, with a chalk stripe. I looked like Lonesome Luke. Even the rag man refused to take it."

Helen laughed. "I don't doubt you were lonesome."

"Well anyway, whatever it was, by the time I snapped out of it, it was too late– there was nothing to do but go through with it."

"She must have been very pretty."

I shrugged. Ruby Alyce had been a pretty girl, once, by prewar standards– plump, rosy-cheeked, and pompadoured. Her looks were already fading. Within a few years, she would probably be the spitting image of her mother. That hadn't had anything to do with our parting though; it was her personality becoming like her mother's that had made life with her unbearable. And then, too, Ruby's chaste, virtuous attitude had continued after we were married.

"I'm probably a disappointment to her. She wanted a stay-at-home type of husband." I said. "I still support her. Separate maintenance, no kids. I expect we'll divorce one of these days. I figured I should let her make the first move on that."

"That's the gentlemanly way." Helen said. "Somehow, though, I suspect she hasn't played exactly fair with you, either."

She poured us some more of champagne and we touched glasses.

"You're a hell of a woman, Helen." I said. "Why me? I'm not classy, or cultured, or any of those things."

"Don't sell yourself short, Avery. You've got charm– genuine charm I mean– you make me laugh, you're good, decent. And I like your looks, your strength." She looked at me across the little table with lowered eyes. "Sometimes, a woman gets tired of being an unprotected female and wants to be taken care of." She put down her glass and licked her lips. "Just now, though, I want to take care of you." she said, and came forward across the rug to rest on her knees in front of me.

I lay in bed with Helen in my arms. Our sex had been savage, more so than even before and I felt spent, completely. Helen reached across my body for a cigarette on the night table and I breathed in her perfume. She snuggled against me. Then, to my shame, I found I was crying. I couldn't stop it happening. I cried like a little child. Helen just held me close, like a mother with a child, not speaking, only murmuring soft, soothing sounds.

"I don't know why I did that." I said when it had finally passed. I sat up with my legs over the edge of the bed, my back to her, not looking at her.

"You needed it. All of it. This has been a terrible time for you. A lesser man would've cracked before now." She lit a cigarette for me, from her own, and handed it to me. "Talk to me about your sister."

I told Helen all about Kit, then– her tomboy childhood, me teaching her to swim and drive a dogcart, and how she loved to sing silly old songs with me on the pianola. And I told her the family secret– that Kit was in fact my half-sister. I only found out after our father died. He had left a letter about Kit for me in his things. She was his daughter by some other woman. An affair. Not the only one, I don't think, but that's just my guess. He was discreet. This woman wouldn't, or couldn't, keep Kit. Father had claimed she was the baby of one of his patients who died, and brought her home for Mother to raise.

"We kids, Kit and I, never had an inkling but Mother knew better, of course." I said. "And to be fair, I think she treated Kit the same as one of her own. Which isn't saying much."

"I can imagine what a beastly shock it must've been to Kit. I hope you broke it to her gently."

"That's the hell of it." I said miserably. "I kept it from her, after I found out. I couldn't tell her. I thought– I don't know– I was afraid she'd think that I'd feel different about her, would think less of her. Kit is more of a sister to me than Bert ever was. I barely know Bert, and what I do know I can't say I like. Kit's worth the lot of them, the whole damn family. I wish I could tell her that."

"You'll have the chance."

"Our– my– mother told her. She blurted it out when Kit told her she was coming here to be a dancer. She said 'blood always tells.'"

"Oh, my God." Helen gasped. "The bitch– I'm sorry."

"You don't need to be. I said the same thing. Kit didn't mention a word about it to me in her letters. I guessed something had happened though, and got the story out of my mother. I'll never forgive her for it. I mean it."

Helen stroked my chest with her long tapering fingertips. I lit another cigarette.

"Ave, do you think– if Kit did go away on her own– this could be why? Finding out like that– who knows what effect it had on her, psychologically, in the sub-conscious maybe. At that age, no longer a girl, not yet a woman, really– you're just starting to figure out who you are, then to have it all blown to hell–"

"I suppose. Although, if it were me, I'd be thrilled to find out I wasn't really related to Mother."

"Oh, Ave– don't joke." Helen said, leaning up on one elbow and watching me, her eyes keen. "I'm serious."

"I know. But Kit would have told me, if she got married, or was– in any trouble."

"Girls don't always tell their brothers everything." Helen said softly, looking away. "We all keep secrets, some of the time."

I awoke to sunlight steaming in the windows and the smell of fresh salt air. Helen was beside me, already awake.

"Good morning." she said, smiling. I thought she looked beautiful, radiant, bare faced with her hair all tumbled wildly about her head. We kissed and she felt for me, smiled. "Uh-huh, I thought so. All yang. And yes, it's very good."

She led me into the bath and ran it, pouring some of her perfume into the water. *Nuit de Chine*, she said. Then she bathed me, leaning over and running the sponge teasingly across my body before getting into the tub with me herself.

After that we had breakfast in the room. The ever-helpful bellhop brought us up some toothbrushes and toilet goods from the drugstore. Our clothes— my suit, and Helen's dress— came back from having been pressed in the laundry, and we reluctantly dressed. Helen finished first and laughed that women wear so little these days, it was easy. "Ten years ago, I'd have still been buttoning my shoes." she said.

I left her to go get a shave in the barber shop downstairs. Then I paid the hotel bill and brought the car around. We drove back to Los Angeles.

We were to have no regrets about our night together, Helen had said when I dropped her at her hotel. We made vague plans to meet again for a late supper some night, nothing specific. She made me promise not to come to the Pink Pagoda again.

I kept the rented car until the afternoon, when I used it to meet Buster at his school. Before that, however, I went in to see his home-room teacher.

She was a pleasant, tall, slightly mannish-looking woman of about forty, a Mrs. Mabel Kerr.

"We're all very fond of Buster here, Mr. Shepard." she said. "He's extremely bright. I'm sure he could easily gain a scholarship one day if he were to keep at it. I have a lot of boys leave school— sometimes they have to, to help support their families, but others just don't care for any more

117

education. Buster, though, loves to learn."

"He says he might not be able to graduate."

She sighed. "The last thing I wish to do is keep him back, but he doesn't have enough credits to advance. He's missed so much school."

"What if he did extra lessons between now and over the Christmas recess– can he make up for it?" I asked.

"Y-yes, I suppose it would be possible." she said, nodding. "But it's a lot to take on. I understand he's on his own, and works to support himself–"

I interrupted. "If you'll give me his lessons, Mrs. Kerr, I'll see he learns them."

"I'd be glad to. I'm so pleased, I can't tell you, Mr. Shepard. I'll certainly be praying for him to succeed." she said.

"Well, between your prayers and his hard work, he ought to have a fighting chance." I replied. We shook hands.

Buster was surprised but glad to see me. I drove to the garage and turned in the hired car then we walked over to Harry's new-old office. Or I should say, I walked and Buster floated. He'd had his date with Harry's girl, Lyric, the afternoon before and still hadn't come down out of the clouds.

We took the elevator to the fourth floor suite where Harry had brought me the other night. The words Price Detective Agency had been lettered in gilded paint across the frosted glass of the door. Inside, the forlorn and cluttered space had been put into some sort of order. Edith, with her auburn hair tied up in a scarf, bustled around in her efficient way, a clip-board in hand, supervising a representative from the telephone company, who appeared to be stringing a line for a couple of extension telephones. Through the inner door, I glimpsed Harry at his desk in his shirtsleeves, chomping a cigar and talking into his telephone. There were fresh flowers on his desk.

"Hello, boys" Edith grinned at us in passing.

A charwoman had been in; the windows had been

washed, the floor was swept and scrubbed, and everything looked and smelled clean. A water cooler had been set up in one corner. File cabinet drawers yawned open, half full of yellow folders. The hardware supply calendar had been replaced by one from Adahor Dairy Farms that featured a cow, presumably female, but not come-hither eyed. Lyric was there, on a stepladder, arranging a set of Britannias in the glass-fronted bookcase; a brawny delivery man in dungarees and a hickory shirt was leaning on his handcart ogling her legs until Edith swept by and pressed a coin into his hand, shooing him on his way. Lyric caught sight of Buster and her face lit up. She wore her middy blouse and skirt having, I supposed, come right from school like he had. Buster went to her, and helped her down the ladder.

"I've got another couple of books for you." she said, giving him two volumes out of a satchel.

He held them, reverently: one was a novel, the other was the life of Jim Corbett, *The Roar of the Crowd.*

"Gee, kid, these are swell." he said. "I've got something for you too." He reached into his jacket and withdrew a small box of what looked like handkerchiefs, and handed it to her. "Because I got yours all bloody yesterday."

"That was sweet of you, Robbie." Lyric said. "They're lovely."

"What's this?" I asked.

"The other guy's blood, not mine." Buster said.

Lyric explained. She'd been waiting for him around the corner from the hotel when a strange boy came along and started teasing her, trying to get at her handbag. She ignored him but it only made him cut up worse, and he'd grabbed hold of her wrist when Buster came up and punched him straight on the jaw, knocked him to the ground, then straddled the would-be thief and punched him in the face some more. They left him there "taking a nap" and went on to the soda fountain.

"He was awfully brave!" Lyric concluded.

"So were you." Buster said. "You didn't faint or anything."

The kids took their books and sat down together on the leather davenport– his dark head and her curly golden one bent over the pages, close together. Edith took me aside. "There's big, big news. I'll see if Harry's finished. He's in a foul mood." she added in a whisper.

"How can you tell?" I muttered.

Harry hung up the telephone and looked at me. I was sure he could tell where I'd spent the night, and with whom. Well, it was none of his business. *I'm free, white and twenty-one*, I thought.

"I tried to reach you before." Harry said. "I've got something. Where is that goddamn file? For Chrissake, Edie, I can't find anything around this place."

"It's right there in front of you, on the blotter." Edith said sweetly.

Harry opened up a yellow file folder but didn't look at it.

"We've found your sister's baggage." he said. "Edith did."

"You did? Where?"

"She checked it at the Southern Pacific Station baggage room here on the ninth of October. A leather suitcase and a hand grip."

"And– they're still there?"

"Not here in Los Angeles. They're in San Francisco."

"You think Kit's in San Francisco, then?"

"No, only her baggage." Edith replied in gentle tones. "The railroad sent it up there. They do that when things go unclaimed after thirty days. It sits up there for another thirty days then it's sold at public auction. We only just got to it in time. Her things would've been sold in the next few days. I got Frank Ricketts to intervene with the railroad– he told them how it's involved in a missing person case and they're sending it back down here."

"If she never called for it then something must have

happened to her."

Edith patted my arm. "Not necessarily. You wouldn't believe how much unclaimed baggage they get down there. Folks move to a smaller place and don't have room for it, or they don't have the money to redeem it, or who knows what all. We'll see when the things get here if there's any clue in them."

I nodded.

"There's one more thing." Harry said.

Edith went to a safe in the corner of Harry's office, opened it, and brought out a black case. I recognized it even before I saw the gold-lettered initials, K.A.S. It was Kit's– a portable phonograph I'd sent her as a present from New York.

"I have a pal at police headquarters on the pawn shop detail." Harry said. "I gave him a description of Miss Shepard's baggage and he kept an eye out for me. They found this, at a shop on West Fourth. It was pawned on the eighth of October."

"Why?" I asked. "Kit had money– her bank account still has a balance. She didn't have to pawn her things. She'd have needed the phonograph for her dancing. Are they sure it was Kit that pawned it? It could have been it was stolen from her."

Edith referred to the report on Harry's desk. "The clerk didn't remember Kit specifically from her photo but he vaguely recalls it was a young woman who brought it in– 'a looker' he said."

Edith and Harry were watching me. I saw sympathy in Edith's eyes; Harry's as usual were unreadable.

Presently, Buster had to leave to get his papers. I left Edith to her organizing and went out with him. When we were alone downstairs, I stopped and faced him.

"Look kid, don't ever let me hear of you pulling a stunt like that again, punching that guy."

He stared at me, open-mouthed. "What? You think I

121

shoulda just stood by and let the cocksucker hurt her?"

"No." I said. "Next time, go for his belly. Sock him in the gut first, and get him down on the ground, then wallop him until he cries like a baby and you put him to sleep. Goddamn it, you could have broken your hand hitting him in the jaw. You've got to protect your hands first, always."

"What else?" Buster asked, sounding enthralled.

"Don't let him hit you. You know what feinting is?"

"Like in *The Three Musketeers*?"

"Sort of. The thing is to wear him out. Then finish him."

We walked along in silence while Buster thought all of this over, his papers forgotten for the moment.

"Your hand's okay, though?" I said. "And you won. That's something."

"Oh, I licked him alright– no foolin'." he said. "Did you ever do any boxing, Ave?"

"A little. I could punch okay but I'm too heavy in the legs. I haven't got enough speed. A good fighter's got to have both."

"Will you show me some of those moves sometime?"

We were out in front of the Rosslyn. I found a quiet corner of the lobby and told him of Doc's offer to get him a try-out for the Athletic Club's boxing team.

He stared at me, a dreamy look in his turquoise eyes. "Do you really think they'd have me, Ave? I know fuck all about the proper form or any of that."

"Don't worry, kid. They'll mostly just want to see how you strip, and if you can use your hands." I said, and promised to show him a few basic moves later, if he wanted.

Kit's bags arrived by express train from up north the following day. Edith and I met Ricketts at his office to go through them.

During the war it had been my job now and then to oversee the packing up of things that belonged to lost or missing men; this was a little like that. Only the men, while I regretted their loss, weren't young women, weren't my sister. Kit hadn't many worldly goods with her. She'd traveled with just a suitcase and a hand grip, intending to send for her trunk later, after Mother had gotten resigned to her remaining in California. There were her clothes, haphazardly packed; books; pieces of inexpensive jewelry; some trinkets, just small mementos that a girl keeps from her childhood; her hairbrushes; my photograph and letters. There was nothing to tell us where she had gone or what had become of her.

CHAPTER 11

When goodness is lost, it is replaced by morality.
—Lao-Tsze, Tao Te Ching

On Thursday afternoon Harry and I took Buster to the Los Angeles Athletic Club for his boxing tryout. Doc had fixed it all up. Buster wore a white sweatshirt and duck trousers with a pair of crepe-soled gym shoes; women on the streets turned their heads to watch him pass by. He hung back outside the grand doors of the entrance, held open for us by the gloved hand of a liveried doorman.

"Holy fuck, I never thought I'd set foot in this place. These guys always tell us kids to scram if we even pass by on this side of the street."

"Don't let Admiral Eberle here bother you any, kid." Harry said. "I remember when he was only Sailor Wallace out at Jack Doyle's place, getting soaked on the mush every Tuesday night."

"Aw, I never did." the doorman scowled.

We were met in the gymnasium by a friendly, clean-cut type fellow not much older than Buster— Royal Johnston, assistant to Mr. Frye, the coach of the boxing team.

He took Buster downstairs to the locker rooms. Buster came back dressed in a blue and white workout uniform emblazoned with the club symbol– a crescent moon and the winged foot of Mercury.

It was the cleanest, brightest gymnasium I'd ever been in, with a massive skylight above and metal truss-work keeping the thing in place so that there were no columns on the floor itself. A gallery ran around the perimeter where several other boys were working the bags and the pulley weights or skipping rope. They paused to look on and razzed Buster good-naturedly.

"Aw, lookit who's stripped for action!"

"He's a tough looking baby, awright."

We looked Buster over the way we would horseflesh. He was skinny but muscular, with a nice reach. He had a slim waist and slender legs, well-built shoulders.

"What do you figure him for– a banty?" I asked.

Harry ran a practiced eye over the boy's form. "Feather, more like. Not for long, the way he eats."

"You called it." Johnston said "He weighed in at one-twenty-five."

"He's still growing." I said.

They would have to take care not to develop his muscles too fast with too much weight-lifting.

"Let's see what you can do with the gloves on." Johnston said and invited Buster to select from a pile of training gloves and leather head-guards piled on a side bench. Then he called to another youth, who'd been shadow boxing in a corner.

"Hey, Jakey! Come and spar with Buster here."

We watched Buster climb into the ring for the first time. He looked as cocksure as usual, leaning against the ropes while the other boy put on one of the helmets, but I could tell he was anxious.

"Remember what I showed you?" I asked him.

"Yeah." Buster said. "Thanks, Ave."

"Just try to keep your ass off the canvas, kid." Harry said.

The two boys faced off.

"You're a newsie?" the other lad sneered.

"Yep."

"Aw, newsies make lousy fighters."

"Oh yeah?"

Johnston, acting as referee and timekeeper, incanted the rules and told them to shake hands and come out fighting.

"C'mere you sap"

"I should worry."

"Be nice, boys, be nice! Break clean!"

"Keep your hands up, McElmon!" I yelled.

Buster seemed to have both speed and a powerful, snappy punch.

After three rounds, Johnston ended the match. The boys stepped out of the ring.

"Say, I was wrong. You're one sweet puncher." the other boy said.

"Wish I had your footwork." Buster replied.

"For Chrissake, will you listen to 'em?" Harry said, chomping down on his cigar. "They sound more like a meeting of the mutual admiration society than fighters."

Johnson dismissed the other boy and escorted Buster downstairs again to the locker room to shower and change back into his street clothes.

We waited in the elevator hallway near the entrance to the locker rooms and steam baths. Members of the club, some trim and fit looking, some fat, some emaciated, wandered by in various states of undress, talking of the stock market and loan yields or the grid battle coming up between Knute Rockne's Fighting Irish and the local team, the Trojans.

Harry nudged me. I followed his gaze to a man of medium height with a receding chin and hairline who had just come off the elevator. What he had left in the way of hair was plastered to his white scalp like an oil slick. I put his age at about forty-five. A bit of a paunch hung over the waistband

126

of his B.V.D.'s, which were of striped silk. He had a bathrobe draped over his shoulders, and wore black socks with Paris garters, and black oxfords.

"That's our man– that's Hillman." Harry said. "Silk drawers– it figures."

I looked at the man again with more interest. He had his thin nose buried in the financial pages of a newspaper. I remembered Buster's newsboy trick of sizing people up by their shoes and looked down. Hillman's were scuffed at the heels and wanted shining. Buster would probably know what to make of it; I didn't.

At first Hillman took no notice of Harry and me. His features contorted in obvious annoyance at something he read and he tossed the paper away into a wastebasket. Just then he looked up and caught sight of Harry.

I'll own Harry's looks could come across as intimidating: his height, combined with the broad shoulders, the proud cheekbones, and the crooked nose, not to mention his scowl– but even so there was no accounting for Hillman's reaction when he saw Harry watching him: his eyes opened wide and his mouth fell slack like something out of the funny papers. He gave a low, strangled yelp, and scurried like a frightened puppy into the sanctity of the steam room.

I turned to Harry, who was watching Hillman's retreating figure with narrowed eyes and a frown.

Before I could think any more about it, Johnston came over to us to shake hands.

"I think we'll make a fine pugilist out of your boy." he said. "He's got heart, and he can sock, alright. He'll be a fine addition to the team."

When Buster was ready we left the athletic club and went down the street to a restaurant, a steak and chop grill, for a late lunch as Buster hadn't eaten before the workout. I watched him tucking into his porterhouse and fried potatoes, followed by a slice of chocolate cake and ice cream, thinking how he wouldn't be able to eat like that much longer, once he had to start making weight.

"Your coaches are going to look out for you." I said. "In the pros, you see some young pugs go out too fast, their managers push them too hard, let them over-train, and ruin them."

"The way they coddle fighters today you might as well wrap 'em up in cotton wool." Harry said. "Take those pillows they use for gloves– and only ten rounds? Hell, you can hardly get going in only ten. You ought to try fifty."

"The only thing is," Buster said slowly, setting down his fork. "They want me there on Saturday morning for my first workout. I don't see how I can. I got the papers to get out."

Harry and I exchanged a glance

"Well, as a matter of fact, that might not be the case much longer." I said. "It's up to you."

Harry spoke up. "Here's what we're proposing, kid. You do your workouts at the club in the mornings, like they tell you. Then you go to school. Afternoons you come over and work for me in the office. Evenings you'll have to do your homework.

"You can live with me, at the Rosslyn." I said. "Starting tonight if you want. But you have to go to class and keep up with your lessons. No more ditching." I told him then about my deal with Mrs. Kerr, and the fact that he might well be able to graduate and go on to high school in the new year.

Buster looked from Harry to me with a stricken expression.

"Isn't charity kid– I'll work you hard." Harry said. "You'll wish you were back hustling sheets."

As Harry strode off to pay the check, Buster burst into tears and swore furiously. I looked away while he blew his nose with his handkerchief and composed himself.

"It all sounds swell." he said. "Does this mean you're gonna stay around here for a while, Ave?" he asked.

"I'm not going anywhere." I said. "So have we got a

deal?"

"Deal."

We shook on it.

Outside the restaurant, a toothless old man begged for the price of a cup of coffee. I kept walking. Harry gave him a coin then fished a dollar bill out of his billfold and gave him that too.

"Get your teeth out of hock with it." he glowered.

We took Buster to a department store across from the athletic club to get him outfitted for his training. Harry and I intended to stake him to it, but Buster would have none of it.

"Uh-uh, nothing doing." he said, his expression set. "I've got some jack saved up."

"You hang onto it, kid.' Harry said. "I may need a loan someday. Don't think I'm kidding."

Buster stood firm. But while he tried on athletic shoes, track pants and the rest of it, Harry and I fixed it up with the clerk for the bill he presented Buster with to be adjusted somewhat, in Buster's favor, without him knowing anything about it.

By the time Buster made his selections and we'd arranged for the parcels to be sent over to the hotel, he had to run off to get his afternoon papers and give notice to his bosses.

Harry bought a cigar from the stand on the corner and lit it.

"Did you mean it about coming to work for me?" he asked.

"Sure I did." I said.

"Then meet me here, at this corner, tonight at half past seven." he said. He strode off with his fast, long-legged gait. I sauntered along at a more leisurely pace back toward my hotel.

It was the popular shopping hour and the streets were thronged with people. Signs outside the department stores warned ominously that there were only twenty-two more shopping days until Christmas. Banks touted their Christmas Club savings plans. Workmen were busy stringing greenery, lights and bells of red and silver and green tinsel from one side of the street to the other, and from streetlamp to streetlamp. Shop windows were edged with white scallops, meant to look like snow, though even the mountains to the north were still bare.

I came to the corner of Sixth and was about to go into the drugstore to buy a toothbrush and a few other things I thought Buster might need when I caught sight of a dapper, goateed gentleman coming out of a steamship line passenger ticket office in the same building. It was the man I'd glimpsed talking to Gladys at the Bamboo Garden, who'd been at her funeral. He carried an umbrella as a makeshift walking stick, and wore the gray sack suit and the gray derby, with spats and chamois gloves. I decided to shadow him. It would be good practice for when I started working for Harry, and besides that, I was frankly curious about the man.

He walked west on Sixth Street. In the crowded sidewalk I had no trouble following him closely without his knowing it, I was sure. He seemed in no hurry, pausing now and then to look into a drugstore or shop front display window.

We came to Grand, and waited at the light together, along with at least a dozen other pedestrians. Kitty corner across the way, on the northwest corner, was the Hotel Savoy. I stuck with him as he crossed Sixth and continued his way west, passing the hotel. We came to Hope Street. Gladys's apartment building was across the street on the southeast corner.

The crowds had thinned out by now so I had less cover. I loitered a few paces away from him, under the awning of the hotel, and lit a cigarette. When the light changed with a clang, he crossed Hope and so did I.

On the corner was an older, two-story building housing a realtor outfit, a photographer's shop and a watch repair shop. My quarry stopped in front of the latter and consulted his pocket watch; since I practically had my hand in his back pocket, I had to choose between halting abruptly and running the risk of attracting his attention or walking on ahead. Walking ahead seemed the wiser of the two, so I passed him.

I ducked inside the entrance alcove of the neighboring building, a shabby, three-story brick hotel with a couple of awning-shaded storefronts on its ground floor I counted to ten then came out again and headed back the way I had come, intending to pass my quarry. The man, however, wasn't there. I figured he must've gone into the photographer's so I pulled my hat down lower over my forehead at a different angle and went inside. There were displays of hand-tinted photographs along one wall, and portraits of all sizes– lots of babies, some wedded couples and elderly folk but overwhelming the subjects were young women. The showroom was empty of any living persons though except for the photographer, a young man with a wisp of a mustache and watery brown eyes behind gold-rimmed spectacles.

"Did a man come in here?" I asked.

"No, sir." he said. "Can I be of any assistance?"

I ignored him and went next door to peer in the watch repair shop; it was empty, closed in fact. There were three men in the realtor's office on the corner. None was the one I sought. They glommed onto me, determined to sell me a fruit orchard or a poultry farm, or better still a poultry farm with a fruit orchard on it. I finally got free and strode back out onto Sixth Street. The goateed man wasn't anywhere.

"Well, shit." I muttered, and threw my cigarette down. I went around to the back of the building, but it wasn't any use. There was an auto park on the adjacent lot, running from Hope all the way north to Flower Street behind the rear facades of the buildings that fronted Sixth. If my quarry had come this way, he was not in sight now. I strolled, defeated, through the auto park and back over to Sixth. At least Harry wouldn't have to know anything about this little venture.

I paused on the corner in front of a hotel café to light a cigarette. I saw it then– an advertising poster in the window, next to a menu board offering an Irish lamb stew and dumplings special.

HAVE YOU TROUBLES?

The Reverend O. M. Seher

Spiritual Advisor

Business   Investments   Love

Marriage   Divorce   Health

Healing Services Ω Full Life Readings

Private Parlors ♦ Strictly Confidential

You Are Invited To Call

9 a.m. to 12 p.m.; 1:30 p.m. to 6 p.m. daily

Sundays 12 p.m. to 3 p.m.

"Seek Ye the Light of Knowledge"

One Who Knows

Success - Wealth - Love - Life

There was a rendering of the Rev. Seher on the poster. His goatee was black not grey, and he wore a kind of turban instead of a derby or homburg. But it was him. The blazing eyes looked straight at the camera, partially closed, and he wore a knowing little smirk. His hands were folded like a church steeple under his chin.

Seher's address was the hotel whose doorway I'd ducked into earlier. Perhaps he had sensed I was shadowing him. In any case, he'd given me the slip and I wondered why. I was sure he was the one who had been Gladys's so-called spiritual advisor. There were always plenty of frauds of his sort in any city, or wherever there are enough vulnerable, gullible people to keep their doors open, but this particular fraud was right in her neighborhood and he had come to her funeral. I decided I would pay him a call.

The consulting parlors took up two rooms on the third floor. I walked in, feeling more like the fly than the spider, and found myself in a small, windowless anteroom arranged as a sort of library and waiting room. There were bookcases along the two of the walls, their shelves sagging under the weight of thick, morocco-bound and gilded volumes. A half-dozen chairs were arranged along the two other walls, and most of them were occupied. There was a young woman in an office dress, a stout and prosperous-looking matron of middle-age in a smart suit and fur scarf, and an old man with long ragged whiskers, studying a mining pamphlet. The three of them turned to stare at me as I came in then hastily looked away and avoided making eye contact with me, or each other.

At one end of the room, near the door to the outside chamber there was a library table, with a portable typewriter on it and stacks of papers. Behind it was a niche that served as a shrine, I supposed, for a large, carved Buddha statue. At the table sat the sullen blond stunner I'd seen leaving with the Rev at the Bamboo Garden.

She was still sulky, and still blonde. Her eyes were a lovely violet-blue, outlined with a kohl pencil and darkly shadowed. She had not been told, or didn't care, that bosoms were out of fashion at the moment, and displayed hers prominently in a tight rose-colored silk dress and no brassiere. Her perfume, a heady, floral scent, wafted up. She had her elbow on the desktop, and her chin cupped in her hand and was reading from a book that lay open in front of her. She looked up as I approached. There was no flicker of recognition in her eyes; I'd clearly made no impression on her at all.

"Do you wish to have a reading?" the girl asked in a flat, petulant tone.

"I dunno." I said. "How much does it cost?"

She narrowed her eyes at me and hissed: "It's five dollars for a private sitting. But if the Reverend's visions help you, you can donate more."

"That sounds fair enough." I said.

She sighed heavily– it was almost, but not quite, worth walking up three flights of stairs to see– and took a sheet of paper from a sheaf of them on the table and handed it to me on clip-board along with a pencil, an envelope, and a piece of notepaper. The latter was blank but for a symbol at the top of it– a triangle, with a sort of sun radiating from it and a thing like an eye in the center of that.

"Fill out the form, then write down your question on the paper and seal it up in here." she said.

"My question?"

"Your problem." She looked me up and down, and spoke slowly as one would to a not particularly bright child. "The thing what it is you want the Rev. to help you with."

The form the blonde secretary wanted me to fill out asked my name, address, age, occupation and annual income. I made up answers for all of the questions and left the piece of paper blank. I sealed it inside the envelope anyway and handed the lot back to the girl.

Then I took a seat in one of the small chairs, taking care to avoid meeting the eyes of my neighbor, and waited.

There were stacks of leaflets on a side table. I picked one up and glanced at it.

HAVE YOU ATTAINED YOUR SOUL CAPACITY?

What is the source of Reverend O. M. Seher's strange and wonderful abilities you may ask?

It is a power of a higher nature– THE SOUL. Every person is possessed of an aura, which tells the history of our past lives as well as OUR FUTURE. Only those possessed of special gifts can see and read this aura. THE REVEREND SEHER takes a mental imprint of your soul, and thusly your aura– with its secrets past and present– is revealed.

IT IS POSSIBLE to realize your greatest ambitions in life, find success in business, and happiness in love, in marriage. Allow the Rev. Seher to remove the impediments that are preventing you from realizing the prosperity and satisfaction that ARE RIGHTFULLY YOURS.

You MAY THINK that $5 is too high a price to pay for such information, that you cannot afford it. WHAT YOU CANNOT AFFORD is this chance to learn your future. The recompense you reap from it will far exceed the cost.

It went on in this vein. Then there were testimonials of unnamed "prominent Los Angeles citizens" who had relied on the Rev. Seher's advice in locating oil wells and were now bathing in the stuff, or had found their "soul mate" through his teachings and their domestic happiness knew no bounds.

The secretary periodically got up and bounced over to get office supplies out of a closet or escort a waiting client into the adjacent room. The girl in the office dress was the first to be called. She remained penned up with Seher approximately twenty minutes, and came out again somewhat flushed, clutching her bag and gloves. The old man went in next, and stayed for only ten minutes at most. He seemed satisfied by whatever Seher had told him, however. The middle-aged matron followed. Her visit lasted no more than fifteen minutes, but she too looked pleased. Then it was my turn. I followed the sullen, bouncing blonde through the inner door.

The blinds were drawn and the room was in semi-darkness. It had the cloying smell of incense. On a table by itself, a brass lamp flickered like a gas flame under a red globe. There were Persian rugs both under foot and on the walls, the latter suspended from brass rods. Against one wall was a pair of carved teakwood Chinese chairs inlaid with pearl, a carved walnut cabinet full of curios between them. In the far corner there was a daybed draped with Turkish rugs and embroidered pillows, with a carved taborette next to it and a tapestry-paneled screen in the other corner. On the wall between this chamber and the anteroom was a bookcase and a large roll-top desk, closed. A small Buddha figurine leered down from the top of it.

Seher stood in front of the desk with his hands folded under his chin in the church steeple position, watching us enter. He had replaced the derby with a tall black hat, and draped an embroidered yellow silk robe over his gray suit, which looked a little incongruous with the spats. The girl went to him and they spoke in low tones for a few moments. I glanced over the bookshelves idly.

Now that I was here, I had no plan. I'd more or less satisfied my curiosity about the man.

"Bring us some tea, please, Zaida." Seher ordered, staring fixedly at the girl. She gave him a sullen look and flounced out, slamming the door closed behind her.

"You are interested in the history of eastern religions, the secrets of the immortals, perhaps?" he asked. His voice was steady, deep, silky. I turned from the bookshelves and met the small black eyes, which almost seemed to flicker like the bulb of the lamp. Up close I saw that, for all their fiery expression, they appeared cold. "My library is quite well known." he went on. "Many famous persons come here to consult it. You might not have heard of it. You are a newcomer to Los Angeles, I believe."

Aren't most people? I thought.

"I think you knew a friend of mine. Gladys Watson. A young girl who worked as a dance instructress. You were at her funeral."

He stroked his goatee and wrinkled his forehead. "Ah, yes. Miss Watson. I was most distressed to read of her death. So unfortunate– a young and vibrant girl struck down in her prime. I can only hope her next life will be a better one." He fingered the Buddha figurine on the desk and stared at the ceiling.

"How long was she a… disciple of yours?"

"Oh– briefly. I have a great many followers among the younger generation. So many these days are lost. Spiritually, that is. I do what I can to help them realize their life potential. I should have known Miss Watson was not long for this world. Her life readings had begun to come up an absolute blank." He made a gesture with his hands, spreading them wide, palms up.

I couldn't help laughing.

His lips turned up in a smile. "Oh– I see. You are a doubter. You have no faith in gifts such as mine because you believe only that which you can see, grasp."

"I know bullshit when I hear it. And I've heard enough."

He stepped closer to me. "You mustn't go yet. You haven't had your reading." He gazed at me with his intense stare. I looked into the empty eyes. "You are a very troubled man. You seek knowledge and don't find it because your mind is closed. I believe I could enlighten you." he said.

He stepped toward me and said, almost inaudibly: "If you have patience, what you search for will find you."

It was a shot in the dark, nothing more than that.

Probably three-quarters of the people who came to him were searching for something or other– money, love, lost property, a pet– or a relation. He was just a charlatan of the lowest type, trading on people's desperate hopes.

I turned on my heel and stalked away. The girl, coming in with a tray, blocked my exit for a moment. I brushed past her into the now empty anteroom.

"That will be five dollars." I heard her call after me crossly. I told her where she could find it.

CHAPTER 12

There are no mysteries any more. If a crime becomes a mystery, it is because it has not been properly handled.
— William J. Burns, 1923

I got back to the hotel in time to see Buster settled in before I had to go out again to meet Harry. An adjoining bedroom would be ready for him tomorrow afternoon but in the meantime, they were going to make up the davenport in the sitting room. I'd asked also for the use of a radio, thinking it would keep him amused. I told him he could listen to it while he had his supper, after he'd finished his homework. I couldn't tell him where I was going, what I was doing, or what time I might be back, because I didn't know myself.

I stood with Harry in an alley that ran between the backs of the Pink Pagoda, the Hillman Building, and some shabby three and four-story brick buildings. Lights twinkled in a few of the Hillman's office windows; the top three floors were dark. Those floors, Harry noted, belonged to the Realty Club. Hillman's syndicate, the Pacific Land & Improvement Company, added them last year, when it bought the building, which had also been completely remodeled and modernized by them inside and out. But Harry hadn't brought me out here for an architecture lesson.

"We're going to have a look around inside the Pagoda."

"How?"

The Pink Pagoda's rear facade presented a blank face to us, unblemished by a single door or window into the alley. Its north wall abutted the Hillman Building.

"There are at least four ways in. Three for sure anyway." Harry began. Then he stopped and listened. Footsteps were approaching, along the alley. Faint, but Harry heard them. I stepped back into the shadows and wished I had brought my gun. Harry stood where he was. I wondered if he had a gun, or at least a blackjack. The footsteps halted. A shot rang out in the dark.

"What the–?" I hissed.

"It was only a car backfiring." Harry said.

A voice whispered in the darkness. "That ye, Harry?"

"Yeah."

A man came up to us wielding a flashlight; it had something over the lens so that only a pinprick of light shone through. He was a tiny and very old man with a sailor watchman's cap pulled low over his forehead. He had a ruddy, wrinkled face with a deep, wedge shaped scar over one cheek and a wide, purple-veined nose. The lid of one eye drooped so much that it barely opened. He wore a dark, high-necked sweater and dungarees with black crepe-soled shoes, and carried a small leather pouch.

"Jockey Sam O'Shea, Ave Shepard." Harry whispered. I shook Sam Shea's gloved hand. It felt like a bag of bones, but the grip was like iron.

"Well let's git on wiff it. I cannae stan' 'ere gabbing like a bunch o' wimmin." Sam said. "Yers ain't me only job tonight."

Harry marched us over to the electrical appliance store next door to the Pink Pagoda. There was a fire escape up the back of it; Harry reached up to grab hold of the metal ladder and pulled it down for Sam, who scrambled up to the first landing as nimbly as a child. He kept going. I went next. At the top floor landing there was a door. Sam crouched down in front of it and shone his flashlight beam on the lock.

"You can handle it, can't you?" Harry asked.

Sam gave him a withering grimace. "This aren't nuffing. A wee child could do it."

He unrolled his leather pouch on the grated metal floor and selected a long, file-like tool, working it in between door jam and the lock. Then he took up a metal pick and something that looked like a bolt puller. Within a few seconds he had the lock disabled. "Whit did I tell ye?"

Harry tried the door, and pulled it open silently. Sam put his tools away and rolled up his pouch again. He and Harry shook hands.

"I'll settle up wiff ye later, Harry. Good luck te ye." Sam said, and vanished silently back down the ladder.

Once inside the back of the building, Harry and I found ourselves in a dark hallway lined with frosted glass office doors. We followed it until we came to an intersecting corridor, where we found the service stairs and took them up to the roof. Once out on the roof, I saw that we were looking at the back of the store's huge electric sign, dark now, that faced Hill Street. Down below us was the narrow gap between the store and the Pink Pagoda; I could see my unlucky fire stairs going up its side. Across the gap it was just a short drop onto the roof of the Pagoda building, its two floors apparently having higher ceilings than this one. Harry nodded to me, then took a flying leap. I heard the dull thud of his landing. His voice hissed, out of the darkness. "C'mon Shepard."

I jumped.

Harry waited while I had a cigarette.

"Why in the hell couldn't we have just come up the Pagoda's fire stairs and had Sam break into their door?" I panted.

"It's no good. Look, that passageway's a blind alley—

only one way out. And from what you said, it sounds like once you're on the other side of it you run the risk of bumping into the bouncers. We can leave that way, though, when we're through here."

"Good."

We found the hatch in the Pagoda's roof that led to a hallway on the second floor and made our way toward the front of the building where the ballroom was. We peered out and could hear the faint sounds of the jazz orchestra tuning up. I explained the layout to Harry, as far as I knew it.

He nodded. "Head for the Sing woman's dressing room."

"What do we do if someone comes?"

"Run like hell." Harry said.

I led Harry around the corner to the red carpeted hallway. The high pitch of young feminine voices came from the girls' resting rooms. We also heard laughter from behind Helen's closed door. Harry tried the knob of the room next to it. It turned, and we went in. Something hit me in the gut. As my eyes adjusted to the dark, I saw that I'd walked into the end of an ironing board. The room was being used as a sewing room– there was a wardrobe against one wall and a sewing machine on another, and there were garments draped over the back of a chair. Harry made his way over to the wall adjacent to Helen's office and pressed his ear to it. I did the same, and heard the girlish voices chattering. It sounded like there were three or four of them.

"…I told him where to get off, awright."

"they gonna have any eats?"

"…one 'a them fresh guys."

"…usually some san'wiches at least."

After a few minutes the hall door opened and a woman in high heels came in.

"Inspection time, girls." she said. It was Helen. "Look sharp."

The girls squealed. Then a man's heavy tread came in.

"Okay– let's see some ankles. You gals is lookin'

good tonight." the man said. I recognized Morelli's voice. "You're a real cute kid, sweetheart. Have I seen you before? You gals wanna stay that way, doncha? Then do whatcher told an' keep quiet about it. Get me? Okay. Doors are opening to the squirrels in ten."

He stomped out.

"...remember– you mustn't say anything to the other girls." Helen was saying "It will only cause jealousy and that will spoil everything for everyone."

The girlish voices rose and fell again all at once.

"...and plenty to drink, too, but I'd advise you to steer clear of it." Helen was saying. "Now– you'd better hurry and finish getting ready. Do any of you need anything pressed or sewn?"

I looked at Harry; he gestured with his eyes to the wardrobe cabinet, but held up his index finger. We waited. The girls murmured.

"Be on the spot– on ten at ten, then." Helen said.

We heard the girls file out. Harry opened the door a sliver and peered out, then closed it again. No sound came from the other side of the wall. At first I thought Helen must've gone out with the girls. But after a couple of minutes there was a woman's heavy sigh, followed by an oath and a loud bang as something hit the wall, followed by a crash of glass breaking. Then the room was silent again. Harry and I stayed put.

I could hardly believe it of Helen– that she would willingly be in league with a man like Morelli. It just didn't wash. Morelli must have had some hold over her, something that he used to get her to do his dirty work for him.

After a little while I heard Helen's high-heeled step cross the room; the door opened and closed and she locked it behind her.

"What are we going to do now?" I asked half-heartedly. I didn't look at Harry.

"We'll get a cab and wait out front. The other girls

won't be coming out until after closing time. There were four girls in that office. When they leave at ten, we'll follow them, see where they go."

With caution, we exited our hiding spot. The Pink Pagoda had opened for business; the band was now going full swing and men's voices rumbled from the foyer. I found our way down the hallway where I'd walked first with Helen then with Cauliflower Ear, and we left the Pink Pagoda by the fire stairs.

Harry secured a cab and had the driver position it across the street where we could see the front doors.

At about half past nine a purple and lavender Cadillac sedan pulled up to the curb in front of the Hillman Building. I had seen it here before; there couldn't be another one like it in Los Angeles– not that color.

The driver switched the big motor off and came around to open the door for the passengers. Three were in dark suits and overcoats, one wore evening dress with a top hat and a white silk scarf around his neck. He was Henry Hillman.

He looked larger than he had in his underwear at the club, but sickly pale under the glare of the streetlight.

The men of his party were older, well-fed and amply jeweled; they laughed and patted each other on the back and talked in loud, carrying voices. They were well-oiled, alright. Hillman was as hearty as the rest, but there was a melodramatic quality about him. His actions seemed forced, affected, and he looked over his shoulder several times.

"We'll see after I get the bills...."

"...not that I would mind it year round...."

"At that price I'd be a fool not to...."

The street seemed almost quiet after the quartet disappeared into the building and out of view.

I turned to Harry to see if he'd noticed what I noticed and found him lost in thought. We sat in silence for a few minutes. Then he suddenly slammed his big hand, palm open, down on the roof of the cab.

"So that's it!" he exclaimed. "I'll be damned."

"Hey, look whacha do to my goddamn cab–" the driver shouted.

Harry leaned in and handed him a bill. "Get out of here before I see how you'd look with your balls for a bowtie."

The cabbie must've decided, wisely, it wasn't healthy to argue with Harry and there was no harm done to the cab, after all. He grabbed the money and sped off in a clash of grinding gears.

"What–"

"The girls. They're going up there."

He pointed up at the Hillman Building.

On the roof, a huge sign with pink, green and white electric lights reading PAC-LAND flashed on and off alternately, each color going dark for a couple of second between intervals before the whole thing started over again.

On the top floor, the tenth, a row of arched windows, high up above Hill Street, dark a moment ago, were now all lit up.

"The Sing woman said 'meet on ten at ten.' She meant exactly that– the tenth floor at ten o'clock."

I stared at him. "And Hillman? What put you on to him?"

"Just a hunch. He's been acting nervy." Harry said. "You saw how it was when we ran into him at the A.C. earlier? I followed him the rest of the afternoon, and made sure he saw me. All I can say is, he acted mighty peculiar. He tried giving me the slip. If he wasn't feeling guilty about something, why wouldn't he come over and demand to know what the hell I was following him for?"

"What are we going to do?" I asked.

"We'll watch and make sure I'm right. Then I'll call a meeting with Doc tomorrow and we'll spill the works, about the Sing woman being part of it, everything."

"We can't stand by and let those girls– and those old men…" I thought of Hillman's flabby, white body and shuddered.

"I don't like it either, but I don't see what we can do about it now. If Hillman's expecting girls and doesn't get them, it's Morelli's hide, then it will be the girls' hides." Harry said.

"We have to do something. Imagine if it was Kit– or your daughter– going up there."

"Goddamn it, Shepard, don't bring my daughter into it." Harry said. He fell silent again.

"The hell with it." Harry said finally, and threw the stub of his cigar in the gutter. "I need a telephone. And a pharmacist. Wait here."

The Realty Club had its private lounges on the top floor, along with a library, a billiard room and a private banquet room, Harry recalled from the newspapers. There was a garden terrace on the roof that they used in the summer months. The two floors below were given over to the club offices, guest bedrooms and other dining and lounging rooms. The elevator cars emptied directly into the club rooms, as only members and their guests were allowed off at those floors. Harry quizzed the elevator operator without the operator realizing re was being quizzed and got him talking about Hillman's parties. Hillman hadn't brought any girls up tonight, he said with a wink. They didn't usually arrive until ten.

We sat in the Hillman Building's plush lobby– all mahogany paneled wainscoting and pink and black marble with beefy bronze hanging lights that might have been plundered from an Italian castle– and waited. For what, I wasn't sure, but hoped it would happen soon.

Then the front doors opened, emitting a blast of traffic noise from the street and a clatter of high heels that echoed across the white travertine floor.

Shit– they're early, I thought.

I looked up to see a blonde and a redhead coming toward us. They made for Harry.

"Well, here we are!" the redhead called. "How do you like us?

They opened their coats and twirled around in front of us. "It's the best we could do on such short notice."

They looked like school girls, dressed in middy blouses and pleated skirts, but with rolled stockings and very high heels. They wore heavy, artfully-applied makeup and it was not until I looked closely that I realized they were probably closer to forty than school girl age– but were damned attractive, shapely women.

The redhead batted her eyelashes in my direction. "Who's yer cute friend?"

Harry introduced me to the women. They were Ida and Pearl.

Pearl, the blonde, said "I swan Harry, this is the weirdest job I ever had. You want us to pretend to make these rich geezers– only pretend?"

"Sure." Harry said. "You know, get some lipstick all over the glasses, leave a garter or two and some hairpins lyin' around– you girls can think what to do better than I can. And slip a dram of this stuff into their drinks."

He held up a little vial of white liquid and gave it to Ida.

"It won't croak 'em, will it?" Pearl asked.

"No. They'll just sleep like babies after a few minutes. They'll wake up in the morning with bad headaches, thinking they've had a grand old time and tell all the boys back in Ohio or wherever they're from what a hot town Los Angeles is."

"I swan– leave it to Harry. Can ya beat it?" Pearl asked me.

"We better run along, hadn't we?" Ida said. "We gotta be back by eleven."

Harry directed them to take the elevator and ask for "ten, as usual."

We watched their swaying forms retreat for a second then I turned to Harry.

"What in the hell? What are they– hookers?"

"I ought to slug you for that, Shepard. They're ponies, from the Burbank Theater. Good girls, and useful to know. Ida's a high stepper– used to be on stage with Edna Goodrich, back when women looked like women not your bookie in a dress."

"But there's only two of them."

"No matter. Hillman and company will be seeing double."

"What are we going to do with the real girls when they arrive?"

"It's your turn to think of something. Use your charm." he said. "Say, how much cash have you got with you? This is turning out to be an expensive night."

Harry and me and the four girls dined on Virginia ham steaks and eggs and coffee at the Barbara Hotel near Westlake Park. Harry, I thought, was awfully generous with my money. Our party would have been just as happy with cold sandwiches at a drugstore counter, and felt more at home. Not that I begrudged the girls any of it, not really. The quartet– Alice, Dorothy, Joyce and Sylvia– ate as enthusiastically as Buster did. In snatches, between giggles and comments on everything from the menus to the little baskets of flowers on the tables, and the waitress's snappy uniforms, we got the whole story. Sylvia, Alice and Dorothy had been to parties at Hillman's before; Joyce was new.

"This spread is better 'n anything we'd get from him." Sylvia said. She was a pretty girl, with brown, bedroom eyes and bottled-blonde hair and an inch or so of face powder attempting to cover an acne-marked completion, but her voice sounded hard.

Alice was also blonde, naturally so, I thought, and much freckled, with a breathy baby-voice and blank china-blue eyes.

Dorothy was a tiny, dark brunette who put away a second helping of ham and two pieces of pie, noting between mouthfuls– to the accompaniment of much eye-rolling from the other girls– that she simply couldn't keep weight on with all the dancing she did and had to get all her things in the children's department of the May Company.

Joyce, a stunner with a brunette bob, full red lips and plump, dusky cheeks, spoke English haltingly and kept pulling at the choker of green beads around her neck.

I gave them each ten dollars and we took them home by cab around one o'clock. Little Dorothy yawned as we dropped her off, and admitted she was glad to be getting in early for a change; she had school in the morning.

Harry and I rode together back downtown. We didn't discuss Helen. Harry asked to be let out at Third and Spring, and said he would see me in the office in the morning. I took that to mean I was working for him.

I went in quietly so as not to wake Buster, but found him stretched out on the davenport bed, in one of his new athletic shirts, reading *Lorna Doone*.

"Hi Ave." he called out.

"Hi yourself." I said. "You ought to be asleep."

"I will. I was waiting up."

"Did you do all your homework?"

"Uh-huh." I offered him a cigarette. He hesitated then shook his head.

"Mr. Johnston at the gym told me I ought to cut 'em out. He said I'll have better wind if I do."

"That's the truth." I said. "Your coaches are going to

help you take care of your body. The only pugs I ever knew who are real top notchers live clean– no drinking, no late hours, no running around with women."

"I'm not going to." he said solemnly. "Say, boxers make a lot of jack don't they?"

"Some of them do." I said cautiously. "Look, Buster– boxing's a good skill for a boy to have, but it doesn't have to be your living. If you study hard in school, Mrs. Kerr thinks you can probably get a scholarship to college. You don't want to miss out on getting a good education while you can. I wish now I hadn't."

He sat up on one elbow. "You, Ave? But you're plenty smart."

"Not book-smart like you are. I never cared about it, much." I said. "Well– you better get some sleep now or you'll fall asleep in class and Mrs. Kerr will have my hide for it."

"Just a little longer– to the end of this chapter?"

"Did you remember to brush your teeth?" He nodded. "Goodnight, then." I said. "No more than five–minutes, not chapters."

Buster called after me on my way to my room. "Say, Ave–"

"Yeah?"

"I'm glad Harry didn't see me bawling today. He'd think I was soft."

"Look– I've seen big, strong men, prizefighters, soldiers, do the same thing." I said. "Anyway, it's possible–just– that Harry might be a little soft himself, but don't tell him I said so."

CHAPTER 13

I got to hand it to him, it's a damned clever set up." Harry was saying. "He's got himself a built-in supply of girls, with new ones coming in all the time, and no one thinks anything of it. He can even advertise for them if they have to. All the while, the dance hall's making money like they're minting it, even with all the palms he has to grease. Hillman, I'm going to bet, pays Morelli a fat fee for supplying the girls, or else has some arrangement with him about the rent. The girls only see a pittance for their end of it. Guys like Hillman probably tip the rubbers at the A.C. more than they give those girls. To them, though, it's a goddamn fortune. Sorry, Doc."

It was just before noon and we were in Doc's office at his high-Victorian church on Figueroa Street near Tenth.

I'd headed to the office that morning at seven-thirty, dressed but not shaved, with my head in a bad way, having stayed up drinking the Rosslyn's bootleg and thinking about Helen long after Buster's light went out. Storekeepers were out sweeping the sidewalks and putting up their awnings. From the drugstores and cafés came the smell of roasting coffee and cooking grease. Men with grubby packs slung over their shoulders came staggering out of rooming houses, blinking into the winter morning light. The theaters, which had a certain lurid glamour at night all lit up, looked worn-out and tawdry at this hour. I thought of Pearl and Ida for some reason and wondered how they had got on.

I found the office locked; a charwoman paused in her task of polishing the brass stair banister to let me in. I sat down at the desk across from Edith's and read the newspaper. Edith came in about half an hour later, carrying a bundle of flowers.

"Good morning, Avery. Chosen your desk already, I see." she smiled, hanging up her hat. I groaned as she pulled the shades up with a jerk. "Honestly– you look like a fugitive from the Keeley Institute!" she laughed. "Late night shadow job with Harry? Never mind– don't tell me. Go on and get yourself a shave. I'll make you some of my coffee– Turkish and strong enough to grow hair on a billiard ball. Very restorative."

"Sounds like something you'd order out of the back pages of *The Police Gazette*." I said.

By nine-thirty I'd been shaved and, fueled by plenty of Edith's coffee, had made it about halfway through a pile of reports she'd given me to examine for one of her cases– a bank job, very dreary, she said. Harry still hadn't come in.

I looked up at Edith.

"Who's Jockey Sam O'Shea?" I asked.

"He's the last of the old time yeggs." she said. "There isn't a safe in this town he hasn't cracked."

Around ten I felt well enough to try to eat something. I went across the street to a drugstore and ordered a cheese sandwich and a slice of hot mince pie. From my counter stool I could see the south window of our office through the drugstore's arched windows. I had just taken a forkful of pie when a red pasteboard square went up in the corner of our window– that was Edith's signal that I was wanted urgently. I left my money on the counter and rushed over without even putting on my coat.

Harry had telephoned, Edith said; I was to leave immediately and meet him at Doc's office.

"I see how it is." I grumbled. "He doesn't tell you what he's doing but when he wants you, you had better hop to it."

"Something like that. It's just his way." Edith said. "Don't forget to keep track of your cab fare– it comes under expenses."

Harry briefed Doc on all we'd learned the night before– how Helen approached each of the girls separately, on different occasions, and asked them certain personal questions. Then one night she'd asked if they didn't want to earn some extra money by going to a "party" with Hillman in his office. They didn't even have to leave the building– there was a connecting door into the lobby of Hillman Building that only the chosen girls were told about– no one but themselves need ever know about the parties. In fact, it was important that they keep them a secret, as all the girls would want to go, but Hillman only wanted them– the prettiest. The setup appealed to the girls; they helped support their families or a boyfriend on their incomes from the dance hall and these dependents knew, practically to the nickel, how much they brought in every week. The bonuses from Hillman went directly into their stockings.

It had been obvious to Harry and me that the girls were afraid of Morelli who, they said, treated the girls "awfully rough." They thought Mrs. Sing was "kinda tough, but fair."

Doc had listened in growing distress and I was glad he didn't have to hear it directly, as we did. The girls had told of going to bed with Hillman in casual tones, even laughing over some of his peculiarities ("He keeps his socks on– can ya beat it?").

"I needn't tell you how disheartened I am by this."

153

Doc said. "I can't bring myself to believe that Mrs. Sing would, of her own free will, betray my trust and the trust of those girls. I can only suppose– could it be– that she is only going along with it to gain this Morelli's deeper trust for some purpose we don't yet know."

"Or Morelli has some hold over her and is blackmailing her." I said.

"Or Morelli offered to pay her more than Doc to keep her mouth shut." Harry said. "Let's get down to brass tacks. The thing that has to be decided is– what do you want me to do now, Doc? We know the vice cops are in this thing up to their necks. Mrs. Sing sees them collecting. The beat cop gets a cut, too, for not reporting what he sees. Why would he? He squawks, all it gets him is fired."

"So why not go over their heads, to the chief of police." I suggested. "You know him?"

"Not really. I remember when he was a patrolman on the Chinatown beat." Harry said. "He was head of vice himself not so long ago. He's only been chief a little while and he's already broken up the central vice squad. A bunch of captains got reassigned and he sent the lower ranks out to the local divisions. I don't know what his motives were but it doesn't bode well for us. Chiefs of police have a funny way of not lasting very long in this city if they get too inquisitive."

"Well, he could hardly just sit on his hands and do nothing if Doc and the other preachers went to him and complained loud enough."

"No– the cops would do something." Harry agreed. "They'd use it as an excuse to raid the little guys, the ones that refuse to pay for protection. They'd make a big show of shutting the joints down and hauling people down to Central on some trumped up charges– selling liquor, or violation of the closing laws– it doesn't matter. They'd maybe even raid Morelli, but they'd send him an engraved invitation that they're coming so he'd have time to hide all of his records. It'd get into all papers– but they'd make damn sure their reporter pals print only the stuff they want printed. People read about the raids the next morning over their ham and eggs and think the police are doing a great job. The boosters can point to it and brag that we don't tolerate crime here like they do in Chicago. They're happy. The preachers are happy, because they think justice has been served. And Morelli is happiest of all, because he has less competition. As soon as the public outcry dies down, his place reopens on the QT, under a different name, or supposedly different management."

I sighed. "So, Morelli and Hillman are just going to get away with it?"

"Not if I have anything to do with it." Doc said, his kindly eyes snapping. He knew everything Harry said was true, and he didn't like it any more than I did.

"For Chrissake, hold on." Harry said, holding up his big paw. "Who said we have to throw in the sponge?" Doc and I looked at him. "We have one card up our sleeve– and that's the District Attorney."

I raised my eyebrows. "He's a good guy?"

"No. He's a crook." Harry said. "One of the worst we've had, and that's saying something. But that could play into our hands just now."

"I don't see how." I said.

"He's attracted some powerful enemies lately. First, he's under attack by the governor, who publicly accused him of being incompetent and derelict in his duties– says he protects vice and has a curious reluctance to prosecute criminals, considering that's the D.A.'s job.

"He's also antagonized the one newspaper in town that can call its soul its own– and its new editor exposed one of the D.As other peculiarities: that is, if he can't avoid charging a criminal altogether, his next best trick is allowing them to plead guilty on a lesser charge. Morelli was brought in on an assault with a deadly weapon rap last fall when he damn near beat a guy to death with the butt of a pistol– you were lucky, Shepard. By the time it gets to court though, it

155

seems Morelli had merely disturbed the peace and he gets off with a fine. If all else fails and he can't help sending an obliging criminal to prison, then he quietly works with the prison board to get him paroled. This paper called the D.A. a puppet of the crook who pulls the strings at the mayor's office, and everybody knows the crime bosses have city hall in their pockets. That, of course, is nothing new. 'He who runeth vice runeth the politicians because he geteth the votes' as the good book says, right, Doc?"

"Well, I don't recall that precise quote." Doc replied. The twinkle in his eye was beginning to return.

"Finally, there's McPherson woman. Ever since the D.A. indicted her she's been firing away at his reputation every chance she gets, and hell hath no fury like a woman who has her own radio station."

The D.A. had dragged his feet over the McPherson case all summer, Harry explained– announcing to the press that he would investigate it fully one day and calling it off the next. His actions had sparked criticism on two fronts– from the evangelist's supporters who decried his persecution as unfair, and those who felt she had perpetuated a hoax and ought to be made to answer for it. In September the D.A. had finally decided to indict McPherson. Then, with her preliminary hearing still underway, the D.A. himself had been indicted on criminal charges for misuse of public funds– funds allotted for investigating liquor and vice cases. The charges had been dismissed; two days later he'd bound McPherson over for trial.

"So," Harry concluded, "if we were to go to him now and say we've got witnesses and solid evidence on Hillman and Morelli and he refuses to investigate– we could threaten to take our information to certain parties who might find that fact very interesting."

"Do we have witnesses and solid information?" I asked.

"We will have, if we can convince the girls to testify. And the Sing woman." Harry said.

I avoided Harry's eyes. "The D.A. would prosecute her, for her part in it, wouldn't he?"

"Her testimony could put this thing over on Morelli and Hillman. We could negotiate a deal for her– say, immunity in exchange for her turning state's evidence." Harry said.

"I should talk to Mrs. Sing before we take any action with the D.A." Doc said. "I'm responsible for getting her into this, after all."

"Let me talk to her." I said. "I think she'll help us, if I ask her to."

"Very well." Doc said. "I'm ready to go to the D.A. as soon as you give the word."

"Are you sure, Doc? You may make yourself a lot of enemies." Harry said.

"I'm not worried about that. They tried to sling mud at me once before, but it didn't stick." Doc said. "I can't– I won't– stand by and let an evil go on, by my silence, if I can do something about it."

He walked us out. The large, rambling, ivy-covered church with its soaring steeple tower must have been something in its day, but now it looked almost quaint in the shadow of a slender, modern skyscraper on the adjacent lot.

Doc noticed me looking at it. "My board of trustees thinks we ought to sell up and build a bigger home in the Wilshire district. They say my voice was meant to fill a much larger auditorium. I can't argue with that. But I like my little church. Best of luck to you, Brother Shepard."

I went back to the office with Harry. Buster arrived after school and Edith put him to work checking a box of office supplies against the bill to make sure it was all there. After that she had an errand for him, and asked him to pick up some sandwiches and coffee from the delicatessen down the street on his return.

"Your pay includes meals, by the way. I don't know about you, but I'm famished." she said. "Oh– and you might go down to Miss Price's streetcar stop and collect her. She could help you carry the food back here."

"Yes, Mrs. Austin." Buster grinned and hopped to it with all the energy he'd put into selling papers.

"So, how did you like your first day on the job?" Edith asked. We sat across from each other at our respective desks, eating the sandwiches. Buster and Lyric reclined on the leather davenport and Harry sat tall in one of the hard back chairs.

"It was kind of rough." I admitted. "But worth it, if Hillman and Morelli get what they deserve."

"It seems to me there would be far fewer devils like Hillman and less need for the services of a Morelli if the sexes were brought up equally." Edith mused. "As it is, daughters are taught to be chaste, and sons are taught to sow their wild oats. And who do they sow them with but somebody's daughter? Maybe things will change now that we women have got the national vote. Mercy, I've got off track! We should have a toast."

Edith stood up and filled our glasses then held hers aloft. "To Avery and Buster– may we have many years of happy toil together."

"I'll drink to that." I said.

The five of us touched glasses.

CHAPTER 14

What blurt is this about virtue and about vice?
Evil propels me, and reform of evil propels me— I stand indifferent;
My gait is no fault-finder's or rejecter's gait;
I moisten the roots of all that has grown.
                                      —Walt Whitman, "Leaves of Grass"

In the end, I didn't have to telephone Helen; she 'phoned me.

I'd just got back to the hotel, having spent the rest of the afternoon comparing witness statements on a case for Harry. Her sweet, musical voice came over the wire.

"I've been given tickets to see Ruth St. Denis perform with her husband— the Denishawn Dancers— at the Philharmonic and wondered if you would care to go? I thought you might like to see what Kit is interested in."

"I– I don't think I could. Thanks just the same."

"Oh, well."

"Look Helen– I was going to call you. I meant to, before tonight, I mean. I need to see you– talk to you– privately. Is there some place we can meet?"

"What– tonight?

"Yes. It's important."

She may have heard the edge to my voice. Her own sounded as calm as ever. "Very well." she said, and agreed to meet me for an early supper at the Victor Hugo. "They don't have a dance band, thank God, so we'll be able to hear ourselves talk."

I met Helen at the restaurant which was done up in the style of Louis Quinze, or one of the Looies anyway— all white and gold and crystal chandeliers, as swank as some of the places I'd seen in France, and it suited Helen down to the ground.

She wore a simple black dinner dress of some sort of sheer fabric with silver accents, long amethyst earrings and a black velvet wrap. Other diners turned to look at her as we passed, following the headwaiter to our table in a quiet corner.

Once we'd ordered and the waiter had gone away, she looked at me across the table.

"You're looking well, Avery." She folded her hands in front of her on the table. "You didn't ask me to come out with you to make small talk, though. What is it?"

I told her, all in a jumble, what Harry and I heard and saw at the Pink Pagoda. Her face paled; her eyes grew tragic and horrified. I felt like a brute, but I kept on.

"So, now you know." she said when I'd finished. Her voice sounded as dead as the expression in her eyes. "You know what I am. There's a word for it. Why don't you use it?"

"Helen, I don't–. Does Morelli have some sort of hold over you? That's what Doc and I believe."

Her eyes were huge; she looked up at me with a wry smile. "But Harry Price doesn't think so."

"It doesn't matter. I believe you wouldn't do those girls wrong without a good reason." I took her hand and told her that Doc would go to the D.A. and seek immunity for her in exchange for her testimony against Morelli, and Hillman.

"Hillman too?"

"Those girls are underage. They're only schoolgirls."

"You don't honestly think the D.A. is going to bring charges against a man worth millions on the word of some taxi-dance hall girls? Darling, be practical. And you think the girls will speak out– will swear out complaints?"

"We hope so. Well, we can try. If you asked them to, they might. They like you. Don't you think you owe that to them at least?"

Our food came but neither of us touched anything. Helen looked down at her soup plate, then back at me.

"Avery, who am I to judge what is right and what is wrong?" she said. Her face was frozen looking, a mask. "I told Dr. Breuner I wanted to turn over a new leaf, go straight. I meant that. I tried. But it's no use. They won't let me."

"They– who? Morelli?"

"Him, men like him. The system. Society."

"We can fight him, his kind."

She smiled. "You're so sure. You see everything clearly as black or white, don't you? Avery– we all chose our own morality, what laws, or morals or creed we'll follow or not follow– how much sin we can accept. Look at us– how many laws did we break the other night? How many sins did we commit, in the eyes of others, if not our own?"

"It's not the same."

"Darling– how can I make you understand? I never pretended I was good. I'm not. I'm not a good person, I'm not noble. I'm not even moral."

"I don't believe that, and neither does Doc. He thinks highly of you, we both do. I know you want to do the right thing. You've fallen into the habit of playing the hard-boiled tough little woman who doesn't give a damn, because it's easier when you have to always be around people like Morelli, but it isn't you. I know you."

"How can you? We hardly know each other."

"I know enough. I know I'm right about this– about you."

She paused. "I told you about Jack when we were at

Long Beach."

"And I told you, I don't hold that against you. I don't think any less of you because of him."

"What I didn't tell you– hoped I would never have to tell you– is that Jack was not my first. Before I ever met him my mother sold me to a man for medical bills and some trinkets, more or less."

"What do you mean?"

She squeezed my hand. "There was another man, before Jack. His father wasn't a millionaire, but they had a lot of money and social position and all the influence that goes with both. I was thirteen, not yet fourteen, he was maybe twenty-eight or twenty-nine– he seemed terribly old to me at the time. I was knocked down in the street one day by an ice wagon, and taken to the emergency hospital. He attended me. After I went home he began calling on us– at first to check on me, he said. After a while it was more than that. At first I thought he was becoming my mother's suitor. Mama told me to be nice to him. It wasn't difficult. He took us out places– for ice cream, candy, amusement places. He bought me shoes, hair ribbons, pretty clothes and gave me a wristwatch and some jewelry. He knew just what would please a young girl. And when we got to places he somehow managed to get me away without Mama. One night he took me out alone, to a resort– a notorious place, I learned later– and got me drunk. After a while we went upstairs. I became hysterical and he gave me something, laudanum probably, to quiet me. Then he had his way with me, and left me there all alone."

"Oh hell. Helen–"

"Mama knew exactly what he was up to, all along. She couldn't pay the medical bills. They must have come to some arrangement over them– her part was to look the other way. She went after him, after that night– swore out a complaint against him with the police and petitioned the medical board to revoke his license. Not because of what he did to me, but because of what he didn't do. She thought he was going to marry me and give her a home. That was the other half of

162

their bargain. She only cared that he reneged on his end.

In the end nothing happened to him. He and Mama came to a financial settlement out of court, the charges were dropped and he went on practicing. In the meantime I got sent to juvenile hall– as if I had done something wrong."

"You hadn't though."

"Hadn't I? There must be something about me that invites attention, of the wrong sort. While I was being held at the juvenile ward a watchman befriended me, and then he got me alone and attacked me. I complained to the matron and the story got in the papers– of course dragging up the whole sordid tale about me and the doctor and making me out to sound like a little tramp. The man was let go, then got reinstated, quietly, a couple of weeks later.

"After a while I couldn't live with Mama anymore. We didn't get on. She had me sent to juvenile hall, again, as an 'incorrigible.' for going out dancing and drinking with some soldiers– this was nineteen-eighteen. When I got out I found a job at a cider stand but they fired me when they found out I was underage.

"I ran out of money. That's when I found out the wristwatch the doctor had given me was a cheap one from the drugstore, and the jewelry was fake. I tried to pawn them.

"I went on the stage not long after that, dancing in a cheap vaudeville. There, again I was told to be nice to men. When your salary won't stretch to two meals a day and you think you'll have to go hungry, and a man comes up to you backstage and says he likes your dancing and asks you out for a little supper– it takes a stronger girl than I am to say no. And of course, it isn't just supper...."

She looked up at me for the first time since starting her story. Her eyes were huge, deep, intelligent, tearless.

"Look at me Avery. Look at me and tell me you still think I'm a good person."

"Helen, none of that means you're bad. Adults– people who should have protected you did wrong. That

163

bitch–"

"I know I ought to blame Mama but the fact is I don't. She was still very young herself, not much older than I am now, and very childish. It was different for women then. She hadn't been taught to do anything except to be pleasant to men, marry well and look decorative– all three of which she accomplished admirably until she was widowed with a baby and there was no more money. Father left some but she let it slip through her fingers– she'd set out to pay the grocer and come back with a pair of kid gloves she hadn't been able to resist– she had tiny hands, back when hands were admired. She had no people, father had no people except an ancient uncle, who was well off, if not rich, and a bachelor. Mama thought he might do something for us but he didn't approve of her. He left everything to the foundling home for cats. Mama honestly thought she was doing the best she could for me. We were so poor. We lived in dingy rooms, always moving because we couldn't pay the rent, the next place always a little more squalid than the last."

"It's no excuse, what she did. And that bastard– the doctor– ought to have had his balls cut off. Sorry. I mean it, though. I'd do the job myself."

She smiled at me. "The thing is, I had rather enjoyed the doctor's attentions. At first I didn't understand. I'd never been to a doctor before. When he examined me at home– I thought it was… usual. I liked how it felt. I thought the doctor was terribly handsome, even if he was old. He was tall and had wavy black hair, and dark eyes, dressed well, and drove a Kissel roadster– he seemed so dashing. Eventually I came to know, in some way, what he was up to, that he was attracted to me. When we were out places I'd brush my arm against his or something like that, and look up to see his reaction. He'd be practically panting. I enjoyed the power of it. I didn't know what I was doing. Not really. It was only that night, when we got upstairs that I realized what I'd been playing at and I was frightened and wanted to go home. He was so nasty then and called me a tease and all sorts of filthy names and that it was my fault."

"It wasn't." I took her hands in mine. She had her mother's hands, apparently– tiny, fragile. "None of it."

"But you'll forgive me–"

"I forgive you anything."

"– forgive me if I have no confidence in the police, or the justice system, especially when it comes to wealthy men. One of the times when I got out of the juvenile police court, there was a woman there, who'd been watching the proceedings. She followed me, and said she could get me a job, she knew a place that hired 'fallen girls.' You know what kind of a place she meant. I did too, by that time. I called her a filthy thing and went away, with my nose in the air. I got the job in the theater, and then I met Jack and went off with him. I got to thinking, later, of those little suppers and wondered if what I was doing was so very different than what that woman wanted me to do, wondered if I hadn't been a fool not to go with her."

"No, Helen. That's not so. But how could you–"

"Sell out girls to their fate the way I'd been sold out?" she finished for me. After a moment she went on. "Do you know, in China, fathers in poor families will sell their daughters into service in the sing-song houses, if they haven't already drowned them in the river. They exist purely for the amusement of wealthy men."

"It sounds sordid."

"I agree. Yet what choice do they have? It's either that or watch their children slowly starve to death. What chance do the girls have? Their fate is as bound by their poverty as their feet are by tradition. Are poor girls here any better off? My girls from the club, who went to the parties at Hillman's– they're so poor, so uneducated. Alice, who you met, has six siblings, four under the age of ten. Darling, you can't know what it's like, that kind of poverty. Your home may not have been a happy one, but you didn't have to worry about basic comforts like heat and food on the table. It has a demoralizing effect on you, after a while.

At least– at least the girls I approached had a choice. I didn't. I chose my girls very, very carefully. I picked only those that I thought would be suited to the job. Meaning ones who were experienced shall we say, but who could act virginal if that's what was wanted. I didn't force anyone into a lifestyle that they didn't want. I used girls I thought would ultimately better off, who needed the money and might otherwise wind up doing something else to get it, something worse."

"Like what?"

"You know. They could be in houses, or walking the streets. It's not like they can earn a decent wage as hat checkers or waitresses. Have you seen the price of a decent coat lately?"

I remembered Gladys and her longing for a genuine beaverette coat. "Was Gladys– was she one of your girls too?"

"Yes." Helen looked me in the eye. "That was a mistake on my part, and I am truly sorry about Gladys. I sent her to Hillman's one time. I knew she'd been married before, and she liked to present herself to the other girls as quite experienced. She certainly looked mature, physically. But she wasn't, emotionally. She didn't end up doing anything with Hillman– she ran out. I calmed her down in my room, reasoned with her. She wanted to keep her job as a dancer, so I gave her five dollars and said I would smooth things over with Morelli. I had no idea she was so young– and a mother."

"Neither did I." I sighed. "I thought she was a sweet kid. Tell me about Hillman."

"I don't know much. He doesn't like to use professionals. The girls could only go to him a handful of times before he tired of them. He constantly demanded more girls, different girls, younger. It's gotten worse in the last couple weeks or so, more demands, more parties–"

"Was Morelli supplying girls to any other men besides Hillman?"

166

"Possibly, but not through the Pagoda. I'm sure he has other irons in the fire. The Pagoda and the deal with Hillman are just sidelines. Very profitable ones."

"Helen– don't you want to help– to punish him for what he's done to those girls?"

"Harry and Dr. Breuner mean well but I know better. The men will get their shyster lawyers and hire shyster private detectives to buy off the D.A., and the jury too if it comes to that, which it probably won't. The D.A. will double-cross me. Hillman's lawyer will say it was all my doing, that Hillman is innocent. He– or she– will bring up my past, my dope habit. And I did things then that were none too savory. I don't care what they say about me– I can take it. But the result will be that I, no one else, end up getting punished. You can bet on it. It's always the woman who pays."

"They can't very well refute your story if the girls back you up. They'll tell– that they had relations with Hillman."

"Yes– and the defense will rip their reputations to shreds and drag the pieces through the mud. Sylvia, one of the other girls you met, has a 'feller' that she's been intimate with. She talked about it quite frankly in the girls' resting room. I can only imagine what the jury– and the newspapers– would make of that, the finger wagging and pontificating on what modern youth is coming to. The girls would be totally discredited as witnesses. And once branded as fallen girls, what do you think is going to happen to them? What decent person is going to hire them? Would any of the good Christian ladies of Dr. Breuner's church? I think not. They'd draw back their skirts– if skirts were long enough to draw back. Woman's inhumanity to woman is to be feared almost as much as Morelli."

"You're not afraid of Morelli, are you? You don't have to be. If he's put away he can't hurt anyone anymore. I know you to be a hell of a brave woman, Helen, and I know you don't need a man to protect you, but all the same, I'm not going to let anything happen to you."

She smiled into my eyes. "I don't believe you would. But look at the facts– you've no evidence other than my say so that Morelli was involved in the Hillman business."

"Harry and I overheard him. And he must keep records."

"Which he'll destroy before anyone can get to them. If Morelli is charged at all– which I doubt– he'll walk on bail and make sure that I either get put out of the way for a stretch at San Quentin or he'll take me for a ride– isn't that what they say in Chicago?– to keep me from talking. I've been looking out for myself for a long time. I know what I'm up against."

"You really won't testify, then?"

"I'm sorry Avery. Please don't pursue this with Hillman. It will only make the girls' lives miserable when it gets out in the papers. For all the talk about the supposed freedom of the 'new woman,' when it comes to female virtue, things really aren't all that different than when I was a girl. And it's not as if it will prevent Hillman, or other Hillmans, from starting up again after it's all over. There always will be girls for hire as long as there are men who want to hire them, and there always will be. It's a rotten system, but an old one."

I couldn't argue with her on that. Edith had more or less said the same thing the other day in the office.

"There aren't any parties at Hillman's tonight are there?" I asked.

"No– nor tomorrow night either, thank God. He's opening his new beach club on the coast. That little party last night was for his top investors, in fact. He's down there now– with his wife."

"Tell me you'll at least think it over some more."

She nodded. "Don't expect too much from me, Avery."

When we left the restaurant, our food untouched, I

168

found us a cab and asked Helen where to.

"I have to go to work." she said.

"You're not going back there? It isn't safe for you."

"I'm in no danger– not yet. I have to go. Just for tonight and tomorrow. Then I'll fold my tent and silently steel away."

I went cold. "You'll leave Los Angeles? And go where?"

She stared blankly out across the sidewalk, and her gaze fell on some of the travel posters in the window of a Thomas Cook & Son ticket office.

"There's always that tramp steamer to the South Seas." she said softly.

"Helen– please– promise you won't leave town without seeing me first."

"Very well. I promise."

I kissed her, and she kissed me back. We kept on kissing, frantically, like a couple of high school kids at a petting party, until the cab pulled up at the Rosslyn.

I got out and held the door for her but she shook her head. "Goodnight, Avery."

"You could come up for a little while and er, see my etchings."

"I've seen them." Helen said, and smiled as the cab pulled away.

I lay in bed, smoking endless cigarettes, not able to sleep. I'd long finished the hospitality bottle from the hotel and had got another one from Harry's bootlegger. That bottle was nearly half gone. I thought about everything Helen had said, and the position we were putting her in: either she testified like we wanted her to and became an enemy of Hillman and Morelli, or we went ahead without her, in which case she'd be arrested alongside the two of them and face a prison sentence. Even Harry had had doubts about the whole

169

thing. It was a lot to ask of her, too much. I recalled the girls—young, yes, but sitting there in the restaurant coolly discussing their bedroom activities and the things they'd buy with their money, and saw exactly what Helen meant about how they would go over with a jury, and what the papers would make of them. About two o'clock I decided I had to talk to Helen again, and went into the sitting room in my pajamas to put in a call to her hotel.

The flat, nasal voice of the switchboard operator came through. "I'm sawwrree, sir but your party doesn't answer."

"Okay– can you try it again later?"

The voice went away and came back on the line a few moments later.

"The party you are trying to reach has checked out of the hotel."

I hung up the receiver and sat, or stumbled rather, down on the davenport. There was a buzzing in my head and I felt worse than I had after being pushed down the Pink Pagoda's stairs. I half-sat, half-reclined there for I don't know how long. I must have dozed a little, because I woke up at the sound of a tapping on the hallway door. I opened it a crack and found Helen standing there, in black trousers, shivering in her polo coat.

"Okay, you win." she said, looking up at me. "I'll do whatever you want."

Her arms went around my neck. I lifted her up. She wrapped her legs around my middle and whispered a two word request in my ear. Her soft cheek pressed up against my rough, unshaven one and her scent– a mix of her *Nuit de Chine* perfume, her brand of cigarettes, her face powder and her own skin– made me dizzier than the whiskey I'd had earlier. I carried her inside.

CHAPTER 15

Try to change it and you will ruin it. Try to hold it and you will lose it.
—Lao-Tsze, Tao Te Ching

The next morning Helen was up with the sun, wearing my bathrobe and no makeup, pouring out strong coffee for us in the sitting room. Buster came out of his room dressed in track pants and a sweat-shirt, ready for his workout at the athletic club, and looked at Helen, shyly. I introduced them. Helen curled up on the davenport and asked him some intriguing and intelligent questions about boxing and soon had him at his ease. I ordered breakfast sent up for me and Helen; Buster said he was too nervous to eat, which was really something.

"Don't worry." I told him. "You're going to do fine."

"Thanks Ave." He surprised me my throwing his long arms around me in a hug. "So long. G'bye, Mrs. Sing." he added.

Lying with Helen in my arms later, I looked at my watch on the bedside table and noted that I had better dress and go get a shave. Harry, Doc and I were to meet with the D.A. Harry thought it best not to bring Helen forward until the D.A. had agreed to immunity for her.

"If you're really sure?" I asked.

Helen shivered. I stroked her hair, looking into her dark eyes. Their return gaze was steady. "I'm sure."

Helen had gone to work at the Pink Pagoda as usual after leaving me the night before; nothing had seemed amiss. She no longer felt safe at her hotel, however. Morelli and Hillman knew where she was, and if Harry and I carried out our plans, soon the D.A. would also. She'd checked out and gone to another hotel, a small one, out of the way. Then she'd changed her mind and came to me.

I met Harry at the corner of Fifth and Broadway. The Hall of Justice was shining in the winter sunshine. Doc was waiting for us at the North Broadway entrance and we went upstairs to the office of a Deputy D.A. Joseph P. Gill.

Gill was about my age, a short man, stocky without being fat, with deeply arched eyebrows like exclamation marks over his dark eyes, and an ink-black pompadour swept back from a pale, melancholy face. He wore a polka-dot tie with his gray herringbone wool suit and two-toned tan leather oxfords not unlike my own. I noticed a golf putter propped up against the wall next to a bookcase. A cap, a heavy fur-collared overcoat, and a knitted muffler of crimson and gold stripes hung from the hat rack in the corner.

A stenographer with a pad came to the door and eyed Gill questioningly; he waved her away and she left us, closing the door behind her.

"Hello, Joe." Doc said, shaking hands. "How's your lovely bride?"

"Can't complain." Gill said. I thought I heard the hint of a New York burr to his voice.

He invited us to sit then listened, with his upper lip pinched between two fingers, nodding now and then, while Doc told Helen's story, Harry adding the relevant details of his own investigation.

"So what we want to know," Doc finished, "is

172

whether the D.A. would be willing to prosecute Mr. Hillman, as well as Mr. Morelli."

Gill stood up behind his desk and faced us, frowning. "If this is true, it's an outrage." he said finally. Then he sighed. "The fact is we can't go poking into the affairs of a respected citizen without cause."

"You mean a rich citizen, who donated plenty to the D.A's election campaign." Harry said.

"If you're implying that we treat the rich any different–" Gill shouted.

"I'm not implying that at all. I thought I stated it rather plainly."

"Look, it would be different if the girls, or their parents, would come forward and swear out a complaint. But the fact is, the injured parties are hardly ever willing to do so in these cases."

"At least one of the parents is willing." Harry said. Doc and I glanced at each other on the sly then back at Gill, who looked like he'd swallowed a collar button.

"And the daughter– she'd back it up?"

"Yes. She and two others, maybe more. We could give you at least a dozen names."

I didn't dare look over at Doc again, but gripped my hat tighter and tried to look as confident as Harry sounded.

"You can produce these witnesses?"

"Yes."

"I'll need to question them. And we would probably have to hold them in protective custody."

There was a knock on the door, and the stenographer came in again, followed by a heavyset middle-aged woman in a heavy cloth coat and a Queen Mary turban. She entered the room hesitantly but her plain, jowly face looked set, determined. Her small eyes flitted around at all of us, settling on Harry, who nodded.

"Mrs. Gillette." the stenographer announced. Harry

got up and gave Mrs. Gillette his chair. She, it turned out, was the mother of Alice Gillette, one of the girls we'd met. Her daughter had told her everything, and she, Mrs. Gillette, wanted Hillman punished for it. She had come downtown to swear out a complaint against him.

Gill looked like he had swallowed a collar button and a set of dress studs this time but he recovered and shook hands with Mrs. Gillette, and nodded to the stenographer to escort Mrs. Gillette out to take care of the business.

"Now, what about Mrs. Sing?" Doc asked.

"This Mrs. Sing will testify in court?"

"She would– but only if the D.A. will guarantee a deal for her: immunity in exchange for her turning State's witness." Harry said. His eyes were steely, unblinking. It was the same look he wore when he was playing cards.

"She has cooperated fully with the investigation. She placed herself in a great deal of danger. If Mr. Morelli found out that she has been working for me–." Doc added.

"Yes." Gill said. "We'd have to hold her too– for her own protection."

"Mrs. Sing is in hiding for her own protection," Harry said, "but I can bring produce her at any time."

Gill rolled his eyes to the ceiling as if looking for divine guidance and pinched his top lip again. "It's highly irregular–"

"This whole thing is highly irregular. Why a gangster like Morelli has been allowed to operate a dance hall in the heart of downtown with the full knowledge of the police department is the most irregular thing of all." Harry said.

"Now look here, Price–" Gill said, his eyes bulging.

"With Mrs. Sing's testimony you might be able to put Morelli away for a nice long stretch, prove to the folks of Los Angeles that the D.A. won't tolerate criminals masquerading as honest businessmen." Harry said. "The D.A. can always pardon him later."

The corners of Gills mouth turned up, for half a second. He tilted his head back and looked at the ceiling again. Then he said: "The D.A. is out of town at the moment. I'll have to get with the chief deputy and discuss it with him. I think— we'll be able to come to an arrangement for Mrs. Sing."

"What about Mr. Hillman?" Doc asked.

"After we've talked to the witnesses— and if their stories bear out— we'll bring him in for questioning. You have the addresses of these young women?"

Harry nodded. "And Morelli?"

"Obviously we'll have to tread carefully with him. My office has no influence over the city police, of course— but I might suggest to certain parties that a timely license violation inspection of Mr. Morelli's establishment is in order. No hint of the other business until we're ready with a warrant. I realize it would be dangerous for Mrs. Sing if word leaked out about that."

"Only the four of us in this room know anything about this as of today. Let's keep it that way." Harry said.

"As you say. We'll have to work fast." Gill said. He sighed, and glanced longingly at his overcoat and scarf.

Back out on North Broadway we walked Doc to his car and saw him off to the cozy bungalow where there would be a pleasant lunch and the football game on his radio.

Harry and I went back to the office, which was empty, the blinds still down. "Where's Edith?" I asked.

"I thought she was looking a little peaked." Harry said, snapping on his desk lamp. "So I sent her to the seashore for the weekend."

At noon I took Buster and Lyric Christmas shopping. They had pooled their money and wanted to buy some things for Charley. We went to a large department store, The Broadway. Crowds of children gaped up at the display

175

windows, which were filled with baby dolls and toy ovens, plush animals, fire trucks and an electric train set against a backdrop of imitation snow and a tree decorated with white and silver orbs and sparking tinsel. Inside, the aisles were festooned with evergreen garlands and plumes of silver bells, and there were wreaths attached to each pillar. Everywhere there were displays of gift baskets and mission figs, harassed looking floor walkers and women balancing piles of string wrapped parcels in their arms. We rode the escalator to the toy department on the fourth floor, where a small army of wide-eyed tots sucked on red and white striped candy canes and stood waiting in line to see Santa Claus.

The kids found the book aisles and agonized over their selections, then again over the toys— finally deciding on a set of Skeezix and Pal dolls, and a soft, mohair toy dog with big brown eyes and a bright red ribbon around its neck. In the infants' wear department they chose a warm padded robe and a set of blankets. Finally, having done well by Charley, we took the elevator to the rooftop café for lunch with chocolate ice cream for dessert, Buster more than making up for having missed his breakfast. Between bites he told us about his boxing workout, how he'd met the rest of the team, and that the coach, Mr. Frye, had taken the boys up on the roof to put them through their paces. Fidel LaBarba and Jackie Fields, both Olympic medalists who were now champions in the pros, were ex-Mercury simon-pures, he said, and had been newsboys once, too. The club was having a ladies' night in February, with athletic contests and a dance afterward and he could hardly wait for Lyric to see it all (*and have a chance to show off in his ring togs,* I thought). The kids counted out their leftover coins on the table and concluded that they had just enough to go to the pictures and go out for a soda afterward.

I spent the rest of the afternoon with Helen back at her hotel. We had coffee and lounged together on the davenport while I briefed her on how things had gone with the D.A.'s office. She was still skeptical, but impressed about Mrs. Gillette coming forward.

Later Helen bathed and got changed for work. I didn't think she should go.

"The police may raid the place any time." I said. "You don't want to get swept up in it."

"They won't do anything tonight– it's too soon. The D.A. would have to arrange it with the chief of police and he would need to appoint a special detail for the job." She put her arms around me. "Don't worry, Ave. I'll be fine. I have to go. I can talk to some of the other girls, get their addresses. That will help, won't it?"

I admitted that it would. Still, I felt uneasy as we rode together in the cab. It dropped me at the Rosslyn.

"Call me as soon as you get home tonight." I said.

Buster and I played cards and practiced some of his newly-learned boxing moves while he chatted about the picture show he and Lyric had seen and generally kept my mind off worrying about Helen. It almost worked. I sent him to bed with a book about ten o'clock. Then I went out for a bit, meeting Frank Ricketts for a drink and a few games of pool.

Leaving him, I didn't feel like going home. I walked, and found myself heading in the direction of the Pink Pagoda.

The streets were cheerful with the sounds of bells and seemed to glow with Christmas lights, looped overhead along the sidewalks and from one side of the block to the other. The department store display windows shone brightly, though the shops were closed, and now and then I caught a glimpse of a lighted Christmas tree in the lobby of a hotel.

As I got about half a block away, I noticed three phaetons parked out in front of the Pink Pagoda at odd angles on the street. They were unmarked but were clearly police vehicles. The next thing I noticed was– like the case of

177

the dog that didn't bark in the night– the absence of jazz pouring out of the windows. It was still some hours before closing; the band should have been blaring away.

I swore and started to run. Men and girls were flooding out of the front doors, some of the girls screaming, others crying, making for automobiles, or a streetcar or running off on foot. A couple of men in suits were bringing some people out and loading them into the phaetons. I strained to see if Helen was among them. I didn't see her or Morelli but they did have my cauliflower-eared friend. Two of the phaetons drove off. I tried to get inside the front doors but was stopped by a third man in a suit, a police detective.

"Sorry Pal, joint's closed."

"What for?"

"Liquor rap."

"Anybody arrested?"

"You'll have to read about it in the papers."

I waited around but after a while it was obvious no more people were being brought downstairs. Helen must have gotten away, from the police anyway. The small crowd that had formed on the sidewalk to watch the proceedings got bored and went back to its business. A fourth detective came out and padlocked the front doors, then left with the other guy in the third phaeton. The only thing to do was to go home and hope that Helen would appear or call.

I took a cab back to the Rosslyn and found Buster awake. His sleep had been disturbed by the telephone, but whoever it was had rung off before he could get to it.

"That's okay, kid. Go on and go back to bed." I said.

I gave the hotel switchboard operator instructions to interrupt with any calls for me, then I called Harry and gave him the news of the raid.

"Goddamn it, that was fast work." he said.

"You think it was Gill's office then?"

"What do you think?"

"That Helen was right not to trust the D.A., and somebody tipped Morelli and he's skipped. I'm worried about Helen." I said.

"Have you tried her hotel?"

"Not yet– I will after we hang up."

Helen hadn't called by the time Harry arrived at my suite.

"They've got her." I said. "I know it. The lousy bastards have got her."

"Who do you mean– Morelli or the D.A.?"

"I don't know." I said. "This isn't the way it was supposed to happen."

At about two o'clock the telephone rang. I snatched it up. The two seconds it took the operator to connect the call seemed like minutes.

"Avery?" a woman's voice came on the line.

"Helen? Helen, where are you?" I shouted.

"I got away." she said, then was silent. She sighed, shuddering.

"Where are you calling from? I'm coming to get you."

"An all-night druggist at Third and Hill. Hurry– please– Avery. I'm frightened."

I left Harry and got a cab downstairs. It only took a moment to reach Helen; I asked the driver to wait and dashed into the drugstore, where I found Helen in the back near the phone booths. She had her hat pulled low over her eyes and the collar of her polo coat up around her neck and there were two hand grips at her feet. I grabbed up the bags and, taking Helen's arm, escorted her out to the cab. Her face looked ravaged. We didn't speak, only embraced until we got back to the Rosslyn. I smuggled her safely upstairs unseen by my friend the house dick and put her bags in the bedroom. Helen sank back into the davenport while Harry poured drinks for the three of us into toothbrush tumblers. Brandy. Good quality. It seemed to revive her and eventually she felt steady enough to tell us what happened.

"I knew something was wrong as soon as I got in tonight. Morelli wasn't there, for one thing. He's always there by eight. His chief goon– he's the one with the cauliflower ear– told me Morelli had 'phoned to say he was sick. About half an hour before closing, the lights went out. It was pandemonium. Women were screaming and I heard glass breaking. Everyone was stampeding for the doors and the elevators. I felt someone grab hold of my arm, but I slipped free and ran. I could hear a man's feet on the tile, chasing after me, but I got away, through the connecting door into the Hillman Building. I walked right out the front doors."

"The only thing is there was a car waiting out front– a big touring car. Somehow– I knew– it was waiting for me, to– to take me away. So I went back inside the Hillman, and wound my way around until I found a service entrance and I got out that way, to the alley. I managed to get a cab, though I must have looked like a mad woman after all that running about. I had it drive around for a while until I was sure I wasn't being followed. I stopped once to try to call you. Then I went to my hotel, packed my things and checked out. I took a cab to the drugstore where you picked me up."

She sighed, breathing hard. She was a tough baby. She wouldn't cry in front of Harry. I put my arm around her and Harry poured her another small brandy.

"Goddamn lousy cops." I said.

"I knew they couldn't be trusted." Helen said. "Morelli was tipped that the raid was happening tonight, obviously."

"I suppose he made off with all of the records." Harry said. "Probably destroyed them by now, if he's smart."

"Well, he didn't get all of it." Helen said. "There's your evidence."

She took a small blue ledger out of her coat pocket and tossed it on the coffee table. Harry raised his eyebrows.

"What is it?" I asked

"Names, dates, and a catalog of Hillman's er–preferences– of a personal nature. All in Morelli's own hand. It's in code, but Harry will work it out." she added. She handed Harry a folded sheet of paper. "Also a few addresses for you, as many of the girls as I could get to before all hell broke loose."

I looked at Harry. "What do we do now?"

"I can't stay here– in Los Angeles." Helen said. "You know what it means if they find me."

Harry thought for a minute then replied slowly. "Can you get Mrs. Sing out of town for a few days– someplace safe where no one can find her? That includes the D.A."

"Of course. Where do you think we should go?" I asked.

Harry suggested the Mount Wilson resort. It wasn't very far out of town, and it had private bungalow cabins, and mail and telegraph service. He would wire us when it was safe to come back.

"When will that be?" Helen asked.

"After we see where all the pieces land." Harry said. "Depends whether they can pick up Morelli– Hillman too; he'll have been warned. And I want to get to Alice Gillette and stash her, somewhere where no one can get to her and try to scare her into not testifying." He nodded at Helen's address list. "This is good work. I'll try to round up some of these girls in the morning, too. They may have scattered to the wind. It'll be a race to try to get to them before Hillman's people do."

"I'm game." I said. I looked at Helen and threaded her hand in mine. "It's really up to you. If you're still willing to trust the D.A., that is."

"I don't trust him at all. But I'm mad as hell at being double-crossed."

"So, what do you say?"

Helen looked up at me through lowered lashes. "I hear the mountains are lovely this time of year."

CHAPTER 16

After Harry left, Helen had a hot bath. I sponged her back for her and we chatted, then went to bed. She slept fitfully. I watched over her, holding her, all night.

In the morning I arranged through another rental outfit to hire a car and had them deliver it to the hotel. I sent a wire to the Mount Wilson resort and reserved a cabin.

Over breakfast we read about the raid on the Pink Pagoda; I hadn't seen any reporters there– they must have gotten their stuff from the police. There was a photograph of Cauliflower Ear– who was in fact a Frank Tufts and the alleged operator of the establishment, as the dance hall license was in his name. He was as an ex-grappler with no known prior criminal record. He was being held, and his license suspended, for allowing liquor on the premises and letting minors into the club. Hillman wasn't mentioned, but Morelli's was, for his "reputed connection" with the club, and the fact that he was being "sought for questioning."

The raid had been one of a sweep of several "known illegal establishments" in the city last night.

"That's all just a smokescreen, so the Pink Pagoda doesn't appear to have been the target." I said, remembering what Harry had said about that at Doc's. I wondered if all the places would reopen after a little while.

We were interrupted by the telephone. It was Edith. Her normally calm voice sounded agitated. "Good morning, Ave– is Harry there? I've been trying everywhere to reach him."

"He must be out gathering up our witnesses already." I said, and briefly told Edith about last night's events. "Where are you?"

"The Ambassador Hotel, now." she said. "Our man has bolted."

"Our man? You mean–"

"Yes." Edith broke in hastily, and I realized she wanted to avoid using Hillman's name, probably thinking of the hotel operator listening in– which she probably was. "He's gone. I was down at his new beach club– just keeping an eye on him."

So that was Harry's idea of giving Edith a rest at the seashore.

"He left there sometime early this morning, by car." Edith went on. "His wife claimed she doesn't know where he went or why he left. Then she packed her things and quietly took herself off. I followed her here, thinking she would lead me to him. If so, there's no sign of him yet. I wonder if Buster could come over here and watch her, while I try to pick up our man's trail?"

I said I would send him over by cab and we hung up.

While Helen got our things together, I took Buster aside and explained what Edith wanted him to do, giving him some cash for the cab ride and expenses.

"You know I've got to go away with Mrs. Sing for a few days." I said. He nodded. "I'll be back here as soon as I can, get me? I mean it. You could come along, only you've got to go to school and keep up with your workouts at the club."

I told him how in the summertime we could all go camping together up in the mountains. Harry knew some goods spot– places where Jack Dempsey and other boxers had once made their training camps. We'd go ocean fishing, too.

"That sounds swell." Buster said. "Are you going to marry Mrs. Sing, Ave?"

"Oh– well– that's– things are pretty unsettled right now." I said.

I didn't think I was setting a very good example for the boy, and thought I ought to try to say something to him, but was damned if I knew what. The situation was rather beyond the vague warnings of the purity and health tracts my father had foisted on me when I was his age.

"You know, Mrs. Sing and I have both been married before. And adults sometimes like each other's company, at night, I mean. But you're a kid, it's different for you. I mean, you might feel like you want– uh, company– yourself sometimes. There's nothing bad about thinking about it– it's healthy– but you know, every girl's somebody's daughter or sister, that's the thing. Has anybody ever talked to you about this stuff before?"

He shook his head, half-grinning, his blue eyes bright. "Can I tell you something Ave? You won't laugh? I'm going to court Lyric proper. And when we're old enough, I'm going to marry her. I don't want anybody else– honest, no foolin'."

"I believe you." I said. "And in that case you better do your homework while I'm gone and make up your credits, or you won't even graduate high school, and how are you going to support her then?"

"I will." He grinned and gave me one of his bear hugs.

"Okay. Well, you need to get going. Do exactly what Mrs. Austin tells you. Got it? And go to school and to the office in the afternoons like usual while I'm gone. Be back here and in bed by ten sharp– no staying up reading all night. And don't forget to brush your teeth. If you need anything, just ask Mrs. Austin."

When Helen and I went down to the car in the early

afternoon, the newsboy who had taken Buster's place– a runty, sandy-haired kid all piercing voice and no personality– was hustling extra editions that carried a headline about Hillman's disappearance. A Cadillac believed to be his had been sighted in a garage at Redondo Beach and the police were now treating it as a missing person case with potential foul play. Helen and I knew this already– Harry had called. He was going down there with Frank Ricketts. He'd dictated a note for me to send with Buster for Edith instructing her to follow up on tracking down the girl witnesses. For my part, I was to stick with Helen as planned. So, I helped Helen into the hire car, a blue Star Four touring model this time, and pointed it toward the still-snowless mountains.

With Helen navigating, we reached the Mount Wilson lodge by teatime and got settled into our quarters in one of the private cabins that were scattered around near the main lodge. In the evening she put galoshes on over her thin evening slippers and we walked to the lodge's rustic dining room for a roast chicken supper. Over our meal I noted that the food, though ample, was clearly not the attraction at this resort.

"No." Helen said. "It's their telescope."

Afterward we ventured to the view point and looked down at the expanse of lights from all of the towns in the valley below.

"To think, somewhere down there is the wicked Angel City." Helen said. I admired her profile as she stared out rather pensively across the horizon. Then she gazed up at the stars.

"'Though rapt at gaze with eyes of light; looked forth the seraph seers; the vast and wandering dream of night; rolled on above our tears.'" she quoted.

I took hold of her hand.

"Doesn't it make you feel small, to think of all of the

heavenly bodies up there, all that we don't even know anything about– will likely never know?" she asked.

I made a corny joke about heavenly bodies closer to home. It made her laugh and she twirled around for me. The spangles of her gown twinkled like stars themselves in the moonlight.

The next afternoon we drove back down the narrow toll road as far as the town of Pasadena and stopped at the Hotel Maryland where I got a real shave and Helen visited the beauty parlor. We enjoyed a very good lunch in the dining room, festive with Christmas greenery and potted poinsettia plants, and afterward went shopping. Helen bought an armful of magazines at the newsstand. I bought her handmade French lingerie, a lacey negligee and a snakeskin handbag at a women's shop and she chided me for being so frivolous but her eyes told me that she was pleased. She selected warm, outdoorsy clothing: corduroy breeches and a sweater, striped wool socks and gloves, and a red cashmere tam with matching scarf. Then she had me drive down the big wide boulevard to a men's shop where she picked out some of the same type gear for me.

That evening Helen tried on her gifts and modeled them for me, teasing, brushing my skin with the soft silk and lace, then darting just out of reach, refusing to let me touch.

"Wait, my yang man." she said. "I have a gift for you, too." She went to her overnight case and came back with something cupped in her hand, which she placed in my palm. It was a man's ring, an exquisite one of white gold, with a red-orange stone.

"It's red jade." she whispered in my ear. "Jade is a talisman. It's supposed to bring long life and drive away worry. The red jade symbolizes vitality and strength– and those admirable qualities of yours– and is also a reminder of our passion."

"As if I could forget that. God, Helen, it's beautiful."

"I hope you'll wear it always."

"I will." I said. I slipped off my signet ring and put on Helen's red jade one. She tried on a pair of apricot silk French panties next, with flared legs inset with lace, and came to stand in front of me where I reclined on the bed.

"*Monsieur* has excellent taste" she purred, imitating the saleswoman from the shop. "Just feel that silk. Non– this silk, here." she guided my hand. "You like, *oui*? *Regarde*– how easily they come off. *Alors*– did you learn anything of French ways while you were over there?"

CHAPTER 17

Our days were almost idyllic. It was like a honeymoon, Helen said, without any bitterness. Other guests smiled at us and waved, calling Helen 'Mrs. Shepard,' of course, because that's how we had to register. The weather stayed fine. We slept late and went for long walks after breakfast. Once we walked up to the observatory museum, where we saw the hundred-inch telescope and Helen talked easily with an astronomer on duty about Einstein's theory and the latest pictures being made of planet Mars. Another day we hiked a trail to the summit. I marveled at Helen– a tomboyish, healthy figure, shapely in her breeches with a rosy glow to her cheeks and boundless energy. It was me who grew winded first and wanted to turn back, but Helen urged me on.

"You know me by now Ave– when I see something big, I want to climb it." she said, looking at me with a saucy grin before racing off up the trail.

In the late afternoons we had coffee on the porch of the lodge, with its sweeping views. Helen read *American Mercury* and *Vogue* and I read the news from town: a Japanese ship almost sank at Los Angeles harbor; the D.A. of San Diego County was on trial, accused of taking a bribe in a murder case; Scotland Yard was baffled by the disappearance of a lady mystery writer; and Dempsey started training for a return bout with Tunney. There were developments about Hillman, too. The evening papers our first night here had carried the news about the purple Cadillac found parked and locked in a public garage at Redondo Beach. It was Hillman's, of course. The attendant couldn't recall anything about the driver. The police had looked it over and saw no signs of a struggle in or outside of the vehicle. The following day we read that a coat bearing Hillman's name on an inside label and a cigarette case with his monogram on it had been found on the Redondo pier. Vargas' paper quoted Ricketts as saying the police had not uncovered any blood or other signs of foul play near the scene, and were investigating the idea that Hillman may have drowned himself. Tonight I read:

BODY FLOATING IN SURF NOT THAT OF MISSING BROKER

REDONDO BEACH, Dec. 7. Police have concluded that the body of a man found floating in the ocean near Redondo Beach pier at 7:00 this morning by a fisherman is definitely not that of Henry J. Hillman, the Los Angeles property and oil man missing since Sunday morning. Mrs. Hillman, though prostrate with worry and said to be near collapse, motored to the beach city but failed to identify the body as that of her husband. The man appears to have been about 35 years old....

PRIVATE DETECTIVE TO SEEK HILLMAN

According to Det. F. L. Ricketts of the Missing Persons detail, authorities are now satisfied that the disappearance of Mr. Hillman is not a police matter. Los Angeles County Dist. A Los Angeles private detective who has been assisting Det. Ricketts in his inquiries believes the missing man may have travelled south to San Diego or Mexico, and will concentrate a private search for the missing man there at the behest of a client, whose identity is being kept confidential.

Edith wrote us her own news. Wherever Hillman was, he hadn't joined his wife, who played bridge, danced and entertained friends at the Ambassador with gay abandon. ["So much for being 'prostrate with worry'" Helen murmured]. The D.A. had an investigator watching her now, just in case. Gill's officers had interviewed Alice Gillette and placed her in technical custody as a material witness, but let her remain at home with her mother. Edith herself had decoded the record book of Morelli's that Helen had liberated, and was now trying to round up more of the girl witnesses as well as parents who would swear out complaints against Hillman. She enlisted Buster and Lyric to ask around school campuses of some of the other girls.

Tufts, Morelli's cauliflower-eared henchman, was still in custody facing liquor charges as the so-called proprietor of the Pink Pagoda. He hadn't been able to make his bail. Morelli remained at liberty, seemingly carefree; D.A. investigators were shadowing him as well.

I also had a letter from Buster himself. It was just like him— articulate, profane, entertaining as hell. I read it after dinner, when we were sitting before the great stone fireplace. He wrote that he and Lyric had been to see Ruth St. Denis and her troop, who were spectacular and did oriental dances. Edith and Lyric had knitted some woolen booties, a sweater and a cap for little Charley and yesterday they'd taken them, along with the basket of his other presents, out to Gladys's mother's— a little cottage near Westlake Park. Charley had seemed well cared for. Mrs. Watson had given them a couple

190

of Gladys's books in return. They didn't want to hurt her feelings so they took them– but they were "awful drool."

He was doing his homework and brushing his teeth. He hadn't stayed out past ten except when they went to see the dancers, "but Mrs. Austin said it was okay because it was a Cultural Experience, and besides that I wrote an essay about it for extra credit." He had lots of books and isn't lonesome at all, but missed me all the same.

I chuckled to myself, and caught Helen's eye; she was watching me over the top of her magazine; the expression in her eyes was wistful.

"What is it?" I asked softly.

"Nothing, darling. I like to see you enjoying yourself. What's so funny?"

"Just something the boy wrote." I read her the passage. She smiled.

That night our ardor was especially fierce and left us both gasping for breath. When we were finally sated, for the time being, we lay entwined together on the bed, looking out at the sky over the treetops.

"I wish we could stay up here in the stars forever." Helen said dreamily. "I know we can't though."

"Look, Helen." I said, tracing the curve of her hip with my palm. "I'm going to get a divorce. I should have done it a long time ago."

"Avery!"

"I wrote to Ruby Alyce and told her I want her to go ahead with it or I would. Don't worry–" I added at her look of alarm. "I didn't use any names, but I told her I meant it. If she won't– I'll get a Mexican decree. I should have done it a long time ago."

Helen held my face in her hands, caressed it. "Avery– we don't know what's going to happen with the D.A. – he may still decide to charge me."

"Whatever comes, I want to cut all my home ties and start again. Los Angeles seems to me the kind of place where you can do that. Nobody asks you what your father did, or who your mother's people were. Kit's there somewhere. I'm twenty-seven. I want to settle down."

"You are settled," she said. "You've got that boy– you care for him like a son already."

"We can move out of the hotel. Get a little house, with an orange tree right outside the window."

She burst out with a laugh. "Oh, Ave! Can you picture me in a bungalow apron?"

"Sure." I said. "Why not?"

"It sounds like a dream. A beautiful one." Helen said. She kissed my neck, my ear, and my lips, then straddled me. "I just need to feel you again, Ave." she whispered. We stayed that way, with our bodies joined, for some time; Helen somehow kept me just on the brink of orgasm again and again until we finally let go and climaxed together.

On our last day in the mountains, it snowed. The resort turned into a wonderland as the green treetops and brown hills disappeared under piles of white. Helen and I made snowballs and commandeered a toboggan; I pulled her around on it until it smashed up on a rock and dumped her, laughing, into a drift.

It continued all day. Hoards came up from the city for the day by auto stage or in their private motors.

When it got too cold we went indoors and had coffee in front of the fire.

"Ave, I've been thinking." Helen said. She sat curled up in her chair, like a kitten, with her chin in her palm, staring into the fire. "About the girls, maybe something could be done for them, the way you're helping Buster, to give him his start. Dorothy has quite a nice voice– I bet if she had some training she could get work on the radio. Sylvia isn't very bright, and she's lazy, but she loves to sew. I've seen some chemises and step-ins she made for herself. They can't compare to the things you gave me from Magnin's, but the handwork was exquisite. It might seem hopeless to them at first, but I don't know–?"

I leaned over to kiss her.

An old timer walking past scowled and muttered to himself, "Huh– damn newlyweds."

We burst out laughing.

The lodge manager found us then with a telegram that had come for me. Helen looked at me, and folded her hand in mine, touching the red jade talisman. We both knew that, whatever it might say, it meant that our honeymoon idyll was ended.

The message read simply:

REQUEST YOUR PARTY RETURN LOS ANGELES AT ONCE= H.P.

We got hold of what papers there were scattered around. Vargas' rag carried the story on its front page.

HILLMAN MYSTERY DEEPENS
WEALTHY BROKER CHARGED IN
TAXI GIRL ATTACK

A warrant was issued today for the arrest of Henry J. Hillman charging him with two counts of criminal attacks on Alice Gillette, one of several minor girls who, it is alleged, attended "wild parties" hosted by Hillman in the sumptuous rooftop clubrooms of the Realty Club. Alcoholic beverages and lascivious dancing are also said to have played a part in these "parties." The whereabouts of the wealthy broker, who has been missing since last Sunday morning, ostensibly remains a mystery. Hillman's attorney, George Zeigler, has assured authorities that his client will turn himself in as soon as it is advisable for him to do so. Mr. Zeigler added that the charges against his client are of course completely false and are the work of "unscrupulous persons who wish to ruin the good name" of his client. He declined to name the wealthy broker's alleged enemies.

Mrs. Hillman could not be reached for comment. She remains in seclusion and is said to be under a doctor's care.

The Dist. Attorney's office revealed that it has placed a second girl involved in the case into technical custody as a material witness. It is unknown whether her testimony will result in additional charges against Hillman, although it was intimated that further shocking revelations and likely more arrests are imminent.

Vargas must have gotten his stuff from Harry, or the D.A.'s office itself. The other papers had little to add, so they padded their stories with reminders of Hillman's good works, calling him a "civic leader," and a "noted philanthropist," ballyhooing his recent contributions to the city's skyline, and generous gifts to the Milk Fund, the Community Chest, the Children's Home Society, the Y.M.C.A., the W.C.T.U., the Tuberculosis and Veteran's associations, rescue missions, hospitals...." One ran a photograph of Hillman from last fall attending a benefit concert for the Grand Opera Association. We threw him onto the fire and went to get changed for supper.

That night, our lovemaking was tender– still passionate, but without the earlier abandon. Helen's kissed my scars and asked me how I got them.

"Besides the ones from being chucked down the stairs at your place you mean? Well, one of them's a war wound. The nurses over there were really tough on a fellow. That faint one's from fighting as a kid. I used to get picked on a lot on account of I was short until about the time I got to high school. I finally got to be six foot, according to my army records. I got better at brawling too."

I thought that would make her laugh, but was horrified instead to find that tears were running down her cheeks. I pulled her close and kissed her.

"What did I do? Did I say something? Helen—"

"The two most damnable words in the English language are 'if only.'"

She wouldn't say anything more and was inconsolable. I held her while she sobbed, as she'd done with me over Kit. Eventually she lay quiet and calm. I thought she was sleeping and started to arrange her more comfortably and pull the quilt up over us.

"Don't let go of me, Ave." she'd murmured. "I never felt so safe anywhere as when I'm in your arms."

I held her to me and we looked out at the blanket of white.

CHAPTER 18

What is done out of love always takes place beyond good and evil.
　　　　　　　　　 —Friedrich Nietzsche, *Beyond Good and Evil*

The sky in the morning was gray and threatening, but the snow had let up. After a quiet breakfast, where we held hands under the table and said little, we packed our things and Helen bundled into her polo coat for the cold drive back to Los Angeles. I folded the robe over Helen's knees. We stopped at the service station down the mountain and I put the side curtains on the car.

Between the bad weather and too much traffic, it was a slow and fairly treacherous ride. Rain pounded against the curtains and the wiper, fairly useless anyway, finally gave up and blew upward off the windshield altogether. We got back to the city environs to find a full-blown storm in progress. Though only mid-afternoon, it was already almost dark. I parked the car as close to the Rosslyn as I could get and, taking Helen's hand, dashed for it.

Edith and Harry were waiting for us in my suite.

"Thank God. I was so worried— such weather to be driving in!" Edith said.

She helped us out of our wet coats and I presented Helen to her.

There were sandwiches, but neither Helen nor I felt

much like eating. Harry seemed downcast, but then, he always did. But Edith didn't seem her usual cheery self, either.

"What's the news?" I asked. "Did you find Hillman in Mexico? The papers said his lawyer knows where he is."

"Zeigler is sticking to that story about Mexico but I think Hillman's right here in town." Harry said.

Whatever the papers had said, Harry and Ricketts dismissed at once the idea that foul play had been involved in Hillman's disappearance or that he had drowned himself.

I agreed. The whole thing, from Hillman's impossible-to-miss Cadillac left in plain sight, to the coat and cigarette case bearing clear evidence of their owner's identity left on the pier, did sound like something right out of Nick Carter.

No, Harry believed Hillman had left the car as he did to keep the police looking for him on the coast, and planted the other items to further divert attention. In addition, though it hadn't been reported in the papers, a portion of a timetable for trains to San Diego and a tourist brochure about Tijuana had been found in the pocket of the coat. Harry fed the information about San Diego and Mexico to the press to let Hillman think his clumsy bait had taken. Ricketts and Harry had gone not to Mexico, however, but back to the El Rancho Beach Club where Hillman had been celebrating before his flight. They sorted through the wastebaskets in Hillman's rooms but found nothing. They returned to the city and over the protests of Hillman's stenographer, searched his offices in the Hillman Building. There they'd found items indicating Hillman had gone to San Francisco by steamer and engaged rooms at the Plaza Hotel there.

"So you think he's in San Francisco."

"I'm not really concerned about where he is." Harry said. "I think he will show himself as soon as Zeigler and the D.A. come to terms about a nice cozy nest for him to land in."

"I don't know what they think they can do. Isn't it true the D.A. has another witness besides Alice?"

"Oh yes." Edith nodded. "I found her." She poured us some coffee and filled us in on the investigation.

The girls, as Harry predicted the night of the Pink Pagoda raid, had fled the city or went into hiding, afraid to talk or else the other side had gotten to them first and bought their silence.

"Someone, Hillman most likely, has a private detective of his own out searching for the girls. His methods are not very scrupulous but they're effective."

Of those who still lived at home with their families, Edith had met with cold receptions from mothers, fathers or brothers of the girls and had doors slammed in her face. Finally her patience and persistence paid off, however, and she found one of the girls living in a cheap room west of the Third Street tunnel– Sylvia Hoskins– one of the four girls Harry and I met. Edith had initially placed her in care of a friend of Doc's who ran a small hotel for Christian women. The D.A. was now putting her up at the Rosslyn, in the Annex across the street, with a woman officer chaperoning her.

Helen knew a little about Sylvia.

"She left school a couple of years ago, has no folks that I know of, and works in a laundry during the day. Hillman asked for her several times. I found her rather– case-hardened."

"Yes– she doesn't exactly come across as school-girlish." Edith agreed. Once caught, the girl had spoken freely to Edith. She thought Hillman was "a limp rag" but liked going to his swell parties, and getting some extra dough, and the Pink Pagoda had been a swell place to work– she got paid to listen to jazz, and sometimes met interesting men who took her out to swell places and bought her things.

"What about Morelli?"

"He couldn't believe it when they picked him up. According to Gill he went positively pink with rage and broke out in spots." Edith said.

"He boasted about his pals at City Hall and swore his lawyer would have him out in an hour. He wasn't too far off the mark. He was arraigned this morning and released on bail." Edith said.

"What in hell?"

"Some mysterious benefactor posted his bond. The bondsman isn't saying who but we can guess." Harry replied.

"Any more good news?" I asked.

"Actually, there is—" Edith said. "I'm very upset about this. The D.A.'s office has been raising holy hell since finding Helen checked out of her hotel. They want to bring her in and charge her as an accessory."

"What? Hell no. Goddamn it— they agreed." I yelled. "Immunity for Helen's testimony— that was the deal. Why'd you call us back? We've got to get out of here."

"Hear her out, Avery." Helen said.

"Gill says that it would only be a formality. They would book Helen then release her on her own recognizance. She'd be in technical custody, like Alice. The immunity deal still stands. They just want Helen safe."

"She'd be safe if they hadn't let Morelli go and brought Hillman in instead of letting his lawyer lead them around by the nose."

"It's alright, Avery." Helen said, putting her hand over mine. She turned to Edith. "We were having such a nice time while you were down here having a lot of trouble over me on top of everything else. It's fine— phone Gill and tell him we're here."

Edith made the call and said Gill would be over about five o'clock. Helen would be released before supper.

Helen set her coffee cup down and wondered if she could take a bath and have a rest in the meantime. "I'm exhausted." she said.

"You do look all in, my dear." Edith said. "I— wasn't sure what the, er— sleeping arrangements should be." she said. Under the circumstances, she had gone ahead and engaged the adjoining room and bath for Helen. "But if necessary I'll muss up the bed every morning so the chambermaid won't be scandalized."

I grinned at her and thought, not for the first time, that Victorian women were just as broad-minded as the so-called new women– they just didn't go around telling the whole world about it.

Helen looked at Edith gratefully and asked me to wake her in a couple hours.

"Okay, kid." I said. I held her hand; she touched my ring and smiled up at me. The expression in her eyes said all the things we couldn't say in front of the others.

Buster and Lyric came in then and there were hugs and happy greetings all around.

A little while later the bellman knocked on the door, bringing our bags.

I took my grip, and indicated Helen's white pigskin cases. "Those two go next door."

"Yeah– I knocked there, mister, but no one came to the door." he said.

"That's because the lady's taking a bath." I said.

"I'll take them in to her." Edith volunteered. "She'll want her dressing gown and hairbrush and things."

Buster and Lyric wolfed down the last of the sandwiches and asked me all about the mountains. I told them how pretty the snow had been yesterday, and about the tobogganing. Lyric had just asked whether we'd been able to look through the telescope when Edith came bursting into the room. Her knot of hair had come loose from its pins and fluttered down past her shoulders. She held her sides, breathing hard.

"She– isn't– there." Edith gasped. "Helen. Gone."

"What in the hell?"

"Sonofabitch!"

"Holy fuck!"

I raced out of the room like a mad man, Harry and Buster at my heels.

200

The door of the adjoining room was ajar, as Edith had left it.

I could hear water running in the bath and the light was on. But Helen was gone.

"Oh God!"

I had my gun in my coat pocket. I'd forgotten about it, having kept it with me for the drive down the mountain. I heard Harry yell at Buster to have Edith call the house detective while he and I searched the hotel. I took the elevator to the lobby and scanned it. There was no sign of Helen. I ran outside onto the street. The rain was still coming down in sheets. It was as dark as dusk already. Cars had their headlights on. People hurried by huddled under black umbrellas, their legs wet to the knees. Across the street on Fifth, a big, black Lincoln touring car idling at the curb with its curtains up caught my eye, then a yellow streetcar went by and blocked my view. By the time it had passed, the Lincoln was pulling away, heading west. I glanced at it, and my heart stopped for a second as I caught a glimpse of Helen's face, white and pale, in the oval of the rear window.

Blindly, stupidly, I ran after the car, which couldn't get up any speed owing to the traffic light at Spring. Without thinking, I took out my gun, aimed it at one of its tires and fired. The sound was mostly drowned out by the rain and the traffic noise and the shot went wild, hitting the rear fender on the passenger side. The big car leapt forward like a wounded animal, going through the still-red traffic signal and careening drunkenly for a moment. Then it straightened itself out, just in time to swerve around a slower-moving car in front of it. I ran after it again.

An auto horn blared behind me and I turned to see Buster at the wheel of the Star Four, which I'd left sitting at the curb on Main; he must've gotten the keys from the bellhop. I jumped on the running board and held on to the door frame as Buster maneuvered the machine through traffic, ignoring the signals and the cusses of pedestrians and the indignant ahoogaing of other drivers.

The Lincoln was only about a block and a half ahead of us. Then there was a huge bang– as loud as gunfire. For a second I thought we'd been hit, but then felt the Star pulling to the left, despite Buster's frantic steering to try to keep it straight. He maneuvered it to the curb and got out of the car, swearing and kicking the flat front tire. I ran up the street, hopelessly.

The Lincoln was nothing but a black blur now. I watched its taillight disappearing in the distance, until it became a pinpoint and finally vanished altogether.

PART II

CHAPTER 19

The three days after Helen disappeared in that car were like my time in combat- rarely thought of and best forgotten. I know we turned the city upside down looking for her. The papers ran a description of her and the car. The county sheriff and the police cooperated, setting up dragnets on the main roads and were checking all ships, trains and auto stages leaving the city.

Deputy D.A. Joe Gill, on being informed of what had happened, had rushed over to the Rosslyn where he and I hurled accusations at each other. He raged that if I hadn't spirited his witness out of sight in the first place, she wouldn't be missing.

I shot back that he'd not only been derelict in his duty by releasing Morelli on bail, he'd tipped Morelli that the Pink Pagoda was about to be raided. "Mrs. Sing said all along she didn't trust you and she was right." I said.

"I'm as frustrated about that raid as you are, Shepard." Gill said. "Somebody else tipped him, not us. I'm as keen to put Morelli away as you are."

"Put him away, my ass. You're the one who let him go. I'm surprised you aren't arresting me on a gunplay rap for trying to stop that car getting away. And if you did, I bet I'd do more time than Morelli or Hillman ever will."

"Don't tempt me Shepard." he said.

Things happened quickly after that. The first was that Alice Gillette disappeared, the evening of Helen's own vanishing act. Gill took all of the blame for that one; his people hadn't watched her closely enough, he owned frankly, and let her slip through their fingers.

According to Mrs. Gillette, her daughter had been restless- she was used to dancing every night and going to parties and automobile rides. I gathered that quiet nights at home with her family didn't suit. After nearly a week of it, last night Alice rebelled and insisted she was going to the pictures. She didn't come back from the show and Mrs. Gillette hadn't seen her since. Alice had, in the words of one of her young brothers "hoofed it." Edith didn't believe a word of it; she was convinced that Mrs. Gillette knew exactly where Alice was but wouldn't say.

A frustrated Gill brought Morelli in for questioning about the fortuitous disappearances of two key witnesses for the case against him and Hillman. Morelli had been sneering, defiant, Gill told us later, and denied all knowledge of Helen and Alice's whereabouts. He'd been home all day and night with his wife. Gill could ask her.

"I've no doubt she'd confirm everything word for word- or else." Gill had said bitterly. In the end he held an outraged Morelli on charges of witness tampering and hoped that this time there would be no bail. He was going to suggest that the D.A. call for a grand jury investigation into the matter.

"Meanwhile, if they should happen to drop him on his face a few times on the way to and from his cell it wouldn't break my heart." Gill said. I started to think he might be a decent fellow after all.

That afternoon Edith waylaid the postman at the Gillette house. While he hadn't let her handle the mail, he had looked away while Edith glanced over his shoulder. She saw the postmark- San Francisco- and the corner of a return address. Hotel stationary- started with a "C." Gill enlisted the San Francisco authorities to help find her and planned to send one of his own investigators up there with a bench warrant. Harry went up himself on the overnight train.

"Father will find Alice and bring her back here, Avery, I'm sure of it." Lyric had said to me, her big womanly eyes full of sympathy and understanding.

People crowded the sidewalks, doing their Christmas shopping. Shows closed, new ones opened. The soapbox orators in the park warned that the end was near. Buster went to his boxing workout on Saturday; he spent the rest of the weekend at his studies and generally moping, not leaving the hotel unless I sent him on an errand- for with Harry up north, Lyric had been sent to stay with her grandmother in Hollywood. There were no sightings of Helen. Hillman and Alice Gillette remained at large.

Monday morning, early, the hotel operator rang with a long distance call for me.

I'd been half awake, having slept fitfully, thinking of how it had been with Helen here with me, remembering the delicate pressure of her hands on me, the heat of her, her taste, and her scent. The linen had long since been changed; there was no trace of her now. A week earlier we'd been enjoying our frolic in the mountains. Two weeks before, we'd been together for the first time at Long Beach.

The telephone bell took me out of further reverie.

It was several seconds while the operator at my end talked to the operator at the other end, then put the call through. I waited through the usual series of clicks and exhaled sharply as a man's voice came over the wire.

"…can't hear anything on this goddamn thing. Shepard, are you there?"

"Yeah, Harry- I'm here."

"I'm catching the train back to Los Angeles in a few minutes."

I could hear a woman's voice in the background, and a man's. Someone laughed. What in the hell? It sounded like he was having a party. "You and your pal Ricketts might want to be at the Southern Pacific depot when the 'Frisco train gets in this morning. He'll have one less missing person case on his books."

I hung up and phoned Frank Ricketts at his rooming house, passing on Harry's message and inviting him to come up here for breakfast. While I waited for Ricketts I went over Buster's lessons with him. He was catching up with his class already.

Ricketts picked me up in his borrowed flivver and we drove to the Southern Pacific station. It was just short of a month ago that he'd picked me up there and took me to view the body of the unknown girl who wasn't Kit. I wasn't any closer to finding her today. In a roundabout way, she'd led me to Helen, and now I had lost Helen too.

The streets were empty and quiet at that hour of the morning, before the shops and banks and theaters opened. The station was wide awake, however. Passengers were dashing to catch the morning outbound trains; others like us were there to meet early arrivals from the north and the east. We crossed the waiting room and went underneath the tracks to the platform where the southbound train would be arriving. I figured Alice Gillette was on it; the arrival of Gill and another man on the platform confirmed it.

The headlight of the big locomotive came into view piercing the low fog that hung over everything. The train glided to a halt and the red caps sprang into action. People came off the cars, mostly businessmen in heavy overcoats and black derbies. There were a few women- middle-aged matron in a fur coat traveling with an older woman and a little boy, and an old woman and her small granddaughter. There was no sign of Alice. A businessman in a grey wool suit and black overcoat stepped off- I knew him. So did Ricketts. Gill and the other man stepped forward and placed Henry Hillman under arrest.

CHAPTER 20

Hillman had not been the least bit surprised by the presence of the authorities; he had expected it. This meeting was arranged for him by his lawyer and the D.A., after they'd come to an agreement on the terms of Hillman's surrender. His arraignment would be held immediately; he would do no jail time.

He was charged with three counts of statutory rape against minor girls: Sylvia had given two dates that she was with him, Alice one. He and Morelli were charged with conspiracy to commit a felony, and multiple counts of contributing to the delinquency of a minor.

Ricketts and I followed the entourage to the Hall of Justice; its white façade was shrouded in fog this morning, which also blotted out the view of the mountains. We waited in the courtroom on the eighth floor, along with a throng of bail bondsmen, reporters and photographers who'd gotten wind of the case. I recognized the reporter Vargas; he caught my eye and made his way through the crowd to us. He was wearing the same old hat and his suit looked slept-in, as was apparently usual.

"You know Stubby?" Ricketts asked, gesturing at Vargas.

"Sure, we're old pals." Vargas replied for me.

"Still work for the same rag?"

Vargas shrugged. "Somebody's got to report the news. The other papers are giving Hillman the soft soap. I got onto the idea there was a woman behind this disappearing act of his. I smelled something down at the beach- and it wasn't the salt air. But Harry Price asked me not to print anything about it yet. He gave me lots of other good dope with promises of more to come, so I can't complain. But I'd like to know what the hell's really going on."

"Oh, you'll get your scoop alright." Ricketts said, trying to look wise; the truth was we didn't know much more than Vargas. "What makes you think your boss will have the guts to print it though?"

"Oh, I dunno- he might. He says the public likes to see a millionaire get it in the neck every once in a while. We're about due for one."

"Maybe he'll give you a raise and you can get a decent hat." I said.

"Hey, don't knock my hat. I only just got it the way I like it." Vargas said, in injured tones.

In all, Hillman spent almost as much time riding up and down in the elevators as he did in the courtroom. He appeared before the judge. The date of his preliminary hearing was set for the twenty-third of the month. Then he ducked out again in the company of his lawyer, trailed by the reporters and photographers and the more persistent of the bail bondsmen.

A few favored press men- Vargas not among them- were invited to accompany Hillman to the sanctuary of his executive offices in the Hillman Building where, in the comforting presence of his lawyer, he granted interviews. I wondered if any of them thought about what had gone on right over their heads.

The story dominated all the afternoon papers. Hillman dismissed the charges against him as ridiculous. The papers quoted him at length:

As for these trumped-up accusations, I need hardly say they are absolutely false. For weeks I have been the victim of unscrupulous parties who would take advantage of my wealth and position, knowing that I would rather pay for their silence than have my family shamed by their vicious and false accusations. I was forced into hiding by brazen and dishonorable private detectives who dogged my steps in the hope of having the opportunity to manufacture evidence against me to substantiate these false claims.

Regarding the allegations that illegal activities were occurring on the premises of one of my buildings with my knowledge and consent, the fact is I own dozens of properties in this city. It's absurd to expect that I could possibly know what kind of businesses all of my tenants are conducting. Mr. Morelli is not one of my tenants in any case. If the dance hall was violating the terms of its license, no one brought it to my attention, and it is only right that it should be shut down.

While they are at it, they ought to reform the detective license law so that these practitioners who are little more than sanctioned con men will not be permitted to terrorize honest citizenry."

Edith and I read them all in disgust at the office while waiting for Harry, who was due in at about eight-thirty. We were to meet him at the Rosslyn in the suite engaged for Sylvia Hoskins and the woman D.A. staying with her. We'd visited her earlier, bringing lunch from the delicatessen. Sylvia was not only restless and bored but resentful that the dance hall's closing had deprived her of her main livelihood. The only thing she was glad about was that she'd been "sprung" from the women's hotel where she had been staying.

"The old lady that ran it was always moralizin' at me." Sylvia said. "An' if that ain't enough, she felt sorry for me. Ugh! And I couldn't smoke or go to the pit'chers or listen to music or do nothin'. Nothin' fun that is."

She had dyed the bottle-blonde locks that I remembered and now had bright red, hennaed hair. The acne marks on her face, bare of any face powder, stood out angrily, matching her general mood. "How much longer do I gotta stay cooped up here? I'm sick of the sight of this rag I been wearing."

When we returned in the evening, Edith brought her one of her own dresses to wear- the fit would be less than ideal here and there, Edith mused, but it would be a change, anyway. I recalled Helen saying Sylvia liked to sew; Edith had produced a work basket and Sylvia was contently occupied for the moment. We also brought cigarettes, a pack of playing cards, a pile of confession and movie magazines, and some crossword puzzles. Sylvia distained the latter but Mary Parsons, the woman deputy, pounced on them.

Gill came along to the suite not long after we did. There were purple bruise-like circles under his eyes and the black shadow of beard stubble across his jaws and chin. Mary brought him some coffee, which revived him a little. In a voice hoarse from shouting, he relayed Hillman's official version of his story:

Hillman owned that there had been parties in the clubrooms, with some drinking, but maintained that nothing untoward had occurred- there had certainly not been any improper relations with under-aged girls. He denied knowing

Morelli and claimed he had never heard of Helen Sing or Alice Gillette and of course knew nothing about their disappearances.

Hillman at first explained his own disappearance by saying he'd been under a strain from the opening of his beach club and just wanted a rest. He'd had no idea anyone was looking for him until he read it in the papers.

Under further questioning, he admitted that he'd bolted because someone had been following him around Los Angeles for days and he suspected it was a detective hired by his wife, trying to frame him on a morals charge so she could get a divorce and marry somebody else. Hillman needed to sell stock in his beach club and couldn't afford a scandal. He confessed that he'd left his car and the items on the pier in order to throw this detective off his tracks, and then took the steamship *Harvard* up to San Francisco.

When he'd read about the warrant out for his arrest, he'd immediately gotten in touch with his lawyer and arranged to turn himself in. Zeigler, the lawyer, emphasized that his client had cooperated with the D.A. in every way.

"I'm beginning to wonder what exactly he means by that." Gill said. He looked anxious, as well as drained.

"Our case is solid, isn't it? We can refute anything he says."

"Sure, Shepard." Gill said. "I worry too much is all."

When Harry arrived at last, he wasn't alone. There was a grinning, gum-chewing young man with him, dressed in a pair of brown corduroy trousers and a bright red patterned sweater; a pair of rather sheepish-looking older men in conservative, banker-type suits and derbies; and a middle-aged man with spectacles, a brown mustache and dull brown hair parted in the middle. The party also included two women: one I recognized as Alice Gillette, the other he introduced as Elsa Kopenschlag. Elsa was a brunette stunner with full, red lips and a nervous habit of pulling at a bead choker necklace around her neck. I had seen her before, with Harry, that night at the Barbara Hotel- only we'd met her as

Joyce. Her brown eyes were somber and, as before, she spoke very little.

Sylvia and Alice collapsed on each other's necks in a squealing, enthusiastic reunion, whispering and giving the young man sidelong, flirtatious glances. "Sweet poppa-in-law, who's he? Sylvia asked. "He looks kinda like Bobby Vernon, don't he?"

Harry introduced the others and told his story.

The young man was a Harry Daniels, of late a bellhop at the Plaza Hotel, San Francisco. The two older men were operatives of the Burns International Detective Agency, Los Angeles chapter. The spectacled man was an investigator of the Los Angeles County D.A.

When Harry went north to find Alice Gillette, he'd soon noticed he wasn't alone. A couple of men were shadowing him. He assumed they were operatives of the opposition, paid for by Hillman or Morelli to make sure he didn't get to Alice and convince her to "squeal." So Harry had dodged them, leading them on quite a chase all over the bay city. He couldn't shake them though, and after a while the doubling back and retracing his steps got tiresome. Besides, he needed to wrap things up and get back to Los Angeles with Alice. So he decided to have a showdown and confronted the two men. He'd been right- they were detectives and they were working for Hillman.

Not Henry Hillman, but Mrs. Estelle Hillman.

Henry Hillman's story about his wife, a detective and a frame up had some basis in fact, Harry said, only it had happened a few years ago, and it wasn't Mrs. Hillman trying to frame her husband, but the other way around. Hillman himself had hired a detective to try to manufacture false evidence that Mrs. Hillman was having an affair, in order to mask his own dalliances and have a basis for a counter-suit should Mrs. Hillman ever succeed in bringing her own case. The detective had lured Mrs. Hillman out to a roadhouse on some ruse and slipped something in her drink; she came to, however, before the man could get any compromising

215

photographs so the effort failed.

At the beach club opening Mrs. Hillman became suspicious that something of the sort might be afoot again. Hillman was acting nervous and strange. Then- she saw a detective lurking about the club, an auburn-haired woman. *Ah!* she thought. Mrs. Hillman knew exactly what was supposed to happen: the woman would befriend her and invite her up to her room on the pretext of a friendly bridge party or something; then the woman would excuse herself "just for a moment, dearie!" and slip out the back, sending in a half-dressed male colleague- that's when Hillman and his witnesses would burst in. Mrs. Hillman had read of such a case in *Flynn's Weekly*. Well, Mrs. Hillman was having none of it. She hired her own detectives, the Burns men, then departed for the comforts of the Ambassador Hotel. The Burns men picked up the trail of "Hillman's" detective- noting that Hillman was now using a male operative. The Burns men followed this detective down the coast. When he realized Mrs. Hillman had given him the slip and doubled back into the city to look for her, they'd shadowed him. When he boarded a train to San Francisco, they were on it too.

Once they got identities sorted out and realized they were, in a way, allies, the three detectives, together with the full resources of the Burns San Francisco office, had easily found Alice Gillette living at a small out-of-the-way hotel not far from the waterfront, the Commodore Arms.

Alice led them to Joyce Bradley, alias Elsa Kopenschlag, alias Mrs. Elsa Hillman. The latter was how she had registered on the steamship *Harvard*. At the Plaza Hotel in San Francisco, she and her "husband" had registered as Mr. and Mrs. Bradley.

Young Daniels had carried the Bradley's luggage up to them when they arrived. He'd also brought up some whiskey for them, and had later seen "Mrs. Bradley" in the bed with no clothes on, and "Mr. Bradley" in only his drawers.

"Silk, they were." Daniels added, snapping his chewing gum.

Sure, the lady Harry called Joyce Bradley was the one he knew as Mrs. Bradley. He would testify to it in court and had happily come south with Harry. He wanted to make a change anyway, maybe break into the pictures.

The other man with Harry's party was Gill's own investigator, sent up to retrieve Alice Gillette.

"Hell, if I'd known I was going to have this mob with me I'd have hired a goddamn auto stage." Harry said. "It would've been cheaper."

Hillman, Harry concluded, at first wanted nothing more than a last weekend away with his cutie. His story about mistaking Harry for one of his wife's detectives was probably true, but once he thought he'd given Harry the slip, he got sloppy and didn't even try to cover his tracks. They had his passage with the girl on the *Harvard*, besides the hotel evidence. He'd probably read of the Pink Pagoda raid but didn't seem unduly concerned. "Why would he? He knows Morelli can't say anything without incriminating himself. The prosecution's key witness, the Sing woman, is safely out of the picture, and so was Alice- so he thinks. He didn't know we had Sylvia, and he's so blinded by his own arrogance, I bet he thinks no one will ever even find out about Joyce." Harry said.

"That might be at least another count of statutory rape if he was carrying on with her here." Gill said.

"You really think Hillman had something to do with Hel- uh, Mrs. Sing's disappearance?" I asked.

"I think he or Morelli probably made it worth her while to leave town. Why stick around and put her own neck on the chopping block? Mrs. Sing has a talent for self preservation. As for Alice, she slipped away and went up there because Joyce sent for her on the sly. She's in trouble- Joyce, that is. I mean Elsa."

217

"What? Oh hell. But Joyce said that night she'd never been to a party at Hillman's before." I said.

"Yeah, well, don't be too shocked, but she was lying to us. She and Hillman have been carrying on for weeks. The dumbbell really thought he was going to get a divorce and marry her. When she told him about being pregnant, he took her up north and left her there with cash and the name of a doctor- after spending the night with her."

"Bastard. I'd like to throttle him and cut off his balls."

"That goes double for me." Gill said.

"Get in line." Harry said.

CHAPTER 21

The next day I helped Harry round up other witnesses, including the elevator boy from the Hillman Building. Of our other witnesses, Elsa Kopenschlag had been admitted to the hospital of the county jail so her condition could be monitored. She was resigned to testifying but not very willing. Sylvia and Alice, united in misery, sulked at missing all the Christmas fun and not being allowed to go anywhere.

"Why are we bein' treated like criminals? Hillman's the one that done wrong. He ain't even in jail." Alice said.

It was a fair point; we had no answer. In exasperation, Mary, their guard, agreed to take them out in the evening to a picture show and supper at a cafeteria afterward. Edith brought them some jazz records Buster and Lyric had picked out from a music store on Broadway. My contribution was the loan of Kit's portable phonograph to play them on.

Later, alone back in the suite, I sorted through the mail that had piled up, and tossed out some old newspapers that we'd finished with. Under them, on the lamp table, I noticed a couple of books and picked them up. One was *Love Bound: A Story of Gilded Kisses*, the other was *Chickie*.

Going by those titles and the lurid paper covers, neither seemed like the kind of thing Buster or Lyric usually read. I realized these must be the books of Gladys's that Mrs. Watson gave them when they visited Charley, the ones Buster had called "drool." I picked them up. Alice and Sylvia weren't big readers but they might like these. Something fluttered out from one of the pages. A slip of paper. There was typing on it, but what caught my eye was a symbol at the top of it: a triangle, a sun and an eyeball. I had seen it before, in the consulting rooms of the Rev. Seher. The paper read:

> My dear child, I don't know what you think you saw, but I assure you there is nothing to it. The girl is new to the city. She expressed an interest in oriental dances and I invited her to view my library. I took it upon myself to help a fellow soul and aid her in her quest for employment. She is very attractive, I grant you– but I remain quite devoted to you, my Princess. How can you have doubt of it? Have I not gazed into your soul and read what is printed there– that you are my one and only destined one? If only you would let me see...

I sat down with the note in hand, thinking. Gladys had recognized Kit's photo when I showed it to her. But Kit never worked at the Pink Pagoda. Gladys had been a devotee of Seher's. There were lots of girls in Los Angeles, I supposed, who might be interested in oriental dances; no doubt many of them were strangers in town. It was just a hunch. But Harry told me a detective should trust his hunches. It fit. I could imagine Kit, alone, fretting maybe about what Mother had told her. She goes for walks, window shopping. She encounters Seher somewhere while out looking for a job. He strikes up an acquaintance, talks to her about dancing. Mrs. Earl mentioned the man's knack for knowing what would interest a person. Maybe she went to see him, out of politeness, or curiosity. If so, had he advised her? Did he tell her something that made her go away– abandon her ideas about dancing? I decided I would pay O. M. Seher another call.

I found the anteroom of the consulting rooms on Sixth Street open but empty. The sulky secretary was not at her post. I tried the connecting door to the inner sanctum; it was locked. I pressed my ear to the glass and thought I heard a sound from within. It sounded like a groan. I shouldered the door once, then again and it gave.

The blinds were drawn as before and the room was in semi-darkness. At first I thought I'd been wrong, that it was unoccupied after all, but as my eyes adjusted to the gloom I could someone lying on the day bed in the corner. It was the blonde girl. I crossed over to her. She reclined languidly, with one arm curled under her head, her lower half covered by a paisley shawl. She looked up at me, her expression as sullen as ever.

"Remember me?" I said. "I'm looking for–."

"I know. Th' girl." she murmured.

"Where's your boss? Where's Seher?"

"Otho's gone 'way. First her, then th' oth'r one, an' now him." Her words were slurred, like she was still sleepy, or drunk.

"You mean the dancing girl? Do you know where she is?"

"Gone 'way." she said, turning to face the wall.

"She's gone away? Where?"

"...he's gone." she mumbled.

I jerked open the two window-shades and knelt down next to the couch to look at her in the light. Her face looked even whiter and more mask-like, and the pupils of her eyes were so large I could barely see any blue around them. Her ruby lipstick was smeared all around her mouth like a gash. She closed her eyes and I bent over her and slapped her cheeks lightly, like I'd done that night to Gladys. Just like Gladys.

Through the long, tight, embroidered sleeves of her garment, I felt for a pulse. The wrist was wet, sticky– and red. At first it looked to me like she'd rubbed it across her mouth, but it had to be blood. Not a lot, and I didn't find a wound on her.

I glanced around for the telephone. There wasn't one. But I saw something else– more blood. It was spattered against the arched top of Seher's roll-top desk and smeared across the chair back. I noticed there were papers scattered around on the floor, and the Buddha statue lay on its side. The girl's eyes were still closed. I left her to go downstairs again and found the manager's office.

I interrupted him dozing in a rocker in front of the radiator.

"Need the telephone– quick." I said. I lifted the receiver, jiggled the handle until I got the operator and told her where to send a police ambulance.

"Somebody sick?" the manager asked.

"Yeah, Seher's girl." I said. "She's alone upstairs. Do you know where he might be?"

"Him the one that tells fortunes? I thought he were in a bit ago. Maybe that were yesterday. 'Spose he could be at home."

"Where's that?"

"Be in my rent book. That drawer, there."

I found the book and flipped through it until I found what I wanted: The Rev. Otho M. and Zaida Seher. Rubaiyat Apartments, South Hope Street, Bunker Hill.

The cab dropped me off in front of the address, a pre-war apartment house of cream-colored brick built right up to the sidewalk. The street was on an incline, so much so that the building appeared three-stories in height from the front, but from the side it was revealed as fully five stories. I could see the public library, with its central tower and bright, peaked roof, looming to the south. As the crow flies it wasn't very far from here to Seher's consulting rooms; walking, the crow would have to trudge up and down quite an incline. The Castle Towers, Kit's place, was right around the corner. Had Seher glimpsed her there and watched her, coveting her? Or had they simply met walking up the hill one day?

I went in to the lobby, a forest of potted ferns and mahogany woodwork with Parish prints on the walls and dark Axminsters underfoot. In the parlor to my right a young man and an older man, clearly father and son, were playing pool. The father said he thought the "psychic chappie" was in, and I'd find his room on the third floor, end of the hall toward the back.

I went up the stairs and along a narrow hallway until I came to the last door on the left. I knocked but got no answer. I tried it again, louder.

Across the hall, another apartment door flew open and a sturdy looking woman stood there in a pongee wrapper and a sleeping cap.

"Good Lord, you don't have to shake the place down." she said. "Obviously he'd have heard you the first time if he was in."

"I thought maybe he was in a trance." I said. "They told me downstairs he was in."

The woman rolled her eyes. "Well, he is in alright. He woke me. It sounded like he was tossing the furniture around."

I tried the doorknob; it turned. But Seher was not in the room. There was a golden oak writing desk against one wall with a Remington typewriter and a brass reading lamp on it. A golden oak dresser on the other wall, covered with a stained linen scarf, held a woman's pink celluloid hairbrush and mirror set and a bottle of Ashes of Roses toilet water. The bed had been slept in. I went around it and went through a dressing room, where a couple articles of men's and several items of woman's clothing hung from the clothing rod, and into the bath. A shaving kit and a bottle of restorative hair tonic rested on the shelf above the sink next to a tin of bath salts. A wet towel lay pooled on the floor next to the tub. There were dark red splotches all over the tile floor and the rug– blood.

I went back into the bedroom, looking down at the floor. There was more blood out here, trailing across the floorboards. The largest amount I found on the carpet next to the bed, as if he'd stood or knelt there for some time.

The woman from across the hall had followed me over and stood in the frame of the door, looking into the room with keen interest.

"I wouldn't go in there." I said hastily. "There's a bunch of blood–"

"I've seen blood before." she said. "I'm a nurse. Does he need help?"

"He isn't there."

She went in and looked around. "Looks like someone was bleeding from a cut, a pretty bad one, I'd say."

Now that we were looking for it, I spotted more blood out in the hall.

"How long ago did you hear Seher?"

"Right before you came. I thought you were him, starting up that racket again."

We went to the window that gave out onto the fire escape attached to the rear of the building. I couldn't see any blood on the dark metal. Looking down I saw the service yard and a gray concrete terrace that extended across the back of the building. The chalky hillside sloped beyond it, covered with scrub brush and litter. The air smelled foul, acrid. Out of the corner of my eye I caught a glimpse of something moving below on the terrace.

"Ugh– it's the incinerator. Some fool is burning trash." The woman said. "Close that window, will you?"

I ignored her and ran outside where I found a set of concrete steps leading down the side of the building to the terrace. At one end was a squatty concrete incinerator, belching smoke. What I'd seen from up above– a man in a gray wool sack suit– was half-crouched in front of it. The

Rev. Seher heard me coming and snatched an armful of something out of a grip that yawned open next to him, tossed it into the grate. As I drew near he dove toward me and tried to grab my ankles, missed and fell forward onto his knees. I jerked him up by the collar none too gently and saw the blood on him. It had soaked through a towel pressed against his middle and was smeared around the cuffs of his dress shirt and coat. I also saw what he'd been burning, and dropped him. He doubled over with a groan. I grabbed a spade leaning up against the side of the incinerator and used it scrape out the grate, stamping on the flames to put them out.

I turned to Seher again. "What did you do with my sister? Tell me, or I'll finish you right now, you sack of shit. Where is she?"

For a half second Seher looked up at me, his black eyes unfocussed. I'd seen that look on the faces of boxers just before they went down for the count. He didn't fall though. In a sudden move he dashed the few feet to the far edge of the terrace, jumped from it to the ground. He made for a path worn into the scrubby brush of the hillside beyond the building and ran north, toward the Castle Towers. The bluff got steeper here; geraniums and morning glory vines grown wild tumbled down the side of it. Down below, looking very small, was a line of cars in an auto park. I had Seher within arm's reach and grabbed for him. He stumbled over a tree root and started rolling headlong down the embankment, grasping at the vines and brush, failing to break his fall; he tumbled down, past rusted tin cans and empty bottles, a corroded mattress spring, and discarded tires, until coming to rest in a gray heap at the bottom. I couldn't see any way down, except to fall the way he had, so I went back up the hill to the apartment.

The woman from upstairs was on the terrace, dressed with her nurse's cape wrapped around her shoulders. I told her to telephone for an ambulance; she already had.

I nodded. "Good. Unfortunately I need him alive."

She showed me the way to go, to get down to him. We found him in a vacant lot next to the auto park I'd seen. Looming high above us I could see the Castle Towers. The woman knelt over Seher's crumpled form, established that he lived.

He lay on his back half in the dirt. His limbs were contorted, reminding me of Gladys's flapper doll. His middle was dark red with blood. It had soaked through the towel and his suit coat. There was a fresh gash on the side of his head.

"Have you got a handkerchief?" she asked. I nodded. "Hold it here and keep pressure on it. Good. Keep doing that. I'll go wait and guide the ambulance." she said.

"You don't have much time left. Better talk fast, you bastard." I said when she'd gone. Seher coughed but nothing. "You did something to my sister and Gladys saw you."

Seher kept silent. I pressed harder against his temple. He groaned.

"I'll give you one more shot: Kit Shepard– where is she? If you don't tell me the girl will– she's alive you know. I found her in time. Did you try to poison her– like you poisoned Gladys?"

Seher looked up at me. The black eyes were void of emotion– no alarm, guilt, or even pain.

He still didn't speak but gazed past my shoulders up at the sky. He gasped and I heard the terrible rattle in his breath; it had been a familiar sound to me, eight years ago. I knew what it meant. I cursed and rose to my feet. I kicked at his blood-soaked shoulder. The Rev. O. M. Seher didn't feel it. The Rev. Seher was no more.

CHAPTER 22

The girl, the self-styled Zaida Seher, did live to tell her part of the story– enough of it anyway. Frank Ricketts and I, with Det. Lt. Hoyt of the homicide division, interviewed her in her room in the receiving hospital as soon as the doctor allowed it.

"You haven't a lot of time." he said grimly.

The doctor didn't know what exactly was wrong with her. All he could say for certain was that she had swallowed some sort of poison and wasn't expected to pull through. Detectives were combing Seher's consulting parlors for traces of whatever it was.

There wasn't a single wound of any kind on her; the blood I'd found on her and splattered all over the desk was apparently Seher's. According to Zaida, she'd threatened to cut her own throat with a little Chinese dagger that he kept on his desk as a letter opener– had held it up to her body, but when he hadn't tried to stop her– had in fact, given her his serene little smirk– she'd turned it on him instead, she said. I could hardly blame her there; that smirk really was annoying.

They'd met when she responded to Seher's advertisement for secretarial help. His interview technique, she admitted, had not involved much in the way of note pads and dictation. He told her that her true name was Zaida and she was his soul mate. He asked her to marry him, right then.

He confided that he had palaces in Shanghai that he'd been forced to flee them during the conflicts there— but he would return soon, with her. She would live as his princess with servants to do her bidding and have the finest silks and rubies and pearls. She happily accepted. Seher had married them himself. They consummated the union there in the consulting parlors.

Ricketts and I exchanged a glance; he rolled his eyes.

"Why were you threatening to harm yourself earlier?" Hoyt asked gently. "Did you two have a quarrel?"

"He was going away without me." Zaida said. "There was only one."

"One what?"

"One steamship ticket. I found it in his coat pocket. He was sailing to Hawaii on Saturday. Alone." she repeated in her flat, sullen monotone. "He tried to poison me. All because of her."

"Her who?" Ricketts prompted.

"You mean this girl? The dancer?" I held up the photograph of Kit.

"She wasn't a dancer. The other one was the dancer."

"Gladys Watson?"

Patching Zaida's version of events together, we gathered that dreams of royal riches aside, life as the Rev. Otho Seher's consort was not exactly a paradise. Seher brought in new women followers constantly, and then there was Gladys, his previous amour who, as Zaida put it, continued to bother Seher, coming around and lurking about his lodgings and the consulting rooms at all hours even though he had made it clear he was finished with her. To the three of us it seemed obvious that it was Seher who continued to pursue Gladys— although supposedly married to Zaida— not the other way around and that Zaida's jealousy drove her to keep close tabs on Gladys. Zaida admitted she often went to the Pink Pagoda at night, coming and going by way of the passage between it and the Hillman Building. Yes, she knew all about that— she'd overheard Gladys telling Seher of going to Hillman's party with the others.

"She was a harlot, that Gladys. You see that don't you? I tried to tell him."

"She wasn't, actually." I said evenly. "So was it you who pushed me down the stairs?"

Zaida looked up at me with her eyes at half-mast. "You were asking questions, looking for her– the other girl. You'd have set the police on Otho. He didn't do anything. It was an accident."

The voices and other sounds in the room became dull and there was a ringing in my ears like they did in the war after a shelling.

Hoyt kept his voice flat and said "Sure– we know it was an accident. He didn't mean her any harm. How'd he meet her?"

"Oh– around. Otho felt sorry for her. She was a hick from somewhere. She was always pestering him. Just like Gladys. She came around that morning. Otho took her into the parlor– I went to watch through the hidey-hole. I could see everything that went on in there."

"What did you see this time?"

"Otho asked to make a life reading of her. 'No thank you' she says, all haughty and superior. 'I just need to know where to go, to report for work– the dance instructress job. Your message said I could start today?'"

Zaida then heard Seher saying that there was plenty of time. He would take her to meet her new boss in half an hour.

'I'll just run to the bank and the post office, then.' she'd said, and tried to go. Seher rushed at her and held her hands, saying he loved her, that she was the most beautiful girl he's ever seen, his true destined one. She backed away and was saying 'No, no– oh, leave me alone.' They struggled and she pushed him away. Seher came at her again and she ran for the door but he tripped her and she fell. She hit her head on the valve of the radiator.

We three were silent.

"Did you call for an ambulance then? Or the police?" Ricketts asked after a moment, barely audible.

"No." Zaida said. Her toneless voice wavered, but only a little. "An ambulance wouldn't have done any good. She wasn't breathing. The police would've said Otho did it on purpose, and hung him for murder. He fell at my feet and begged me to help him."

"What did you do?"

"We got some old clothes and put them on her, and Otho had me cut her hair. When it got dark, I helped him carry her downstairs out back."

"What then?"

"We had her pocketbook. There was a postcard in it she hadn't mailed. Otho said we could make people think she was still alive. When they found the body, they wouldn't know who it was, and no one would've reported her missing."

Ricketts and I exchanged another glance.

"So what did you do?" Hoyt asked in his soothing voice.

"I got dressed in her clothes and went to her apartment late at night. Then I sneaked out again in the early morning. I did that every night for a week. Then Otho mailed the postcard and I packed up all of her things and took them away."

"How?"

"What?"

"How did you get them away?"

"Otho met me at the side door. We went the back way 'cross the field, back to our apartment."

"You pawned her phonograph." I said.

"Yes." she shrugged.

"What did you do with her other things?"

"I checked them at the railway express. Otho said the police would find them and think she had gone away. She had no connection to Otho. She wasn't one of his clients. We

230

were safe. We were going away. Then he came around asking about her." The lowered eyes glared in my direction.

"You weren't safe, though, were you? Gladys Watson saw them together, didn't she?" I asked.

"I told you she was always creeping around, spying. She saw Seher walking with the girl by his apartments, and she found out later that the girl was missing because you told her."

"And Gladys told Seher that the girl's brother was looking for her?" Hoyt asked.

"She said Otho ought to use his gift to help him find his sister. It was a threat– you see? She must've been spying that night, saw us, with her."

"So you gave Gladys something, in her drink. You were there that night, at the Bamboo Garden."

"Otho didn't do anything." Zaida said petulantly. "He told her they were through for good, that we were married."

Ricketts scoffed.

"We were!" she hissed. "Gladys said she didn't want to live anymore, that nobody loved her."

"You're wrong. Gladys Watson had a baby and a family who loved her. Just like Kit Shepard had a brother who loved her."

"I don't want to talk to you anymore." Zaida said, sullenly. She shut her eyes and turned her head to the wall.

CHAPTER 23

There was no time to mourn for Kit. Not then, not yet, with her body to be found. Ricketts and I dug through his records like mad men. He hadn't looked at any cases of missing women before October 8, because as far as I or anyone else knew, Kit had been alive up until that date. We now poured over the entries of "Jane Doe" cases from the morgues for that preceding week.

Of several, only one fit:

> October 1, 1926. 4:30 a.m. Female, age 16 to 21, 5 foot 2 inches, about 115 pounds. Hazel eyes, attractive features, light brown hair, cut short. Hands well kept, nails manicured; Feet callused. No distinguishing blemishes on body. Dressed in a cheap cotton shirt and blouse with lisle hose, blue felt hat. Low-heeled black leather shoes, worn. No labels or markings on garments. Blow on right side of head. Deep cut above right ear. Found in rear yard of apartment hotel, 534 Flower St.

The location was north of Seher's consulting parlors, across the auto park I'd walked through on the day I shadowed him.

The body had been taken to a Breese Brothers

Mortuary, where it went unclaimed. It had then been transferred to the county hospital. An autopsy revealed the blow to the head to be the cause of death. The inquest determined the death to be accidental, likely caused by a fall.

I had to go there to identify the body, just as before, except this time I had to say: "Yes. That is Katherine."

All this time, the weeks that I'd been in Los Angeles, and weeks before that, she'd been here, her body unclaimed, just like her baggage.

If we'd been much later in finding her she'd have been transferred to the county crematorium where her ashes would sit on a shelf in a metal box for however long– two, three years. If still unclaimed, she would have been interred at the county cemetery there with others who were unidentified or had no one who would or could claim them– a mass grave, marked only by the year of death, mourned only by a few cemetery employees, if at all.

I went to see Doc at his office.

He'd been sitting at his desk with his head bowed, but he looked up as I came in and came around to clasp my hand in both of his. "My heart is heavy for you, Brother Shepard. How are you bearing up?"

"I hardly know." I said. "I keep asking myself, why the hell didn't I come get her and make her go home? She'd still be alive."

"Is that the life she would have wished?"

"I don't care."

"I know you to be a strong man. It's hard for you to accept that in some matters, you are helpless."

"Don't tell me the Lord works in mysterious ways and all of that–" I said.

"I'm not talking to you as a pastor, I'm talking as your friend. I hope that you consider me one, anyway."

"Sure I do, Doc. I didn't mean to be rude."

"Be as rude or as angry as you want, if it helps. You've got other friends here, too. They're rallying around you."

It was true. I'd had kind notes from Joe Gill, Ricketts, even Vargas; Miss Emily, Lena Parrish, and the others of "the Castle menagerie" had written also. Buster ran errands and sent wires for me, saw to it that I ate. Lyric and Edith shopped for a dress for Kit to be buried in; they picked out a pretty pale blue one, just the kind of thing she might have chosen herself. Harry was gruffer than usual and kept me busy working. I didn't have time to mourn. Not until Kit was properly laid to rest.

"Is there anything I can do for you, Brother Shepard?"

"I came to ask you for a favor, Doc, as a matter of fact."

I asked if he would arrange the services for Kit, in his church.

"I'd be honored." Doc said.

"The Monday after Christmas okay?" I said. I knew Doc would be rushed off his feet before then, with Christmas services; besides that I wanted to have the Hillman hearing behind us first, and there had to be time for Mother and Roberta to come out– if they would.

"Fine." Doc nodded. There was a troubled look in his blue eyes.

"Something wrong Doc?"

"No, Brother Shepard. I was just thinking it's fitting that the service for your sister, who was fond of old-fashioned things, shall be my last in this old-fashioned church of mine."

The church, he said, was to be sold, and would no doubt be pulled down before very long. The board of trustees had voted on it last night.

"But I won't be here to see it go." he said. "I sent my resignation to the board this morning and they accepted it."

"Are they forcing you to out?"

Doc's last sermon, delivered the Sunday after Hillman's arrest, had been printed in the papers. Titled "Let us put the blame where it belongs," it reproached property owners who allowed illegal businesses of all kinds to operate in their buildings, the police for not being diligent enough in enforcing the vice ordinances, and the D.A. for failing to prosecute certain criminals.

"No, no. This has been a long time coming." Doc said. "They think I'm as outmoded as this building. Perhaps I am."

"You're not leaving Los Angeles?"

"Yes, but I'm not going far. I've been offered a little church in Hollywood. I understand there are a lot of souls there in need of salvation." His eyes twinkled again. "I'll still be rooting for the Seraphs, though. Maybe you and I could take in a game come summer."

"I'd like that, Doc." I said.

CHAPTER 24

But Thou, O Lord, shalt bring them down into destruction.
Bloody and deceitful men shall not live out half their days.

–David, Psalm 55

Harry threw a party of sorts in his suite on Christmas Eve. He and his cronies from the Spring Street club played poker in the dining room while Edith and I decorated a tree I'd brought for Lyric. There was a fire going in the fireplace, and carols on the radio– Harry's gift to Lyric. Trays of salted nuts, mission figs and candied fruits were spread out on the coffee table. Harry had supper sent up, Virginia ham and Yorkshire sauce with sweet potatoes and pumpkin pie. Harry's bootlegger, a good-looking Italian guy of my own age or thereabouts, had brought him a case of booze for a present. Harry, he said, was one of his best customers.

Yesterday morning had started off with a bad storm that hit town bringing an icy rain, tying up traffic and flooding certain streets as we made our way through a sea of black umbrellas to the Hall of Justice for the preliminary hearing of Hillman and Morelli.

The papers had been full of the case for the past two

weeks and opinions seemed divided. There were those that denounced modern youth and its declining morals as evidenced, they said, by girls selling their virtue, not for life's necessities but for luxuries and pretty clothes.

There was censure of Hillman, to be sure, but much of it tended to make light of his offenses. A woman newspaper columnist called him "Daddy Hillman." Her allusion to the aged New York millionaire realty man– whose nuptials to, honeymoon with, and separation from "Peaches," his sixteen-year-old bride, had titillated tabloid readers for months– was intended more as a jest than a jibe.

The title of a popular play being staged at the theater of a local women's club provided more fodder. I remember it had been running in New York when I was there but I hadn't seen it: *Cradle Snatchers*. The plot involved three middle-aged wives whose husbands are addicted to chasing young flappers, so the women hire three young college boys to romance them. It was of course, Edith said with no small amount of bitterness, a farce.

Vargas' paper ran a daily barrage on the rampant graft in city hall, the D.A.'s office, and the police department, that allowed vice to flourish and gave wealthy businessmen like Hillman and gangsters like Morelli free rein over the city.

That the hearing was proceeding at all had been a victory for our side; lawyers for the defense had made every attempt to get it postponed until after the holidays, if not indefinitely.

Not that there hadn't been bad news. Gill came to see us at the office late one afternoon, his face like thunder. He flopped down on the leather davenport and loosened his tie, which, for Gill, I'd by now come to realize, was wildly dishabille during business hours.

"We've lost Elsa Kopenschlag." he said.

"What?" I'd gotten up from my desk but fell back onto my chair. "For Chrissake, how? Wasn't she being watched?"

"I mean she's no good to us a witness." Gill said, his black eyes vexed. "We're not going to call her."

Elsa, he said, might be going to have a baby someday, but it wouldn't be in the next nine months. The jail doctor who examined her didn't believe there had ever been one. Gill had questioned her then and she'd broken down, admitted she'd made up the story to try to hold Hillman and make him divorce his wife to marry her, like he'd promised her he would. She became petulant and demanded to be released from technical custody. It was almost Christmas. She wanted to go home. Gill went downstairs to his office to think it over. The defense might not find out about Elsa's condition until after the preliminary hearing, but he didn't want to go into court with a lie on his lips. He resolved to let her go. Before he could act, Elsa's father was ushered into his office. He had Elsa's birth certificate with him. Whatever she'd told Hillman about her age, she was in fact twenty-three. Not a minor. Mr. Kopenschlag wanted his daughter released. He was ill and couldn't work; he was dependent on Elsa's earnings. Gill released her.

The storm the morning of the hearing hadn't kept reporters away, or the hordes of spectators who thronged the hallways and shoehorned themselves into the courtroom.

Gill sat behind the gate at the prosecution table, dressed in a custom-tailored dark blue suit and crimson and gold striped tie, his pompadour as slick and glossy as his oxfords today. I went over to wish him good luck. His face screwed up and his thick black brows nearly met in the middle.

"I'm worried, Shepard."

"About what?"

"I don't quite know. But something's up."

"What?"

"The chief deputy called me up at home last night, says he doesn't think we can win the case. He wanted me to drop the charges. Said he'd talked it over with the D.A. himself. The D.A.'s been out of town on so-called personal business– I don't even know where he is."

"What did you tell him?"

"What do you think? I said the hell I would."

"Think there's been a fix?" I asked. I glanced over at Hillman and Morelli, seated at the defense table with their lawyers. They wore expensive, well-cut suits and looked unconcerned, relaxed.

"To tell you the truth, I don't know what to think, Shepard. I used to think the D.A. was a square guy. Well, I've had Hail Mary cases before and won. I'll do my best."

We shook hands and I took my seat next to Edith, with Harry and Doc.

Edith pointed out Mrs. Gillette, Alice's mother, in the crowd. She had a blonde, husky youth with her, Alice's brother Tom, Edith said.

We rose as the judge entered. He looked around the courtroom and threatened to order the curious spectators removed if there were any outbursts. Then Gill called his first witness: a handwriting expert, who would testify that entries in a blue ledger were in Mr. Morelli's hand. The audience, poised for sensations, settled down, disappointed. It perked up slightly at the mention of Hillman's name in the ledger, along with dollar figures and the names of young girls.

Morelli's lawyer made short work of the witness. Mr. Morelli, he drawled, took over the dance hall license in what he thought was a legal transfer. Mr. Hillman, therefore, was his client's landlord. The girls were his employees. He failed to see anything particularly conspiratorial in the keeping of records to show when he had paid his employees' wages due them, and when he had paid his landlord rents due him.

Gill called Alice Gillette next. She wore a plaid wool suit with her blonde curls hidden under a wide green hat. At Gill's prompting she gave her age as seventeen. She lived with her mother and went to high school. Yes, she'd worked at the Pink Pagoda. She'd been a dance instructress there until it was closed down. A Mrs. Sing at the dance hall and Mr. Morelli had asked her if she wouldn't like to earn some extra money. She'd said sure.

Several women, including Mrs. Gillette and a lady reporter, left the room when Alice started in on her testimony, detailing the parties in Hillman's clubrooms in her breathy baby-voice. I'd heard it before but it was no less foul in the retelling.

Under questioning by Zeigler, Hillman's lawyer, Alice admitted it had been Mrs. Sing, not Mr. Morelli, who approached her and who had paid her this extra cash. Zeigler then asked her to identify a document.

"Is that your signature?" Zeigler asked.

"Y-yes." Alice replied in a whisper.

"I admit into evidence this employment application" Zeigler said. "Signed by Miss Gillette, declaring her age to be twenty-one."

Alice's eyes darted from Morelli to Gill and back at Zeigler.

Yes, she had given her age as twenty-one, but only because they told her at the dance hall that's how old she had to be to get the job. She'd been sixteen then.

"So, you have lied about your age when it suits you, is that right Miss Gillette?" Zeigler asked. "One more thing: how have you supported yourself since the Pink Pagoda closed down?"

"I ain't been. How can I?" Alice shrugged. "First I was kept at home, then Syl and me been at the Rosslyn."

"So, the D.A. has paid your lodgings, your meals, bought you clothing, phonograph records, took you to shows– is that right?"

"Well, sure– one show. I guess we acted pretty bad to Miss Parsons. She was only tryin' to be nice. Them two gave us some of the stuff." she added, looking at Edith and me.

Zeigler raised his eyebrows to the ceiling. He didn't use the word bribe, but implied that the D.A. and "private parties" seemed to have a "quite unusual" interest in keeping the witnesses happy, at considerable cost to the taxpayers.

Sylvia took the stand next. She'd been dressed demurely in a simple, dark green dress with low-heeled shoes and a smart brown hat. Her acne-spotted skin looked pale but her brown eyes gazed out over the heads of the crowd and she raised her chin. She answered Gill's questions easily enough, at first. Her age was seventeen. She lived on her own, had done since coming to Los Angeles about two years ago. She'd worked in a glove factory, then a laundry. Nights she'd been a dance instructress at the Pink Pagoda, same as Alice.

"And while you were there, did anyone approach you about making any extra money?"

"Yeah." Sylvia said. "One of the gals asked me to sew her up some scanties out of a few old lace bits she had. I did and she paid me a buck for it."

"Uh, well– er, were you asked about any other work?" Gill asked

"I'm not sure I know whatcha mean." Sylvia said.

Edith and Harry and I looked at each other, and back at Gill.

"Did Mrs. Sing and Mr. Morelli invite you to go to parties upstairs in Mr. Hillman's clubrooms, for money?"

Sylvia pursed her lips and looked down to inspect her nails. "I don't remember anything like that." she said finally.

The court erupted in chaos. Edith's jaw actually dropped, and even Harry looked baffled. The judge threatened to clear the court if order wasn't restored.

Gill tried again with Sylvia.

Yes, she admitted, she had gone a couple times to parties upstairs in the Hillman Building. But when Gill asked if anyone had offered her any money for it, she couldn't remember; she didn't think so, though. Her memory also failed her when asked if she had gone into one of the bedrooms with Hillman. Gill finally gave up. Zeigler had no questions for the witness. The judge dismissed her and Sylvia stepped down, blinking as the photographers took flashlight pictures. Zeigler requested that Miss Gillette and Miss

Hoskins remain in the courtroom as Gill called his next witness, the night elevator boy from the Hillman Building to the stand. Sure, he recalled taking girls up in his car to the tenth floor, quite often. Yes, those occasions always coincided with him having first taken Mr. Hillman and other men up to the tenth floor. Yes, the cars there opened directly into the clubrooms; there was no possibility that Hillman or the girls had been headed anywhere but to the Realty Club.

Zeigler took over questioning the lad. He asked him if he could point out in the courtroom any of the girls he'd carried up in his elevator. The youth squinted into the audience, scrutinizing the female faces. He took a pair of spectacles out of his coat pocket and put them on, looked again. His gaze lingered for a second on a girl sitting across the aisle from us, and another somewhere behind us. My own glance went to Sylvia and Alice, sitting– one nervous and one defiant– to the left of the judge. They looked very different, and much younger, without their makeup. A couple people looked "kinda familiar," the lad said, shamefaced, but he couldn't say for sure.

The court burst out again. A couple of reporters dashed out of the room. The judge rang his gavel down and demanded order.

"Your honor," Zeigler began, "given that the State is unable to introduce any evidence against my client, has failed utterly to produce any credible witnesses nor demonstrated that any felony conspiracy took place, I ask that the charges against him be dropped. My client has admitted to inviting girls to his parties, and though he believed them to be of age, if it is true that they are the ages they now claim to be, he is willing to plead guilty to the contributing to the delinquency of a minor charges and pay any fine he has coming to him."

The judge, frowning, looked to Gill, whose hands were balled into fists at his side. "What say you, Mr. Gill? Has the State any other evidence to add? Or will it accept the defendant's plea to the lesser charge?"

In the end, Gill had no choice but to accept it. The

statutory charges against Hillman were dismissed. As to the conspiracy counts pending against Hillman and Morelli, their counsel argued that the D.A. had no evidence to prove there had been any such conspiracy. The charges were dropped. The photographers' flashlights went off like fireworks on the Fourth of July. Reporters dashed away. Morelli and Hillman, all smiles, stood and shook hands with their counsel. They would walk out of the courtroom, free men.

CHAPTER 25

*I think that there are certain crimes which the law cannot touch, and
which therefore, to some extent, justify private revenge.*
–Conan Doyle, *The Adventure of Charles Augustus Milverton*

I was nobbled and that's all there is to it." Joe had fumed
when he'd stopped by Harry's party earlier, bringing a
box of cigars for us. "And they obviously got to the
Hoskins girl. I can't think what else accounts for her
sudden lapse of memory. At least they picked up Morelli."

That had been a surprise. As Morelli, fat and smug,
strolled out the courtroom, two men came forward flashing
the badges of Department of Justice agents and took him
away with them. Morelli's response had, as the papers would
say, been unprintable.

"The worst thing that happened to Hillman in all of
this was running into the Gillette girl's brother." Gill said.

That had been our only other bright spot: Alice's
brother Tom had barreled up to Hillman and socked him in
the gut; Hillman had gone down like old Ruby Robert landing
his legendary solar plexus on Corbett. But, in fact, Joe was
wrong. The worst thing to happen to Hillman was meeting
Harry Price.

The night of the trial, last night, Harry had me meet
him just after supper. The rain had let up but it was cloudy
out and dark as midnight. Crowds of merry theater goers,

diners, people doing their last minute Christmas shopping hurried along the slick, wet sidewalks. Bells rang out from the corners, and carols blared from radios and phonographs in all the shops. Harry strode on, his hands jammed into his overcoat pockets. He didn't speak, had not spoken more than ten words since the hearing.

I knew Harry well enough by now that I wasn't even surprised when we stopped in front of the Hillman Building. The windows of the eighth floor were lit up.

The Pink Pagoda was still dark and padlocked. The hat shop on the ground floor advertised the fantastic bargains to be had at its removal sale.

We went around to the alley, where Jockey Sam O'Shea stepped out of the shadows and opened a door for us at the back of the Hillman. "It weren't nuffin." he said, and left us again.

I followed Harry up the service stairs to the eighth floor where Hillman had his offices.

His secretary had gone for the evening but we let ourselves through.

It was a handsome room, paneled in walnut glowing in the soft light of a dual pair of bronze sconces. There were Persian rugs over a tiled floor and oil paintings on the walls. Two green leather wing chairs flanked a massive walnut desk.

Hillman sat behind the desk. He'd changed into evening clothes but he didn't look like a man celebrating his freedom; he was slumped over holding his bare, oil-slick head in his hands. The face he turned up to us when he heard our step looked haggard.

"Get up." Harry said. He held an oblong object in his overcoat pocket and aimed it toward Hillman.

Hillman stood. "Wha– what do you want? Money?"

"Shut up." Harry said. "Walk."

He marched Hillman out into the hall and back toward the service stairs. Hillman hung back, hesitating. Harry gave him a shove with his pocket. Hillman went up the stairs, Harry and I trailing at his ankles. We passed the tenth floor landing and came to the door that let out onto the roof. Hillman hesitated again.

"Go on." Harry said.

We stepped out onto the roof.

The huge electric PAC-LAND sign towered above us. I could feel the warmth of it. It was double-sided, facing both east and west. The words flashed pink for a span of about three seconds, then went dark. They flashed green, then went dark, flashed white, then dark. All three colors illuminated for a few seconds then went dark for a few more seconds. After that the whole flashing sequence started up again.

The sign flashed green. Hillman, in its glare, looked bilious.

"What do you want?" he whined.

Harry said nothing. The sign went dark. I heard a scream— a ghastly, high-pitched sound. With the clouds overhead and no moon, it was pitch black. The sign flashed white. I saw Harry over at the parapet. Hillman dangled over the edge of it; Harry held his ankles in his massive hands. The sign went dark.

"I got no use for men who like to fuck little girls." Harry said.

The sign came on in all three colors. I looked over the parapet. Far below was the flat roof of the Pink Pagoda. I could see the white glare of Hillman's dress shirt.

"Be a shame if you dropped him." I said as the sign went dark. "They might not find him 'til tomorrow and the homicide boys wouldn't get to be home with their families."

I heard sounds in the darkness. When the sign flashed pink, Hillman lay sprawled on the roof by my feet like a salmon on the deck of a fishing barge. Harry loomed over him.

"He isn't worth it." Harry said.

Hillman made great, gasping breaths. "I'll— call— the— police." he rasped.

"Go ahead." Harry said. "Who do you think told me

where to find you tonight?"

The sign went dark.

Harry and I took the service stairs down to the ground floor but left the building by the main lobby. The night watchman opened the front doors for us and wished us a merry Christmas. I wished him the same as Harry pressed a bill into his outstretched hand.

The kids came in, with red cheeks and sparkling eyes, having been ice skating and to witness the lighting of a giant Christmas tree in the park across the street. They spotted our little tree and went to it, laughing over the playing cards, cigar bands and other bits of nonsense we'd tied to the branches.

Lyric clapped her hands. "I love it– thank you!"

Buster wore his new blue cashmere suit, an early Christmas present from me along with some casual things for everyday. When he started high school in the new year, I wanted him to be dressed like the other boys, which from what I'd seen meant filthy white corduroys with pull-over V-necked sweaters most of the time.

For he would be graduating with his class; he'd made up the work, sooner than expected. Mrs. Kerr from the junior high sent me the good news in a Christmas card.

I stood in front of the window, watching the lights twinkling around the three sides of the park: red, blue and green Christmas bulbs, the orange glow of a theater's electric sign, and all the regular white lights of the city. A boys' choir on the radio sang *"Adeste Fideles."*

Edith came alongside with a toddy for me and one for herself. We touched glasses.

"My dear mother passed nine years ago." she said after a moment. "She took sick. It came on sudden and I didn't get here in time to say goodbye– I had a war job in Washington. I miss her all the year, but at Christmastime most of all, somehow. It makes me think of when we were young, all at home."

"Does it ever get any better?"

Edith was quiet for a moment. "Not better, exactly. The pain of the loss wanes, at times. Then out of the blue it comes back as strong as ever. I almost don't mind it. To not hurt would be to forget her, and that, I think, would be worse." She gave my hand a friendly squeeze.

I turned and Buster caught my eye.

"Time to go, Ave?" he asked.

"Yeah." I said. "Get your coats on."

We were going for a drive in my new car. The Buick dealer had delivered it today. Since I would be staying in Los Angeles, I had to have a car. Or so people told me. It was a beauty– a blue four passenger sport roadster. It would have to stretch to five tonight. We were going to collect Edith's boy Arthur from his grandparents, Edith's former in-laws, in Pasadena. Then we would drive out to Altadena to see the street of lighted Christmas trees, which was, Edith had on good authority from Arthur, the dog's derby.

I helped Edith into the front seat and tucked the robe around her knees. Buster held Lyric's hand as she balanced herself nimbly on the fender step, then he climbed into the rumble seat next to her; it would be a brisk ride for them but they didn't seem to mind.

Their love story was just beginning.

My own, mine and Helen's, had never really begun. We'd been lovers but hadn't actually spoken of love. Maybe there hadn't been time. For a while I thought she might be hiding somewhere near, watching to see how the trial proceeded, and that one day I might see her again. I didn't really care if I did. I told myself that sooner or later I would stop wearing her red jade ring, and then, someday, I would drop it into the blue Pacific. By that time I would hardly remember her at all.

CHAPTER 26

I want to dance always, to be good and not evil, and when it is all over
not to have the feeling that I might have done it better.

—Ruth St. Denis

We had Kit's service by candlelight with the winter
sunshine projecting images of the stained glass
across the floor. There were old hymns Kit had
loved: "Lead Kindly Light," "Abide with Me."
There was dancing too, performed by a young woman in the
Denishawn style. The Castle folks were all there. Miss Emily
played the organ. A Miss Smith read a verse of her own
composition, strange but kind of lovely, about the sea foam.
There were other neighbors from the Hill too, glad to have
known Kit if only briefly: the postman, a couple who ran a
small laundry, an old woman whose overgrown garden Kit
had called romantic.

The home folks had not come out. Mother, Roberta
said, was too frail to travel. They sent a large wreath of
carnations. It stood on an easel, stiff and formal next to the
other tributes: evergreens and yellow daffodils, violets and
pink roses, pansies and lilies of the valley.

Lena Parrish designed a sculpture for Kit's grave
marker: a barefooted woman with flowing robes and hair, her
arms arched above her head. At the base of it she'd carved

the words:

> *And what her voice did sing her dancing feet*
> *Seemed ever to repeat.*

EPILOGUE

It seemed fitting, to me anyway, that the fate Kit's killers had intended for her became theirs: an unmarked mass grave in the potter's field. No friend, no relation came forward to identify or claim either of their remains, and the authorities here were never able to learn the true names of Seher or Zaida, where he had lived before coming to Los Angeles, or anything else about either of them. Even fatally wounded, with Zaida dead or dying, Seher had tried to hide his secrets, past and present. He'd run to the apartment with the weapon still stuck in his belly; police recovered it near the base of the high embankment that cut Hope Street off at Fifth. He'd managed to burn who knew how many documents and photographs before I interrupted him. The charred remnants of what I'd salvaged from the incinerator were all that remained.

The photographs were of young women and they were mostly all nude. Some were partially-clad, having been captured in the act of undressing; others while they stood, looking awkward and rather shamefaced, against a patterned backdrop. I recognized it as the oriental screen in Seher's private parlor. They thought he was using mystic powers to take an "imprint of their souls." Hoyt's men found the camera, hidden in plain sight on one of the cluttered bookshelves. Near it was Zaida's "hidey hole," a small opening in the wall where she could watch the illicit goings-on.

The photographer who developed the images had the shop next door to Seher's consulting rooms. Police raided it and confiscated the negatives, threatening him with arrest.

"I didn't know there was anything wrong about them." he'd whined. "I thought they were just some o' them art poses like they print in the camera magazines."

The papers played up the story— referring to the shabby consulting parlor as Seher's "temple of love" and lingering over the salacious details of the photographs. Seher's desk had yielded lists of dozens of women's names. He divided them into two camps— older women whom he hoped to get money out of and young women whom he admired and hoped to go to bed with, some of the latter presumably his unwitting models.

The county chemist was able to determine that the fatal herb concoction Zaida swallowed was the same poison that killed Gladys, but whether Zaida or Seher had been the one to give the stuff to her we could never know for sure. It made little difference to Mrs. Watson, who considered the two equally responsible. Just as well, she said, that she did not have to depend on the legal system to bring her daughter's murderers to justice. A higher power had dealt them what they deserved.

The federal agents who took Morelli away had been acting on an anonymous tip, alleging that Morelli was on the payroll of a vice operation supplying girls to houses in Mexico. The agents had investigated and found evidence to substantiate the claim. They arrested Morelli for violation of the Mann Act, the so-called white slave law. He was arraigned and booked into the county jail. He'd been able to post his five thousand dollar bond, however, and so walked out of the

Hall of Justice that day after all, though not exactly a free man. He promptly jumped bail and vanished. Our government agents traced him to Tijuana. The Mexican authorities found his body in a flophouse there, throat slashed. His death, the papers said, quoting sources south of the border, was believed to be the work of oriental assassins.

Hillman's name still made it into the papers once in a while, but rarely in connection with any philanthropic efforts.

Estelle Hillman filed for divorce on grounds of infidelity, naming Elsa Kopenschlag and nine other unidentified co-respondents. Housewives and reporters battled each other for seats in order to hear Hillman's dirty laundry aired at last– his now-infamous silk drawers and all the rest of it. Harry and I gave testimony. Witnesses who would have been discredited in the criminal case went over big in divorce court. The judge granted Mrs. Hillman an interlocutory decree without hesitation. Her cash settlement was not made public, but rumors put it in the hundred thousand range.

The next time we heard about Hillman was when he and some of the board of his real estate syndicate were arrested and charged in a scam dating back to the sale of stocks for the construction of his beach club. Hillman again avoided doing any jail time, but the syndicate faded out of existence. Los Angeles forgot about Hillman, so much so that when, one day, a man named Henry Hillman was found shot to death in his automobile, by his own hand, the story barely rated a mention on the third page of the papers.

Joe Gill resigned from the D.A.'s office a little less than a year later and went into private law practice. Most of his clients were women and the downtrodden. He became my personal attorney, a sometimes employer, and a pal.

Not long after Gill left the office, the grand jury began an investigation into whether the D.A. had taken a bribe to drop the Hillman case. Meanwhile, the D.A. faced other inquiries into his activities: bail-bond irregularities, allegations of failure to prosecute criminals, and more bribe accusations. One of them finally stuck and the D.A. was charged with willful misconduct in office for fixing acquittals in an oil stock-fraud case, was convicted along with his chief deputy, and went to San Quentin.

We had our reform movements, about every two years, just like Harry said. Somebody would come charging in with a new broom and proclaim loudly to all and sundry that they were going to clean house with it, sweep out all the dirt. Only, they almost always missed some spots in the corners.

AUTHOR'S NOTES

As 1926 came to a close, the population of Los Angeles had grown from 576,673 in 1920 to 1,268,680, making it the fifth largest city in the United States. Los Angeles then as now was a city constantly in the process of reinventing itself, though the building up of new landmarks often came at the expense of old ones. The Los Angeles Avery saw on his arrival in November 1926 would have looked different to him only a few months earlier and would be altered still more in the near future. The energy and optimism wrought by this hub of activity is partly what draws him to the city.

On January 1, 1925 veteran *Los Angeles Times* writer S. Fred Hogue wrote that (jealous) visitors to Los Angeles often disparaged the city for its newness and the state of its civic infrastructure: "You have not even a library building. Your city hall is a dump, your courthouse almost a ruin. Though materially prosperous, the cultural spirit is surely lacking."

"It is true that Los Angeles possesses no crumbling mansions commemorating the culture of a historical period that has itself crumbled." Hogue said in his rebuttal. "This is not a cemetery in which art and culture lie entombed. Its face is not yet scared and wrinkled by time and revolutions."

By November 1926, the critiques Hogue cited were rendered practically moot.

The city's main library occupied its beautiful new building (still in use today) at Fifth and Hope streets, having moved in July from the leased space in the top floors of the Metropolitan Building (at Fifth and Broadway) where it had been since 1914.

Groundbreaking for the now-iconic city hall on First Street between Main, Spring, and Temple streets had commenced in March 1926; its rapidly rising framework would have been be easily visible to Avery. It opened in April 1928. Until then, city hall was an 1888 "dump" in the 200 block of Broadway, demolished (for parking) in 1929.

The beautiful Beaux Arts-style Hall of Justice had opened in February 1926. It housed the county jail on its top floors, most of the county courts, the Sheriff, District Attorney and Coroner's offices, and many other county departments. The 1891 red sandstone county courthouse on Poundcake Hill, architecturally old-fashioned perhaps but hardly a "ruin," continued in use until deemed unsafe in 1933 due to earthquake damage (ironically earthquake damage would close the Hall of Justice in 1994; it reopened in 2014 after undergoing a retrofit and restoration).

Nor could the mansions of late, lost and lamented Bunker Hill yet be called crumbling. Out of my research came the impression of a quiet neighborhood with cheap rents, close to downtown, that at this point was no seedier or more crime-ridden than any other section of the city. It attracted both working-class and retired folks, as well as show people and artists who gave the Hill a certain bohemian quality in the teens and twenties. The wealthy residents who settled here in the 1880s and 1890s had for the most part died off or fled to more fashionable neighborhoods, leaving their eclectic dwellings behind. Many of these once single-family homes were converted to apartments and rooming houses. The Castle Towers apartment had once been the home of Miss Almira Hershey, and was originally located at the northwest corner of Fourth and Grand. In 1907 Miss Hershey had the home cut in half, converted into apartments, and moved to

750 West Fourth Street. The Rubaiyat Apartments around the corner were erected in 1912 on the site of the Dr. John Carl Zahn family home, built in 1890.

One aspect of life in Avery's Los Angeles of 1926 that definitely hasn't changed (except to get worse) is an excess of automobiles and drivers complaining about the traffic. And no wonder: the Automobile Club of Southern California reported in 1926 that, of 1,641,571 cars registered statewide, 560,136 of them were located in Los Angeles County.

While real life people, places and events are mentioned, this book is a novel and anyone with a "speaking part" in it is a fictional character.

The disappearance of pastor Aimee Semple McPherson of the Church of the Foursquare Gospel did occur in May 1926; the resulting investigation and legal fallout lasted into January 1927 when, with her trial for conspiracy to commit fraud underway, Los Angeles County D.A. Asa Keyes abruptly dropped all charges; in 1928 the grand jury investigated reports that his decision had involved a bribe. While nothing came of that allegation, Keyes (along with his chief deputy Harold L. Davis) was eventually found guilty of accepting bribes in another criminal case: the Julian Oil stock fraud.

A novelist is bound to make the details of a story believable; in real life all bets are off. What fiction reader would accept, for example, that the chief witness against a D.A., on trial for "fixing" acquittals, was a guy named Ben Getzoff? You can't make this stuff up.

Research

The background for *Red Jade* is largely based on original research using primary sources including newspapers, magazines and journals, maps, city directories, historical photos, and miscellaneous ephemera. While some of these sources are from my own collection, others are maintained by libraries, archives and historical societies. In particular: the photograph collections at the University of California, Los

Angeles, the Los Angeles Public Library Central Branch (LAPL), the University of Southern California, the Huntington Library, and the California State Library (CSL). The LAPL History & Genealogy Department has a collection of maps, city directories and other resources indispensible for researching local history. That the historical *Los Angeles Times* can be accessed on-line nowadays is a wonderful thing, but other Los Angeles newspapers of the past can be found at the CSL California History Room on microfilm. The California State Archives has useful records from the state board of prison directors.

Selected Reading:

Bahr, Robert. *Least of All Saints: The Story of Aimee Semple McPherson.* Prentice-Hall. 1979.

Blum, Deborah. *The Poisoner's Handbook: Murder and the Birth of Forensic Medicine in Jazz Age New York.* Penguin Press. 2010.

Callis, Tracy and Chuck Johnson. *Boxing in the Los Angeles Area: 1880-2005.* Trafford Publishing. 2009.

Cressey, Paul Goalby. *The Taxi-Dance Hall: A Sociological Study in Commercialized Recreation and City Life.* University of Chicago Press (new edition). 2008.

Greenburg, Michael. *Peaches and Daddy: A Story of the Roaring 20s, the Birth of Tabloid Media, and the Courtship that Captured the Hearts and Imaginations of the American Public.* Overlook Press. 2008.

Henstell, Bruce. *Sunshine & Wealth: Los Angeles in the Twenties and Thirties.* Chronicle Books. 1984.

Historical Society of Long Beach. *The Pike on the Silver Strand. Journal 1982-1983.* 1982.

Kahn, Roger. *A Flame of Pure Fire: Jack Dempsey and the Roaring '20s.* Houghton Mifflin Harcourt. 1999.

Politi, Leo. *Bunker Hill Los Angeles: Reminisces of Bygone Days.* Desert Southwest Inc. 1964.

Shelton, Suzanne. *Divine Dancer: A Biography of Ruth St.*

Denis. Doubleday. 1981.

Sitton, Tom. *Metropolis in the Making: Los Angeles in the 1920s.* University of California Press. 2001.

Starr, Kevin. *Material Dreams: Southern California Through the 1920s.* Oxford University Press. 1991.

Tygiel, Jules. *The Great Los Angeles Swindle: Oil, Stocks, and Scandal During the Roaring Twenties.* Oxford University Press. 1994.

Wagner, Rob Leicester. *Red Ink and White Lies: The Rise and Fall of Los Angeles Newspapers 1920-1962.* Dragonflyer Press. 2000.

Warren, Beth Gates. *Artful Lives: Edward Weston, Margrethe Mather, and the Bohemians of Los Angeles.* J. Paul Getty Museum. 2011.

Acknowledgements:

Many thanks to HJK for the painstaking editing and other support; to my parents; and to my grandfathers and great-grandfathers, who were real-life code heroes and never knew it.

ABOUT THE AUTHOR

J.H. Graham is a third generation Los Angeles native. She has an M.A. in History from California State University and worked as an architectural historian, researcher, and professor of history before starting to write fiction. She now lives in Northern California.

For more about J.H. Graham and old Los Angeles, visit www.jhgraham.com.

www.ingramcontent.com/pod-product-compliance
Lightning Source LLC
Chambersburg PA
CBHW022155170626
46807CB00005B/2214